JOHNSON'S DICTIONARY

ALSO BY DAVID DABYDEEN

Fiction

The Intended
Disappearance
The Counting House
A Harlot's Progress
Our Lady of Demerara
Molly and the Muslim Stick

Poetry

Slave Song
Coolie Odyssey
Turner

Non-Fiction

Hogarth's Blacks
Pak's Britannica

David Dabydeen was born in Guyana. He read English at Cambridge, taught at the University of Warwick, and is presently Guyana's Ambassador to China. His poetry has won the Commonwealth Poetry Prize. His fiction has been shortlisted for the John Llewelyn Rhys Prize, the James Tait Black Memorial Prize and the International Impac Dublin Award, and received the Guyana Prize, the Raja Rao Prize and the Sabga Caribbean Award.

JOHNSON'S DICTIONARY

DAVID DABYDEEN

P E E P A L   T R E E

First published in Great Britain in 2013
Peepal Tree Press Ltd
17 King's Avenue
Leeds LS6 1QS
England

ISBN13: 9781845232184

Supported using public funding by
ARTS COUNCIL
ENGLAND

To Robin and Lucie Tiemeier, with great love,
and in memory of Gudrun Tiemeier.

Acknowledgements

I am most grateful to Jeremy Poynting, Hannah Bannister, Lynne Macedo, Jonathan Morley, Michael Mitchell, Michael Niblett and Joseph Jackson for making this novel possible, and especially Rachel, Moses and Surya Dabydeen. Thanks too to Ma Bole and his restaurant staff.

"Metaphors are anklets to art, they hobble the flow of reality."
– Samuel Johnson

"A metaphor does not run on all four legs." – Shelley

"Legba: the lame voodoo priest stumbling towards the gates of higher truths." – Wilson Harris

PROLOGUE

These things he knew – a calabash scraped of skin and painted in the colours of dusk; an ancient brush of lama branches inherited from his father, and his father before him; and vials containing sidyam juice and the venom of water snakes, which only he could blend, to becalm poison with benevolent fruit, so that when a child was born, he could anoint its forehead with the potion and ordain for it a life of constancy: passion contained within wisdom, anger within forgiveness, sickness within hope, death within the intimation of stars. And only he, Manu, originator of life, could read the scroll of light that was the evening sky. It was his task to bear this knowledge, inherited from his master, and his master before him, and out of such knowledge to name the newly-born and to determine its future.

When a child was born, it was first brought to his hut, for without its naming, it could not be displayed to the tribe. These things he knew, the bawling of babies awaiting their names, the night air stinging their new skin, the night air like cinder in their lungs. And the sudden stillness as he brushed their foreheads clean, applied the potion from the calabash bowl and called them Saba or Tnika or Ellar, signifying that this one would be the village beggar, that one a planter of eddoes, the other a shrimp-seller.

Calabash, vials, brush, potion, and an evening sky textured with stars: these were the measure and security of his life. His place in the village was constant because he had a particular function which only he could discharge. There was the Elder, schooled from childhood in the remembrance of their laws, who sat in judgement over adulterer and thief and gossiper. There was the Sorcerer, the keeper of the secrets of their masks, who knew what colours and patterns their faces must wear for particular ceremonies. And there was Manu, diviner of stars. The three of them maintained the order of the village, governing over farmer and fisherman and weaver of cloth. And all life was contained within the boundaries of the village, the fields of jamoon and guinep trees, and the grasslands for their livestock. Beyond was the habitation of their ancestors, who never appeared to them, not even in dreams. Beyond was unthinkable, for it was the realm of loss.

As unthinkable as the present was clear; the clearly defined tasks and duties and ceremonies of the village. Until one dread night when an infant was brought howling to him, and he scoured the sky for its name, but the stars were shaken from their frames and he was speechless before the chaos, the unexpected sadness of their lives that the brightest star foretold. The child howled and for the first time he felt pity for its pain, knowing that he was unable to determine its future, to moderate its pleasures and its sufferings, so life would become acceptable to it. He brushed its forehead, anointed it, and gave it a false name, for the stars could not be read. The infant continued to cry, and no amount of rocking and singing could comfort it. He knew then that the appearance of the new star presaged their destruction. The ways of their village would be changed forever, and with it his reason for being.

The Elder gave his judgement. "Two cannot govern the village," he told Manu, "there must be three. It has always been so."

"But I must go," Manu insisted.

"There is nowhere to go. Beyond us there is nothing," the Elder adjudicated. Manu pointed to the heavens and to the new star summoning him to an unthinkable fate, but the Elder could not distinguish one light from the next. It was not his role to divine the meaning of stars. The knowledge which once gave pride to Manu became burdensome. He felt trapped by a secret which could not be shared with others.

"Look," he addressed the Elder in a tone of desperation, pointing again to the new star, but what was obvious to Manu was unthinkable to the Elder. He gave his judgement again: "Two cannot govern the village. There must be three. It has always been so." The repetition of verdict which once impressed Manu with its ring of authority now sounded like the stubbornness of the ancient.

"I must go. Someone is born afar and I must name it," Manu protested, for the first time in the history of the village questioning the Elder's ruling. "You cannot go," the Elder commanded, denying him a third time.

So, when everyone was asleep, Manu slipped out of the village, his calabash and brush and vials wrapped in a bundle like a thief's haul. He slipped out of the village with the guilt of a thief. He had stolen their inheritance, their right to be named, and he was taking their inheritance to give to a foreign child in a foreign land.

The orchards and the grasslands gave way to swamp, then to softer earth, which suddenly collapsed into emptiness, absorbing and negating his terrified humanity. Only his possessions remained as tokens of identity, reminding him of his once fixed position within the village. But now he was the loosened nail in a collapsing universe. He clutched at his possessions frantically, to preserve an aspect of his former self, and he called out to the Elder, to the Sorcerer, but no-one answered. He called out his own name but no-one answered. Once more he panicked, but the distress in his throat was stillborn. In the emptiness his cries were rendered inaudible. He no longer mattered. He slipped out of consciousness with the guilt of a thief.

★ ★ ★

In dream they appeared, in profound guise, for their masks were corrupt, signifying no ceremony he recognised. The Elder and the Sorcerer wore battered faces, and their bodies were dressed in chains. They headed a procession of villagers, each chained to each in a coffle of grief. Now and again someone screamed to the crack of a whip upon his back, like the call and response of storytelling, except that the fables were unfamiliar to Manu. A pale man dismounted from his horse and bowed reverentially to Manu. He offered Manu a staff. "Beat them," the man tempted him, but Manu was perplexed by the gift. "Beat them, be their rightful master," the man urged. "Their pain will give you strength. Here, let me show you," and he raised his staff against the nearest slave, breaking his skull. The agony of the dying slave, and the terrified sobbing of the others, inspired the man. "Look how easy it is to kill," he shouted, lashing out ecstatically. He battered them until he grew bored by their hurt. "It is true. After a while, people are not fun, don't you think?" And before Manu could recover his senses, the man clicked his fingers, conjuring forth a troupe of musicians. "People bore me. I give you instead the finest specimen of animal." He clicked his fingers again, and a woman appeared, dancing before Manu, offering magnificent breasts and thighs. "Here is something worth killing for," the man whispered into Manu's ear, pressing the staff again into his hand. He pointed to the slaves who had stopped their wailing, suddenly relieved by the dancing woman. "Kill them all before they rob you of her," the man advised, drawing Manu's attention to their fidgeting. "They will rise up, snap their chains, murder you and devour her," the man warned. Manu felt his hands gripping the staff with intent, but even as he stared longingly at the woman's nakedness his sense of duty revived. He was still the wisdom of the village, determining its future according to the configuration of stars. He let the staff drop from his hands, denying the pale man a second time. "What will you kill for?" the pale man asked in desperation. "Tell me, and I will summon up anything you desire. Shall I bedeck you in gold? Shall I burn frankincense to beguile your senses?"

"Go from me," Manu shouted in unexpected anger and the man retreated, startled by the threat of violence.

"You've already sinned," he accused Manu from a distance. "You have abandoned and broken your people and caused them to be sold into slavery. There is nothing you can do to redeem them." And he mounted his horse, raised his whip over the villagers and drove them to the waiting ships.

★   ★   ★

Still in dream Manu watched them go, knowing that their names would be cast aside. They would be renamed after mules and hoes and hovels. But the star still beckoned, reminding him of a superior purpose. The desire to save the villagers faded. The Elder and the Sorcerer cried out, challenging him to deliver them from evil, but he turned his face away from their distress towards the West, where the star presided.

It was a plainer journey than he imagined, for he encountered no marvels, no bizarre landscapes. There were no epic struggles with his conscience, nor with giants and monsters. No riddles blocked his pathway. In no time at all he arrived and was disappointed not to be greeted. It was a village shabbier than his own, a stretch of dust littered with stones. There were a few huts and a monkey straying among them. He had expected crowds, but the place was still. He followed the monkey to the nearest hut and called out in a stranger's voice, but no-one appeared. He went from hut to hut, announcing himself, but all were deserted, except the last where a groan answered him. He pushed open the door to discover an ancient woman slumped on a bed of straw, as thin as brush-bristle. With great effort she opened her eyes to meet his, but there was no flicker of interest. She lowered her head, closed her eyes and fell asleep. He looked around the hut, seeing nothing, for it was devoid of any sign of presence. Not knowing what else to do he squatted beside the woman, waiting for her to stir. Eventually she awoke, but ignored him, gazing instead at the bag tied to his body.

"Give me the food," she said, stretching a shrivelled hand at the bag.

"I have none," Manu confessed.

"Give me the food," she insisted, the desperation of hunger giving life to her fingers. She ripped the bag from his waist and opened it greedily. She bit off a piece of the calabash and swallowed it without waiting to chew. He snatched the sacred vessel from her before she could eat more of it.

"I need it for the child," he said foolishly. She looked upon him with pity.

"You are like the rest of them," she said, not seeing his black skin, his woolly hair, his alien garments.

"I am from…" he went to explain.

"I don't care where you are from," she interrupted. "Thousands have passed through here recently from all corners of the earth, places you never thought existed. Yellow people, some white, some brown, then you, on horses and camels and asses and on foot, all different but all seeking the one fortune." She spat at his feet, watching the phlegm shimmer on the surface of dust. "They were following some star, they said, and it led them here. A goldrush, but there's nothing here, see for yourself, there's only me, but some of them were so desperate after their long journeys that they'd have me. 'Get off you filthy pagan pigs,' I cursed the lot of them, 'shame on you to try to breed an old woman.'" She thrust her face accusingly at Manu, then relented. "Please, do you have any food in that bag you are carrying?"

"I have no food," Manu confessed a second time.

"I begged them too, but they wouldn't give. They just wanted to take. But there was no treasure here, so they left. True, there was a star singled out, but my eyes were too weak to see it fully. And what's a star to me; I can't eat it."

"Where are your people?" Manu asked, thinking of his own loss.

"My husband was a carpenter. Wolves ate him. I bore children. I grew old. I walked out of the house, through all the phases of the moon, till I reached here, and I knew right away it was the place to die in. Look how loveless it is. But why can't I die? I've been waiting for ever to die but nothing happens. Please, do you have any poison in your bag?"

That night, he sat outside the woman's hut, fingering his vials of poison obsessively. Her sleep was broken by cries of distress. Manu felt useless before the life suckling her breasts, a creature of spite refusing to detach itself and allow her to die. The woman sobbed, challenging him to deliver her from evil, and he searched the night sky for wisdom, but the brightest star had eclipsed the light of other stars, like a life feeding off other, more vulnerable lives. There was nothing he could do but witness the rapacity in heaven and on earth. There was nothing he could do, and there was nothing to go back to. And yet he clung to his bag of instruments as frantically as life clung to the sobbing woman. They were useless, he knew, all their miraculous properties so much myth, but that was all there was. The brightest star was all there was, even though it witnessed nothing but a woman's agony.

★ ★ ★

"What is your name?" Manu asked at first light, giving her victuals he had found outside one of the huts, wine, rice, water, salted fish and coins buried under a heap of stones. He had intended to search the huts, but the stones beckoned, wanting to reveal their secret to him, as if only he was ordained to discover it. Secret stones... He recognised them, but how, he knew not.

"Name, name! Why all the fuss about names? They all come bewailing their names or boasting about them. Call me willow for that is what I have become. I used to be stout as cedar, my pot always brimful with dumplings and cassava, but look at me now, my back curved, I can no longer raise my head to the sky. I wander the village with my gaze fixed to the earth as if I'm searching for the right spot to be buried in."

Manu poured her some water, for her lips were flakes of bark. He went to search underneath the stones for other things to comfort her – an empty rice-sack, dried reeds, the hide of a cow, horns still intact, and a piece of cloth, its dyes still aglow in spite of layers of dust. He spread the cowhide for her to lie on, the rice-sack her blanket. He shook out the cloth and fashioned it into a parasol, breaking up the cot and using the reeds as spokes. "I will shine and carve the cow horns into ornaments to brighten your hut," he offered. She turned in distrust, sucked her teeth and spat. She curved her body away from him. Manu wondered what had befallen her in the past to make her such a stranger to kindness. She must have divined his thoughts for she turned to face him in a sudden and final effort at strength, her parched tongue now a-flow with stories.

PART ONE

Me, Cato, work for Massa Hogarth from the time he come to the colony, fleeing debts or mistresses or zealots, who knows? – I don't care for the gossip, I just think: what a foolish man to want to come to this swamp and snake-place call Demerara. For twenty years or more I work in plantation, but too much trouble – riots, hangings, oh you don't want to hear – and I was so glad when plantation ruin, and me put up for sale, and Massa Hogarth buy me. Oh he is mostly drunk, and he brood, and foul mood catch him, but he never beat, and he summon or send me away with sweet words – "Come here my churl, my cur, my rapscallion," he say, or "Go hither, my beast of burden" – the words sound so England sweet, I learn them by heart but that is not why I glad-bad to work for Massa Hogarth, not for the English words but because he is a painter. Yes, Massa Hogarth has big-big title, "Official Artist of the Colony of Demerara and Contiguous Territories," it say on the scroll which hang in his studio. My ears tingle for days when he read it out for me. I wait till he is drunk-drunk and I beg him, and he feel sorry for his dim boy so he read it out for me. "Official Artist of the Colony of Demerara and Contiguous Territories," it say on the top, and at the bottom, "By Order of His Majesty King George the Second, Protector of the Realm, Defender of…" I can't remember it all, I stop hearing; too many honey bees in my ears.

Massa job is to make record of the factories and the fields and the whitefolk who run the colony. He paint them in the Assembly Hall when they meet for serious talk on how much sugar cane cut that season, how much slaves bite up too bad by mosquito and die from fever, how much tax raise, how much this and that and the other, things that only whitefolk have brains for. Massa has to paint them too, looking jolly, like when they hold party to drink to the latest beating of the Papists in battle, or party for the King's birthday, each with a slave dress only in loin cloth so that the silk of his massa shine bright; each slave hold a union-jack fan of bird-feathers shape like oars so that when they wave all the fans in one, it look like many British victory ships.

Now I don't know these high matters, only what I hear Massa talking to his friends, none of which makes sense to me, but I don't care. All I wish for is to paint like him. He see the craving in my eyes and take pity ("So you want turn Titian?" he laugh-laugh, and then he stop and study me as if he could really titian me), for less than two months I in his service he buy another black, Miriam, a tender young girl, to cook and clean, and he promote me with the title of "painterboy". Oh happy day, how Cato happy! Churl, cur, rapscallion, beast of burden, and now painterboy! All day and the next and for months upon months the bees sing in my ears. Massa show me how to stretch the canvas, how to frame it. I have my own slave, which is my box of tools. If you put all their names together they sound like a Negro gospel choir – tenon saw, dovetail saw, bevel, spindle, chisel, dowel. As to the dyes, they are like the first hallelujahs God utter when He start to make the world: ochre, viridian, sienna, indigo, ultrama-rine. I watch my massa prime the canvas, spread it with animal glue, scrape it with a broad knife, scumble it. He mix the dyes with linseed or poppy-seed oil. He take a brush and he dot and dab, his face light up, he is in a dream, deaf to the sudden downpour, or the horses how they whinny in the stable, or the hissing as Miriam press iron onto clothes. I watch Massa Hogarth before his canvas as if he is before altar, and I know that when he is painting he is worshipping. He is pastor and I am his altar boy. When he is done and gone into his chamber, I wash the brushes and it is like washing the feet of our Lord. I am in truth a blessed Black!

But why is it that at as soon as Massa Hogarth enter his chamber he reach for the rum and quaff all afternoon and night time? Each Sunday, we slaves gather in open field and the one or two who can read find passage from the Bible about folk drunk like swine, who curse up Jehovah and do a thing in Sodom call abomination, and we are so shocked that folk can behave so bad that some of us fall and twist on the ground and start to speak in tongues. I should speak like that to Massa when he is drunk, but I stay silent and judge not, for he has make me his painterboy.

I go to pick him up from the floor and put him to bed and I puzzle over his past. He is a lean man, dark, and his skin rough. Once upon a time he fat-fat, you can tell from loose skin on his neck and stretchmarks on his hip. Some worry waste him for true, but what? He is not nice to look at through lady-eyes. Maybe he never snare a hummingbird, maybe he had to make do in England with plain sparrow, that's why he fret away his sorrow in a rum bottle. And the whiteladies of Demerara are married, or too young and pretty for one like him. And the scars on his body – what fights in England over woman or money or religion cause them? I wipe froth from the side of his mouth, I spread blanket over him, all the time worrying over his scars, and I want to sing a lullaby to ease his misery.

"Miriam, what you think wrong with Massa Hogarth?" I ask her, work done for the day and the two of we in the kitchen eating eddo soup. The best meal of the day, air cool, work done, plenty leftovers. Miriam don't answer. Maybe she just want peace to enjoy the food. Maybe she service so many other massas she don't care no more for whitefolk. She too got scars. And me? Me a grown man, but with no chance for wife and child, for why make family who you can't feed and who can part from you anytime, sell off to another plantation? Me too got scars, but why brood on them? As preacherman say, Christ had them most of all, in He hand, in He foot, where they lash He on the back and where Latinman soldier bore He side. Cato's scars is a small-small loveless story, it don't bear telling.

Howsoever drunk the night before, Massa still get up first light and I am beside him with clean brushes, dyes ground fresh, tools sharp and shine and ready for the act. I like it most when the picture is set in canefield, the factory at the back with chimney smoke, in front the chop-chop-chop of cutlasses, Negroes weeding and manuring the cane, loading punts, whipping the sleepy mules. And, at the edge of canefield, a tree under which some Negroes rest or revel, play tin whistles and tambourines. Oh so much more pretty to see your life in paint, because Massa don't bother to put in the Negro sweat and the hate. Canvas is a special cloth; you can't spoil it with too much real life. Canvas is Christ's miracle. On canvas the lame walk, the hungry get fish and loaves, water turn into wine, work make a man free.

I don't want to talk bad about Massa Hogarth, but a time did come, a year or so on, when he can't bother to wake up early. He sink so deep in the rum bottle that his hand can't reach to push open the cork to greet the sun. He turn into the dregs at the bottom of the bottle. Howsoever I shake the bottle the dregs don't stir. He rise when he want to, spend an hour at the painting, give up, call for the rum. His face is so foul I shout at Miriam to stop whatever slave-job she doing and bring to the chamber one, no two abominations of rum.

What to do? The painting not finish and the client making demands. If the drinking go on, Massa will ruin, then he will have to sell me back to some plantation where I have to mind pig, not pigment, and Miriam will lie on her back all her nights till she grow too old for bed-work. What to do? Up and down I pace the studio, worry for the future, then bam! The answer thunderclap in my head, lightning glow my eyes, I am like Saint Paul when God rollocks him on the road to Damascus. I gird my loins, I still my beating heart, I take up brush. I do the small things, I paint the Assembly Room table, I paint the high chairs, I finish off the walls. Now to the whitefolk... Oh God, I fear to brush their faces, surely they will come to life, dash away my Negro hand and order my whipping. So I start humble, I attend to a foot and give it shoes. I give them all nice legs and shoes. Above the table is chest and arm and face which I can touch up, but a sudden fright catch me, I drop my brush and scoot.

Massa Hogarth, when at last he get up, go to the canvas and complete the work, not sighting my part in it. Maybe his pride stop him giving praise, but he please with me, so I suspect, for the next painting and the next he only do the main parts, then plunge into his rum bottle, hit his head at the bottom and doze. I finish off the small parts of whatever scene it be: cows in the pasture, more shoes, and so on. I come to specialise in animals and whitefolk foot as well as what Massa call still-life – that is table and chair and fruit bowl and hurricane lamp. I pine to do what Massa call portraiture – oh how the word tantalise – but no,

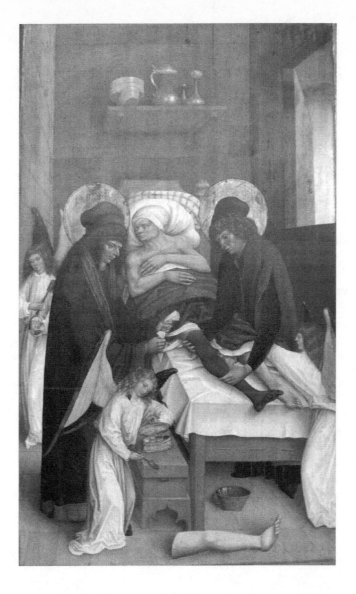

Unknown: *Transplantation of a leg by Saints Cosmas and Damian*
Germany, 16c.

whitefolk face is forbidden to me, like a sin is forbidden, like a wife and child is forbidden. I long for family, I long for portraiture and would damn my soul with sinning. I start to rage against Massa. I dream that the paintbrush in my hand is a torch that will burn down canefield and factory. I paint the cows red, I put a streak of crimson in the sky, I bloody the rocks along the backdam.

God chastise me for my rebellion, God make Massa collapse and catch stroke. I lay him out on his bed, I fan him, I spoon soup in his mouth. My heart soften to his sickness. He is too weak to ship back home, so he nail to his Demerara bed, waiting the end. Miriam and me done for! I distress and distress till salvation enter my head. Let me paint him England, let me do green hills far away, oak trees, ducks in pond, drizzle, pale suns, and all the scenes I hear him talk about when he and other whitefolk used to meet up, quaff and long for home. My art will open his eyes, wake his spirit, make him want to live. I cut a piece of canvas, in size bigger than any painting Massa ever do. I make pigments of every colour you can dream. Don't ask how many hours or days I spend, for when the paint lap and flow time don't be. Paint stop time, paint stop fear of time, because when my hand twirl and dance on the canvas, and rainbows tangle like hoops in my thoughts, and I have to study hard to separate them out, the last thing in my mind become the first, and the first thing become the past and future thing. Time spin and muddle up and then stop altogether. Then there is only beauty left, beauty which is in the colours of the canvas and is forever – mind you, is only forever when you make sure the paint reach the right point of dryness and you apply the proper glaze, for beauty is also technique.

Cato is master of technique, so I tell myself when I hoist the canvas onto an easel at Massa's bedside. The commotion wake him, his eyes open, his brows crease like his mind confuse. Then he close his eyes again but there is a curl in his lips as if he is showing me scorn. I try my best to make England shine but my painting not good enough to revive Massa. Is it the trees? I only *hear* the word beech and oak, I never *see*, so perhaps all my trees wrongheaded. Or is it the stream – a different kind of water? Or the corinna flowers of a different colour? I hurt inside because I fail in paint and will go back to being a field-hand. "Forgive me Massa, I know not what I do, I know not flower and tree and English scene," I whisper to him and leave.

Wait, wait, plot, persist! That is what I do. I take a stroll along the canal, through a meadow of corinnas, through rosebush and hibiscus, the perfume, the songbirds high up the sampan trees, and the water light up like sequins what sew on richfolk clothes, and I get spirit. I take up brush again to rouse Massa, and I do a lady, and God forgive my sinning, I paint her naked white and make her skin shine with ointment and give her gold hair and pretty-pretty small bubbies enough for a mouthful and tiny foot and wrap a rosary round her waist so the cross rest on her lap and cover her patacake. Oh the sinning, but I do it for *he*, not *me*. When I paint, I did not pant for her, only for the loving of the colours, oh the gold against white and the rosary of red beads!

I shake Massa, show him my work but he only snort and fall back to sleep. Is it the bubbies, is it the patacake, is it the waist too small, the foot too fine? How I to know, I never see whitelady naked before till I dream her upon canvas? I go back to the work. I paint her bubbies a rich pink and swell them and put in a blue vein that you can trace your tongue along till you reach the nipple and mountain-top from where to behold and survey the promised land. And more. I try to sweeten her, but how to paint a smell? In desperation I sprinkle sugargrains on the wet paint and rub it in with my naked hand, rub it between her legs and toes and around her hips and behind her ears and along her neck. I do it with love and so thorough; my fingers so linger and my eyes glaze, that if a whiteman walk in and catch me, is hang I hang – lash, pepper-skin and debowel first!

Massa look but not see, see but not look, for he gazing inward. Plus, overnight, rats eat up half the canvas (Oh how I long to stone them to death!), ants crawl over the paint, eat up the sugar and die right there when the paint dry, like pockmarks on the lady's face, like she get pox. Was it the rats and ants that let me down? Or was it the halo I paint round her head to make she into a saint, even though she naked-skin and plump with juice? Maybe I should have left the halo out and present her to Massa as a moll, muck and all, sprinkle her with cow-dung instead of sugar? How I to know?

I used to think me special, how Massa single me out for art and for his disciple, but now I feel like nobody, nobody special.

But wait, wait, victory will come, let me have one last try and thanksgiving for Massa's life, let me show him heaven. I take up brush but this time I will use the colour I know. I will daub the canvas black, then deepen the blackness with a final coat. Whilst it is still wet I will sprinkle charcoal powder over it. There is no technique, but I will say to Massa, "It is still beautiful." I will hold it up to him and say, "Behold black, behold the colour of heaven. Fear not your death for heaven is full of honey bees to sweeten your ears and mouth, and a thousand Miriams to do you virgin service, and a million Catos to ease you through eternity, for heaven is like Demerara, but more." I can't go wrong this time, for I know black, that is all I know and will ever know, but I don't care, for my work will set him free, make him die in peace, and his last word to me before he depart will be "Painterman".

Not to be. He dead without a word before he could see my invention. Gwan, gwan you mangy daag, I curse myself, chasing myself from his bedside, in my mind taking up a cudgel and wielding it over my own head to make my own foot flee faster back to being normal, nobody, even less, minus nothing.

PART TWO

"Liza! Liza! Come in from the dark right now before I strangle you," the mother called from the doorway of her makeshift home – wood, wattle and straw combined by extraordinary cunning to form a dwelling which, over the years, resisted wind and rain. There was no father. One night ruffians came and press-ganged him. The mother followed the captors to the ship begging for mercy but they flung the father onto the deck and took up a cudgel to beat her. All night she remained on the docks, crying out for one last sighting of her husband. Her vigil ended the next day, at noon, when the ship slipped its stays and set sail for another world.

Ships, captives, coarse men and foreign soil: Elizabeth's birthright and destiny. At twelve, she made her first money with a sailor from Poland, in the graveyard, underneath a row of rose bushes. She remembered being enveloped in perfume, and watching the fluted columns, cherubs and the ledgers of the tombs. It was graveyard reserved for aristocracy. Elizabeth resolved to become rich as soon as possible.

She presented the coin to her mother, and a rose which was a little bloodied, for she had dabbed her thighs with it. Her mother threw both to the ground, slapping her so hard that her skin was marked for days. A shrimp-seller her mother, poor as a church mouse and just as sheltered in the presence of altar and cross. A child and already a sinner, her mother shouted, searching the room for a whip before giving in to grief. All night she sobbed, clutching the child to her bosom, thought the child was already lost.

Elizabeth did not mind that the neighbours called her Papist and Jacobite. In fact clients were aroused to a higher degree when they learnt she was Catholic. Men three score or more found new strength, stretching, wrestling, contorting like fairground acro-bats, and at the peak of performance sinking their gums into her flesh. She took to older men for they left no teeth marks on her throat. (Her mother had beaten her when she had come home blemished.)

Her faith and tender age made her a fortune. She specialised in Jews, liking the brushstroke of their beards which she plucked, voided her rheum into, play-acting a child's anger at the lewd assaults. Afterwards they paid her a shilling more than the normal rate and hobbled off to be purified in their special home-wells.

It was such a Jew who accosted her as she moved around Exchange Alley seeking out custom. He singled her out in an area heaving with whores, bawling and gesticulating like stockjobbers. He stepped into the crowd and pulled her onto the pavement. She felt singled out, and resolved to give him a form of pleasure reserved for rare occasions, as when a ship arrived from abroad and its captain proffered a golden nugget. Neither its size nor its gleam mattered. She cherished the thought it had crossed many seas, from a distant land such as her father inhabited. Perhaps he was shackled and put to work in a mine, the nuggets discovered by his own hand. She would save them up to ransom him.

The Jew turned his face when she tiptoed to kiss him. He insisted on accompanying her home. Her mother screamed, crossed herself and hauled Elizabeth away. She boxed her twice, one for the blasphemy of the Jew's presence, the second for conspiring to – conspiring to – (she dared not name the word) in their bed. She raised her hand for a third blow but the Jew stopped her.

"Let her be, she is only a child," he said, the gentleness of his voice stilling her. He looked around the room, at the mattress on the floor, the bench, the bent spoons – everything tarnished but the Bible, its leather cover as bright as the rosary beads resting on it.

"She is a slut, she moves with thieves and tax collectors and –" The mother restrained her tongue from uttering "Jews" for the man before her was smiling kindly at her.

"She is only a child," he repeated. He said this so calmly and with such assurance that the mother wanted to believe him. "She commingles with sinners to distract her from sadness." The mother looked at the child as if for the first time. She went to hug

32

Elizabeth, remembering the tumult of emotions when she was born: the urge to cry, to pray, to praise God, to proclaim her wealth to the world; then, in panic, to hide the child away, to save it from abduction, from sickness, from venery. Elizabeth let herself be hugged, to please her mother and the Jew, who looked so benignly at her. Stupid man, she thought, for not wanting to be pleasured. And even more stupid for saying she needed to be distracted from sadness. She undressed for money, nothing more nor less.

"What do you want of her?" the mother asked, breaking his spell upon her, for he had by his calmness alone persuaded her that in the world outside her cell and sanctuary hurt could be salved, love flourish, the past be forgiven.

"I am in want of her," he said, his voice as composed as ever, hinting at no sin, no subterfuge.

The mother embraced Elizabeth to shield her from his charm.

"I am here to protect her and you. I have wandered the earth, guided by the light of stars and comets, and my journey has brought me here," the Jew said.

Elizabeth spent many hours musing upon the Jew's decision to keep her and her mother in comfort! Even more astonishing was her mother's quick agreement when he asked them to move into his own home; the *sudden* trust in him and betrayal of her religion, though not her marriage for they lived chastely with him. The *sudden* abduction of her father, the *sudden* appearance of the Jew: Elizabeth was perplexed. She decided that she must never-ever be caught unawares by men.

The issue of Jewishness soon faded, for he did not seek to convert them; on the contrary he was happy to see them attend church, furnishing them with shawls appropriate for the worship of their God, and money enough for the collection plate.

"Why are you letting us lodge with you? What do want from us?" Elizabeth asked him. Three weeks had passed; she could no longer suppress her uncertainty. Her mother simply accepted their good fortune but Elizabeth knew the value of money.

"Your mother cleans, washes, cooks to my taste – an indispensable housekeeper. And she still finds time to sell shrimps, and gives me her earnings."

"All that is a bit… you can afford a dozen servants! What more is there?"

The Jew looked at her eyes lit up with animosity and smiled. "It gives me pleasure teaching you, that is all. As soon as I saw you I sensed your brightness."

She was indeed, taking to letters as if they were long-lost family. She could read well within six months. He was delighted, too, at her adeptness with figures.

"You will be my apprentice," he said. "You will enter my profession of book-keeping, a modest but necessary one, for all things must be accounted for."

"But we do not add up, the three of us. We can never be the sum of you."

The stubbornness on her face was a child's. It quickened his heart to think that she could be restored to a childlike state.

Whenever he was away, attending to his clients or at the synagogue, Elizabeth would search his room for some clue to his identity, some hint, if not outright confirmation, of immorality. She found nothing to incriminate him. His workbooks were neatly lined. His papers were mostly pious. A few letters were in an unfamiliar script. Indeed his room was bare of ornamentation, the only property of worth being a Jewish silver candelabrum, and a painting which occupied the whole of a wall. It was peopled with men and women fleeing in all directions. There were fires everywhere; in the centre a huge one engulfed a golden calf. At the far edge of the painting stood a man, one hand outstretched, chasing away the crowd; the other hand clutched a tablet of stone which bore neat rows of writing, as if composed by a book-keeper. Elizabeth stared at the man, recognising in his beard, corrugated forehead and hirsute arms, the features of their Jew – except that the man in the picture was in a rage, so unlike their benefactor who was perpetually calm, no prank, no wilfulness on her part unsettling him. Perhaps the painted man was a portrait of their Jew when he was young, a man prone to cruelty, punishing people, destroying their goods, trading their children as trinkets for men's appetites. Was that why the Jew was keeping them in such comfort, as repentance for the deeds of a heartless youth? Was it the Jew who bought her father, then sold him afar

Hogarth: *Noon*

to be a slave? Folk said all Jews were mean, hoarding their lot, but their Jew seemed to be bent not on saving but on salvation.

He remained an enigma. She wanted to doubt his goodness but it overwhelmed her. He would come back from his clients or synagogue with toys, stopping at the market for a kite or doll or a new bonnet to protect her mother from the sun as she went about selling. "I am too grown for such," Elizabeth complained, throwing the doll to the floor, refusing to be trapped in child-hood. Still she took his offerings, surrendering to his kindness, accepting them as the tokens of a penitent.

A year passed under his supervision. She tired of his benevo-lence. When she turned fifteen she absconded. She missed making her own money, but more the excitement of wandering the alleyways at liberty, making her choice of clients, leading them to spaces she had marked out as her own: an abandoned calf-pen or the sheltered corners of churches which she did not mind sharing with gin-drinkers and tramps. They were too distracted by their own habits to interfere with her business.

Yes, the money mattered, but more exhilarating was the giving of her body in spaces free of surveillance.

And she could leave without guilt, knowing that the Jew would continue to maintain her mother. Could people be kind just for the sake of it? Could people be kind by nature, having no choice in their behaviour, just as she longed for sex? She asked these questions as she removed the graveyard stones under which her savings were buried. Three pounds, and three nuggets worth three pounds each; twelve pounds made in less than two years. If only she could show them to the Jew, then he could adore her even more for her industry! She giggled at the prospect of his beard stroking her neck.

A bundle of clothes, a pouch of coins and nuggets: she was well equipped for adventure. She took a boat to the east end of London, not paying, letting the boatman play with her breasts instead. His rubbing must have conjured up the devil, she thought, for when they moored a huge hand plucked her from the boat and placed her on land. She looked up to see a Negro, a grin stretched across his face like a scar. Bulging cheeks, forehead as flat as a mule's, teeth rotten, hair a carpenter's box of bent nails.

"I have been biding my time for you; what took you so long?" he asked in mild reproach. Without waiting for an answer he led her away. They walked past rows of houses – more rookeries than houses; straw, twigs, and urchins peeping out between gaps like abandoned chicks. She remembered her mother's first home and instinctively pulled her hand from his but he retrieved it, grasped it so tightly that she cried out in pain. "Cry, get accustomed to the noise of crying; it will make our fortune." His words frightened her but there was affection, even pity in his voice, so she let him master her.

She blanched at the sight of his house, a mud and wattle structure leaning towards the ground, certain to topple but for six or so wooden piles organised like crutches along one wall. Her anxiety vanished when she stepped inside. She had never before witnessed such opulence.

"The haul of a year's burglaries, mostly," he said, anticipating her question. "The rest I furnished on credit. I have sold my body in advance of the next ship sailing to Demerara, where I will be a slave. Twelve pounds in all."

"I have twelve pounds, I can redeem you," she said immediately, before wondering at her generosity. Perhaps she *was* kind by nature, like the Jew.

"The ship departs in three months, so there's little time to prepare you for the future," he said, not heeding her offer. "Hurry, set down your belongings, let me bathe you." He led her to the tub.

"I am not a child, I can cleanse myself," she protested, but he undressed her, lifted her into the tub. Quickly he rubbed soap over her body, not hesitating at her breasts and thighs.

"I am Muslim, I was captured in the Niger valley and sold to the Yoruba nation. The Arabs came and took me in a coffle to the coast, where Spaniards bought me to ship me to Brazil, but an Englishman intervened, offered a good price." He paused only to wipe his face and helped her out of the tub.

He towelled her, hurrying on with his story to prevent her speaking.

"I ran away from my master soon after we landed in London. I sought out the company of Catholics, for my master and his friends would often curse them at their dinner-table, calling them 'slaves to religion'. Catholics took me in, took pity on me, taught me to read, baptised me, named me after St Francis of Assisi – birds were always keeping company with me. Wherever I went pigeons would follow, martins and swallows took grain from my hand, even the thrush would drop its caution and hop to me for a treat. The Catholics gave me a choice begging spot, outside White's Tavern. I gained enough money to rent a stall selling shawls but some Anglican Mohawks burnt it down, stoning the church nearby for good measure. I became a tailor but there were so many touting the trade that I needed to specialise. I went after fat folk, learning how best to cut the cloth and place the buttons to flatter them, how to compensate for a hefty neck or Hottentot-sized buttocks. But let me dress you, let us eat. So much to do in such a short time."

Elizabeth was so overwhelmed that she let him lace, stay and stocking her, and showed no surprise when before eating his plate of stew, he closed eyes and uttered "*Pater noster, qui es in caelis…* That is the Catholic tongue, as antique as Jesu self," he explained. He crossed himself. She did the same, involuntarily.

Madness! Unreality! Lunatics let out of Bedlam for the day wandered the alleyways where she used to tout for business, so she was accustomed to their antics. Many were afflicted by religiosity, speaking in tongues, writhing on the ground. She was convinced that the Negro was of their kind, but, out of the prospect of adventure, she surrendered to his will.

He took her a short distance from their abode to a square bordered by rows of dilapidated stalls, a tavern and a park of corinna flowers, the grass a green suit buttoned by daisies. Beggars were stationed beside the stalls, hoping for a portion of change from satisfied customers. "Change," he said heavily but refused to yield to self-pity, recovering in an instant. He sat her on a makeshift bench, grasping her with a steadfast hand, gazing at her with eyes that mesmerised her as he finished his tale.

"Yes, changes in the land as I was taken to the Afric coast. Oh such passing strange sights! I have seen enough deserts, quarries and hills whose heads touch heaven to inspire verse as bewitching as the *Song of Solomon*, but I will not woo your ears with such. I changed because of a simple pinprick, a tailor's everyday hazard, but this one was uncommon. The droplet of blood was as bright as a star. I licked my thumb but the blood kept flowing, down my cheeks, neck, waist, calves, buttocks, my whole body, a Negro turned red, an aberrance of nature. Something monstrous in me was born. I threatened to haemorrhage the earth, I threatened miscarriages, murderation. The priest heard my confession, but his absolution did not stem the flood. Of course it was all a dream, but the white dove was real, appearing from nowhere, making a nest in the eaves of my tailor-shop. There was a rainbow that very day. I gave up my shop to wait at the harbour. Such a long wait until the ark appeared bearing you."

"How did you know I was the one to be singled out?" she asked when at last she found her tongue.

Like the Jew, Francis gave no answer, turning away to look at the crowd gathering for their dusk revelries.

"Wait, wait, watch," he said stroking her chin. "When you grow up you will be free."

"I am already grown and I am not bound to anyone," she objected, but was stilled by his glittering eye.

"Watch, watch, tell me what you see," he said.

The square was a stew of whores, bruises plastered over, some wearing powder and patches to hide the pox but their faces looking sickly all the same.

"You see disease, not so? Look at that woman of meagre and milkless breasts, she feeds her infant gin instead. See the dogs approaching the urchin drunk in sleep – or dead – at her feet. They will pounce, drag the urchin into the park, devour it there, and who will protest? Not the men in lace leading their whores into the park. They will not hear, much less heed, the child's screams, for their own whores would be set a-bawling and a-howling from blows and bloodlust."

Elizabeth saw the sons of the aristocracy strolling into the park, caressing the gilt heads of their canes. They emerged with a smirk on their faces and women in their wake begging to be paid what was promised.

"So many child-whores, too, younger than you," he said, pointing to a gaggle running up to a client, unbuttoning their blouses to give him choice, pushing each other out of the way. Elizabeth remained silent, unsure as to whether Francis was chiding her or expressing care for the children.

"Tell me, what do you see before you?" he asked again, squeezing her hand in encouragement.

"Rakes, dogs, drunks, dirty sluts –"

"Jesu saw otherwise," he interrupted. "If you move the mote from your eyes, you too will see the yearning in their hearts for goodness. Even the rich who seem to wear vicious looks are in want of Him. They crucified Him, each hammer-blow their crying out for forgiveness. But come away, it is late, I will tutor you another time."

★　★　★

He combed her hair in preparation for bed, loosening knots, patting oil into the dent of her head. His hands were persistent; it was futile to resist. He removed her frock, replaced it with a nightdress obviously chosen with care, for it was of cotton softly textured but thick enough to protect her from chill. "The room is unfamiliar and you will be afraid of the dark. I will keep the candles lit, and when you are asleep, I will come back and put them out. Now close your eyes whilst I pray over you." She did as he commanded. He cleared his throat and then broke into prayer in the same alien tongue: *"Ave Maria gratia plena…"*

"Amen" she said, to please him, even as she began to resent her acquiescence to him, a complete stranger, a foreigner. Many shop-signs in London bore images of Negroes: "The Moor's Tobacco Shop", "The Moor's Head", "The Blackamoor's Brandy Shop". The painted Negroes held up sheaves of tobacco, bottles of liquor, sugar loaves and other goods shipped from across the seas. They grinned stupidly; most were half-naked. When she misbehaved with men, her mother would drag her to one of these images, threatening to banish her to the habitation of savages. She pretended to be horrified, knowing that the figures were of mere paint and fixed securely to the signposts which bore them. Francis, though, by some pact with the Devil, had freed himself from paint, stepped off from the signpost, taking flesh onto himself, and speech. Suddenly she was afraid of him. She dared not sleep. She stared at the silver candelabrum, the tapestry of the Madonna, the vases, the porcelain washbowl, the gilt-framed mirror, the mahogany chairs, convinced that they were not a burglar's haul but that he must have made a pact with the Devil, slaved his soul for a Judas sum.

The breakfast table was a feast of food fit for the aristocracy. Before she ate, there was prayer and praise.

"Your golden tresses are already an adornment; rare perfume and jewellery will enhance your majesty." He unlocked two boxes, offering gifts. "Demerara gold," he said, securing a chain around her neck. He uncorked a bottle, dabbed a drop on her forehead. "More fragrant than myrrh, an infusion of uncommon barks."

Once more she was overcome by fright. "What black magic are you practising on me?" She began to cry, wiping her forehead clean and trying to remove the chain but the lock was stubborn.

"Be still and know that I am of God," he said, his sternness yet again subduing her. His voice softened as he wiped away her tear. "It is true that once upon a time I indulged in pagan ceremonies but the jumbie-bead chain decorating my neck is now a rosary. It was Jesu who truly captured me. The slave-coffle was a new congregation and when we reached the coast and sighted sea for the first time in our lives, a song escaped our mouths, like the Magnificat. At the time I was a child, innocent of the true meaning of my captivity. Praise be to the Catholics for removing the mote from my eyes, and teaching me Scripture." He paused, recalling the moment the priest had anointed his own forehead, confirming his belonging to a new faith, a new family.

★　★　★

Six dusks passed watching the world of square and park before he decided she was ready. "A lustful Negro is a fearsome creature and can bring ruin to all of creation," he said, the words flowing smoothly as if he had meditated upon them, rehearsed them as part of a daily prayer. "Praise be to the Catholics who cured me of man-love."

He pressed his hand to his heart to stop its wild beating. She fetched him water. He refused it. "I am already saved, it is my mission to serve you, not you me," he said, looking approvingly at the dress he had prepared for her first outing. "Jesu came to save all mankind, but today we will retrieve a handful, for our means are few." He looked at the cabinet, at the vials containing ointments he had made from herbs blended with juices of cherry, grape, and pear. No African herbs or fruit were available; he had had to compromise.

He was certain of Elizabeth's capacity; if the project failed it would be his fault. A doleful look replaced his grin. She was alarmed on his behalf. In the week's sojourn all he had done was to grin and beam at her, oftentimes his eyes bulging from their sockets when he talked about his conversion to Christ. She listened, not hearing, practised as she was in enduring her mother's zealotry.

"You and my mother would make a right brace of apostles," she said, wanting to tickle his spirit, but his mood darkened. She loosened her shoulder-strap, exposing a breast for his delectation, an instinctive act which always worked with clients who came to her weighed down with cares – an expensive wife, a bullying employer – then departed in peace. Francis turned his face from her. She suddenly understood his previous talk of being cured of man-love, which she had thought was his Negro way of saying "mankind" – that the Catholics had cleansed him from the sins of mankind or at least the Negro part of them.

"It is a man's stubble-thorns tickling your skin or beard stroking your flesh, like the Roman spear scouring Jesu's body, pausing to prod here, there, for the sweetest point of entry," she said. "That is what torments you."

Francis clutched the chair-handle to steady himself. He sat down heavily.

"Fear not, I am come to fulfil the Scriptures," she said, instinctively, having been breastfed in her mother's faith, knowing its phraseology as naturally as a nipple.

"You are truly the daughter of God," he said, rising from the chair, crossing himself, kneeling at her feet. He remained there, the space cloistered and dark enough for confession. In the shop he had once served in, the shawls he tried out on women's shoulders, knotting them at their breasts, were holy garments, he said. The act of fitting out the women was a holy act, causing him no excitement. It was tailoring which was his trial. The men stripped. He measured them, neck to crotch, nape to buttocks, waist to ankle. It was in a daydream of such fleshy parts that the needle pierced his thumb, bringing forth a droplet of blood bright as a star. "Oh the horror! Only I could save my soul. Right away I went to the synagogue by Exchange Alley. Cut me, I said to the Jew. The Jew was taken aback. I told him I was already black; that, as in the Old Testament – I quoted Isaiah and Psalms – he should make a eunuch of me. The Jew was taken aback a second time, wondering how a Negro could be versed in his holy book, but instinctively he took my money and performed the deed."

Elizabeth pitied him, a Negro *sans* the consolation of home, *sans* the wherewithal to replicate family in a foreign land. She consented to his scheme, desperate as it was. Francis's role was to lure men to their abode, eunuch leading sodomite to the boudoir which was fitted out like a room in a luxurious seraglio. The sodomite would be startled to find her there, stretched out on a sofa, cossetted by pillows, naked but for a rosary round her waist, its cross covering the entrance to paradise. Before he could exclaim and make to exit, Francis would cuff him and clap an iron muzzle on his mouth, one of its features a device which pressed down on the tongue, preventing speech. An iron fetter secured his feet. "Saved from Africa days," Francis explained, his eyes threatening to slip their moorings, so excited was he. When Massa brought Francis to London, he had placed him in irons for six days, to season him for his new duties. On the seventh day, he was unfastened, and as soon as Massa went to rest Francis took to his heels with a haul of silver spoons and a vase for sale. He kept the irons to remind him of his pledge to find a passage back to his village as soon as feasible. "But for Jesu I would have gone back to cavorting with savages," he said, addressing the sodomite, checking that the lock was in place. The prologue done, the play began; to Elizabeth's mind a play, but to Francis a solemn ritual. He deliberated upon the Bible before opening it at the Book of Genesis and reading aloud verses on the destruction of Sodom and Gomorrah. There was a minute's respectful silence. The sodomite squirmed. Such was the tension that sweat formed on Elizabeth's brow, though the air was cool, it being a Spring afternoon. Francis replaced the Bible on the shelf, covering it with a white cloth. He reached for the birch resting on the same shelf and for his fob-watch. A full nineteen minutes of frontal flagellation followed; the sodomite was commanded to gaze upon Elizabeth before each lash. She worried for his pain and parted her thighs to let him glimpse the passage to paradise but the sodomite would not be salved, looking instead into Francis's eyes, daring him to persist with the punishment. Francis turned him around, made him lean against the wall, unleashed his righteous wrath upon him, resting the whip only when the sodomite began to sag. Francis made him face Elizabeth again. She fondled herself and smiled, but the sodomite still would not be seduced. It was only when she turned into arabesque pose, offering her back, that a squeak escaped his mouth, defying the device on his tongue. Francis wiped away his sweat and grinned. He rested on the sofa beside her, so panting from his exertion that Elizabeth could hear his heart thumping. The veins on his forearm were excited with blood. He checked his fob-watch: thirty-one minutes in all.

"Are you done? Shall we unshackle him?" she asked, pitying the sodomite.

"There is one more act to perform," Francis said, rising to his feet. In one motion he lifted the sodomite up and placed him on the sofa, with the same ease that he had plucked Elizabeth from the boat. The last rite was the grieving and the anointment, with Elizabeth weeping over the sodomite, dabbing his brow with a special handkerchief whilst applying the contents of Francis's vials to the groin, slowly, purposefully. By the end of the second vial the man was fully risen, taking the handkerchief from Elizabeth and dabbing her own sweat, his eyes grateful, deliquescent, his mouth wanting to call out her name in reverence.

Afterwards the three of them took tea, sitting around the table, sipping, saying nothing. Francis was a master at stewing leaves, adding different quantities of sugar depending on whether it was bohea or green. The sodomite stood up, straightened his wig and brushed a dead fly from his coat, reasserting his dignity. He found his purse, extracted a generous sum. Francis cupped his hand to receive it, a delicate motion, like the unfolding of a corinna flower at dawn. All passion and sweat spent, Francis was now a nosegay. The sodomite bowed, turned, and attempted a dignified exit but his legs buckled, Francis having to support him to the door.

"Did it work? Is he cured?" Elizabeth asked as Francis poured more tea. He did not answer, sitting heavily in his chair stirring, stirring his cup but not spilling a drop, for Francis, even in reverie, knew the value of things, sixteen shillings for an ounce of tea, three for sugar, a spoonful lost by spillage therefore seven pence. An ounce of tea contained forty-seven leaves, an ounce of sugar ninety-eight grains. In an idle hour he had counted out each grain.

"Approximately," he said, coming to his senses. "There is no exact science on the subject of repentance; 'more or less' or 'nearly' is the best we can achieve."

"Is he nearly, more or less, approximately, cured then?" Elizabeth asked, resentful of his constant disregard of her opinions and enquiries. He studied her golden tresses, her fledgling breasts, her tiny feet, her body on the cusp of transformation. His sense of duty returned. He went to fetch a shawl to cover her.

Weeks of Bible-reading, berating and birching followed; the original sodomite brought his friends. News spread about their specialisation. Men forsook the dens they frequented – London teemed with houses catering for every taste – from bondage to bestiality – and flocked to theirs. The new clients included a duke, seven members of parliament, two prelates, the odd puisne judge. There was always tea afterwards and the fee received in the calyx of Francis's palm. He dominated any conversation that arose. They expected nonsense or piffle from his mouth, he being a blackamoor. They were startled by his erudition, for Francis read the *Craftsman* and *Gentlemen's Magazine* regularly. His persistent theme was the fate of Africans. The whip wore them down but even more his arguments, quoting from an array of sources – from the Bible to Adam Smith – to prove the iniquity of the slave trade. When the first reading of a bill to abolish the trade took place, the two bishops and seven parliamentarians voted in favour, not a single abstention, for they regarded Francis with fear and gratitude. "We will solicit help from our friends in the House of Lords to promote the Bill," they told him, and they were true to their promise, membership to the cause swelling in numbers.

★ ★ ★

It was not the sexual nature of the ceremonies which caused their downfall but Francis's loose tongue; his persistent pimping for the cause of Abolition. He still relished the use of whip, restraints and ointments, but true relief only came for him in tea-table talk. Dangerous talk! Parliament was in the control of merchants and planters who were liberal with their bribes. Even by Francis's reckoning, the end of the slave trade would deprive such men of fifty thousand pounds a year. It was dangerous folly to make enemies of them. Still, Francis persisted; persistence was a Catholic habit ("perseverance" they called it) enabling them to survive two centuries of English wrath, but in Francis's case it led to a swift prosecution.

"You used to say 'Wait, wait, freedom will come,' but look at you!" Elizabeth was visiting him in the Fleet prison. The magistrate had sentenced him to seven years' hard labour. Her breasts and child's gurgle as the magistrate fondled them had won *her* reprieve. Seven nights of frolicking for free, the further inducement of the rosary worn around her waist and the protective crucifix (the magistrate had insisted on these, spurning her bribe of the silver candelabrum, though worth two pounds) had gained Francis his own prison cell and promise of fresh straw. He could also be manacled with his own iron implements brought from Africa.

"I am in truth guilty for your fall from grace," he said, his voice flat. "I could have led you along another path." He scratched his skin, brushing off invisible lice. A sudden commotion in the prison courtyard interrupted their conversation. A rat had entered. Some prisoners had blocked its escape. They pelted it. In fright it turned to leap at them, but before it could, a well-aimed stone broke its skull.

"It was not your doing. There was no other path. I was born to my profession. You hoped to use my body for sacred purposes, to

46

save a few befouled sodomite souls and to free your Negro countrymen from slavery. Mr Eliston was my undoing," she sighed.

It was his turn to be forgiving. "Mr Eliston could not be foreseen; you are without sin," he said.

She knew otherwise. Mr Eliston had been their most lucrative client, coming practically every day for curing. He was of slender figure, fine-boned, daintily dressed, face powdered and perfumed. He was all pouting and curtsies and flourish of limp wrists, peeling off his gloves and kissing them before placing them in his pocket. To begin with she treated him like any other sodomite. She stretched, opened her thighs, turned on her back, wept over him, wiped his brow with a handkerchief embroidered with St Veronica's name. It may have been at his sixth or seventh visit that she began to soften towards him. Why, she knew not. He was unctuous, sickly, weak of mind, vulnerable. He would buckle at the first threat, at the first temptation. He was all of these, but more. She sensed a serpent within him as natural to him as harlotry was to her; a serpent all the more dangerous because it resided in his heart, not his loins. Francis's ceremony gave him no pleasure; the serpent slept. Its threat and temptation: it was Elizabeth who yielded to both. As Eliston lay beside her for anointment, she reached for his hand, let it brush aside the crucifix, let his long delicate fingers move within like a playful octopus, suddenly turning into a serpent, spitting, baring its teeth. Quickly she withdrew his hand before Francis could sense her excitement but he was too engrossed with putting away his prized irons to notice. The serpent, aroused, acted swiftly. That very night, Mr Eliston came with constables, a magistrate, and an affidavit from a merchant in the West India trade claiming to be a victim of their fraud. Francis was taken to the Fleet prison, Elizabeth to the magistrate's bed. He, having examined her juvenescence, pronounced her innocent. It was all so sudden, their downfall. She should have anticipated it. More than the money, she missed the mischief of their pantomime, tantalising the men with her beads and crucifix and vulnerable breasts, being thrilled by their worship of her, like the golden calf in the Jew's painting.

"Go to Demerara, continue my mission there," Francis pleaded. "The colony is new but already ripe with sin." He was so excited that his speech was reduced to short bursts. He told of the African slave population, mostly male, forced to seek pleasure with each other, even with lambs. He crossed himself as he pictured the abomination in the canefields, broke into a hymn:

> *I thirst, thou wounded Lamb of God*
> *To wash me in thy cleansing blood*

"So much sin and me in shackles!" he lamented. "And proper tropical herbs too, not my substitutes. The herbs there will certainly cure. You must be my missionary. Cure them, preach freedom. Ruin the colony. Bring Mr Eliston to penury; he has investments in many plantations."

She sold the contents of the house, gathered her money and set sail for Demerara. It was because Francis besought it, but she did it also for the adventure; the spirit which made her escape the conformity of her mother's and then the Jew's households and made her arouse the serpent in Eliston. She had thought of going to her mother, but her farewell gift of money would be dashed to the floor, then a flurry of blows to her head. No, she would return a year later with gold which her mother would accept as acquired by fair means: Demerara was on everyone's tongue because huge quantities of gold were recently discovered and there was a rush into the colony.

Getting a berth was easy though the ship was crammed with migrants seeking their fortune. She merely presented herself to the captain, twirling her golden locks and putting on a face of shyness as she bargained with him: free passage in return for potential access to her. The captain took her to be a daughter of the aristocracy. Mingling with royalty, episcopacy and the Law had made her into such. Her dress, her speech, her manners had a certain quality, impossible to define, which marked her out from the lesser breeds. And there was her freshness of face, roseate skin, delicate frame. The captain surrendered his cabin to her. She never complied with his wants, making excuses, feigning illness or merely staring at him, identifying him as a commoner – wealthy, wielding authority, but still low-bred, unworthy of her favours.

"But you promised," he groaned.

"You took advantage of my youth. You deemed me to be an immature, heartbroken girl escaping the anger of her parents, eloping to Demerara to meet her lover, no doubt a man of your age and society, who had gone in advance to prepare for my coming. In the meantime you would try to seduce me, debauch me!"

The captain realised he was in the presence of a vixen. Visions of being set upon by constables beset him.

She hoped for tempests, sea-monsters and pirates but the voyage was uneventful. She sought out a victim among the passengers, settling on a man whose corpulence, from afar, suggested a surfeit of wealth. She went to converse with him but his wife appeared and led him to a quiet corner of the deck. Elizabeth was relieved: close to him she had noticed a button missing on his coat. He was soaked in sweat. His eyes were sorrowful. His fat was unhealthy, unlike that of the grandees she kept company with, plump from birth in preparation for authority. His wife appeared sickly, too, in need of his supporting arm. They kept to themselves for the duration of the journey, dwelling on their own thoughts, for hardly a word passed between them.

Flying-fish, gulls, and a carnival of dolphins signalled nearness to land. She arrived at Georgetown port in the pink of condition. Black hands helped her to shore, to a coach, to an inn appropriate to her class. She tipped them extravagantly, in Francis's honour. At supper she avoided fellowship, sitting alone and distracting herself by the strange creole victuals on her plate. She stood up to depart for bed. The room was crowded but her eyes alighted on a man sitting by himself at its far end. She felt faint. She leant on the edge of the table to steady herself, but slipped. Hands rushed to redeem her from the ground. When she awoke Dr Gladstone was at her bedside, fanning her, wetting her lips with tea which even in her weak state she recognised as bohea.

"Before you fainted you called out 'father'," he said, propping her up with pillows, ordering a slave-boy to fetch more tea.

"I need to drink much of it. Tea animates the faculties, keeps up the vigour of the spirits, expels the cloudy vapours that darken meditation," she said.

Dr Gladstone was overwhelmed by the choiceness of her diction. A month later he married her.

A year later he was dead. Elizabeth mourned for a respectable period, then shed her weeds. Her inheritance made her wealthy beyond expectation – fair compensation for Dr Gladstone not being her father. The resemblance was uncanny, from what she remembered of her father's face, but the doctor's accent betrayed his Scottishness. Her heart had slumped at his first words. She had drawn the sheet over her head, buried herself in the pillows and sobbed. When she recovered, she had sipped the tea, turned her face away, and looked distant, for she would not betray her anger at his solicitude, his gesture at fatherhood. But far from home, with limited means, she needed the protection of a parent and benefactor. She would tolerate his Scottish speech, barbarous as it was, kindly words meant to soothe her but uttered in rasps and burrs. Such was the nature of the language, he was not to blame.

Her anger, however, did not abate. After marriage she gave him a week's comfort, then moved to another bedroom, deaf to his entreaties. At the dining table, he would tell her stories of his upbringing – the glen, cairns, ceilidhs, cattle, peat-bogs, vandals (English) – but they bored her. As a Catholic, she knew the language of victimhood. Nor was she impressed by his rise from the peasantry to the profession of a physician; she too had elevated herself by unwearied application. He was probably only modestly qualified, a degree or so above a quack, for why else did he end up in the nether region of Demerara instead of in the heart of Edinburgh?

Twenty or so years of frugal living in the colony meant that he had amassed a fortune, not only from the sale of medicine but from investments in a slave-estate. He had spent only a minuscule part of it on relief with Negresses. The rest was destined for her. She never enquired of him why he had never taken a wife. She presumed it was out of meanness and reluctance to be distracted from moneymaking. But the allure of her body and

Hogarth: *The Rake's Progress*, plate 1

speech put an end to his frugal instincts. Two decades and more in advance of her age, he turned rake overnight; shoes with silver buckles, tunics, coats, ornate belts, breeches of the finest cloth, cravats, wigs, watches, handkerchiefs, powders and pomade adorned his body. He took to dice and cockfighting. He bought fashionable paintings, shipped from Italy. Such a show of connoisseurship failed to awe her. As soon as he opened his mouth he was a philistine again. She pressed her hands to her ears to soften the Scottish burr.

Six months into the marriage he was a broken man. He longed to taste her sweetness again, raking over the memory of their honeymoon. He went mad thinking of the cornucopia of promises she had made on the marriage bed. He wilted, refusing to rise from his bed, turning away food. "Physician, heal yourself," she taunted. She waited for a respectable period before dispatching him with poison, her accomplice a young slave to whom she granted her favours.

Oh the prospect of a carefree life! Oh to be a merry widow! She gave her Negro lover Dr Gladstone's clothes. She avoided any attachment to him, not bothering even to discover his name, summoning him to bed only when the urge took her. At the slightest hint of scandal she would sell him and acquire another. In the meantime he presided over the nightly soirées she held for her new companions – the colonial officials, planters, fortune-hunters. She cultivated their desires with sighs, suggestive looks, exposed shoulders, loose hair-ribbons, and the flouncing of her golden locks. They plied her with gifts of money – for which she had no use. Tempting them sufficed her need for mental pleasures. It whetted her appetite for the Negro's exertions.

A perfect life, attended by slaves and suitors, but she found herself wondering what lay beyond the boundaries of the city, a curiosity that turned into a craving. Her Negro organised expeditions into the jungle, a party of a dozen or so adventurers sailing upriver to a suitable clearing and setting up camp. In the morning she shot a deer, in the afternoon a labba, minor triumphs which gained great applause from the men who were more experienced with the gun, dispatching before nightfall seven bush-hogs, six parrots, five kingfishers, four anteaters, three armadillos, two squirrel monkeys and a cockatoo in a pear tree, none of which they retrieved, for the slaves had brought cured meats for their repast. She fell asleep but only after many hours of wakefulness, even though her Negro, having first sweated her (her flesh red and black and blue with the dyes of his lust, as in a Titian painting), was guarding the tent from snake and scorpion.

The thrill of seeing birds stopped in flight waned. At first it was a spectacle for the birds were full of colour but when they fell from the sky they looked like Easter kites when their strings broke. She winced at the childhood memory of climbing trees or wading through gutters to retrieve kites, then restringing them, selling them to hawkers for a penny or two, enough for a handful of shrimps for that day's meal. She suppressed the memory, ended the expeditions.

The craving for…? She knew not what, but it persisted. She fed it as if it were a wild animal, warily, from afar, flinging meat to it, ready to club it to death should it rear up at her. She gave it to another Negro to create tension with the original, which resulted in fistfights. The violence was not sufficient. She gave it to a planter, a magistrate, a tailor, an English tar, a foreign tar, folk from high-life, folk from low, but this gamut still did not satisfy. She sought refuge in prayer, resolving to fulfil her promise to Francis to become a liberator of slaves. Once free, she would wean them off their passion for field animals. She was in the midst of buying bibles when salvation came. It was the fat man's doing, her fellow passenger on the ship to Demerara. His sickly wife had died, a month before his promotion from overseer to manager. If only his wife had lived to share his good fortune! His elevation, so long sought after, held no joy. He blamed the slaves for breeding the disease which killed her. They lacked hygiene, not washing their hands and defecating everywhere, even in the corners of their huts. He took revenge, relieved his grief by reducing their rations, extending their work hours, whipping them on a whim. They rebelled, burned down the Great House and the factory. The fat man fled. The soldiery shot twenty slaves. The rebellion spread, reaching Elizabeth's region. Her two Negro favourites remained steadfast, though the rest of the household ran away into the jungle. The two took her to the safety of a ship bound for England. They scrubbed and disinfected her quarters to expel the stench of nigger sweat, for the ship had just discharged its cargo. Sugar was loaded into the hold. By the time it reached London she was sure the aroma would have soaked into her skin. She would step on land like a perfumed vapour and, adorned with the gold of El Dorado, would inspire gasps and startled looks from all those who came to greet the ship.

★　★　★

Three years had passed. Her mother had begun to come to terms with her loss, thinking Elizabeth (given the company she kept) to have been a victim of rape and murder. She was overjoyed at her daughter's homecoming. The Jew squeezed her so tightly that she feared for her bones. They stayed up all night as Elizabeth fabricated her adventures in Demerara, telling how she had borrowed money and purchased a cheap plot of land at the edge of the river; how she kicked over some stones and found gold nuggets; how she sold the plot for a huge profit; how she spent the rest of her stay wandering through the colony, searching for her father, until she came across his grave, coconut and cuckrit trees encroaching on it, many choked with vines; how she paid for a new headstone, the clearing of vines, the felling of trees, the planting of flowers, converting the desolate spot into a scented garden.

Her mother wept. Elizabeth continued, telling of how the moneylender in Demerara, by whose kindness she was able to purchase the plot of land, had been cheated by clients, had gone to London in pursuit of them, but was now penniless and languishing in the Fleet prison. "We must save him, we must bring him into our family," Elizabeth said. Her mother nodded, wept freshly. At the height of her sorrow, when she was at her weakest, Elizabeth said, "He is a Negro." And just in case horror at his blackness restored her mother to her senses, she added, "a Catholic, chaste of heart, christened and named after St Francis no less. And such devotion to the Lord that his massa set him free in Demerara, with an allowance too! To think he lent me all he was worth in the world to buy my plot of land…"

The new family: mother, daughter, Negro, with the Jew as

patriarch. Prison had broken Francis. The magistrate had reneged on his promise of fresh supplies of clean straw and a cell to himself. Francis had been bundled together with lunatics, killers. Years of abuse had followed.

Now he hardly spoke, preferring to coo to the pigeons Elizabeth bought him, spending all his time cleaning their cages, feeding them seeds soaked in a special preparation of oil stored in vials Elizabeth had inherited from Dr Gladstone (she had kept only the silver ones). At dusk he secured the roost with a padlock and chain from his African days.

The new family had enough money to live happily ever after. Elizabeth went out each morning with her mother to buy shrimps, which were donated to orphanages, alms-houses. The habit of walking with a basket on her head remained with the mother in spite of their changed fortune. In the afternoon, Elizabeth swept the house before setting out to buy fresh straw for Francis (prison had deprived him of the idea of the comfort of a bed). At night she sat quietly beside the Jew, watching him tally the day's expenses, another unbroken habit.

Shrimps, straw, broom, ledger-book… Boredom set in, against her best efforts. On her way to buy provisions for Francis, she found her feet taking her in another direction, towards the square and park. The corinna flowers were blushful as ever, the grass buttoned with daisies. A man was attempting to gather some of the corinna. He did so with clumsy hands and when he stooped, he threatened to topple over. She rushed to steady him, not for his sake but to stop him crushing the flowers.

"Fatman," she gasped.

He turned to thank her. His eyes were milky like a snake's, unseeing; he leaned close to her face but seemed not to recognise her.

"My wife," he said, pointing to the flowers. "She was as dainty as these. Tell me, what colours are they? I can only scent them." She began to describe the flowers but Fatman interrupted. "Is it Sunday? Is it afternoon? I only come on Sundays, at specific hours, to remember her."

"I am your wife," Elizabeth said on impulse, squeezing his hand to reassure him.

"My wife? You are my wife? But she is dead; is that not the

truth? They told me she was dead. Did I not bury her myself under an olive tree in Demerara?" He leaned again as if to study her face.

"I am your wife and full of life, you foolish man!" she said, her voice playful in spite of the pity in her heart.

"Yes, yes, so you are" he said. "What did I just say? Was I speaking? Oh the sweetness! Can you sense it?" A breeze had ruffled the flowers, releasing more perfume. "What did I ask? Am I here or in that frightful place?"

"Come," she said, letting him lean on her arm. "Soon it will be dark; we must go home." It was a *sudden* offer. In the past suddenness had broken, but also profited her. She would take a gamble with Fatman. Perhaps he would end up in true companionship with her mother. Or perhaps Francis would become her mother's paramour (assuming the Jew had not already claimed her, in spite of his persona of chastity).

Jew, Negro, Fatman (mind wrecked, sight gone), mother and daughter (pretending to be Fatman's wife to stop his babbling). Happily ever after. Happily ever after.

Elizabeth escaped to the docks from which her father had been wrenched. Every day she spent a solitary hour watching the ships come and go. She relished the memory of Demerara. It saved her from the boredom of happiness and family. Above the clamour of sailors and stevedores she heard the call of the colony – gunshots breaking the silence of the jungle; screeches and croaks as birds dropped; grunts, sobs, sighs, hollers, as slaves made love or felt the whip; the noises fermenting and distilling in the heat, making sounds so strong that she could smell them: the stink and aroma of a Demerara ship; no, stronger, more like the stink of cannibals. She craved to express the call of Demerara, but could not. It was as if she had so devoured its heart and drunk herself to senselessness on the darkness of the place that a fusillade of hunting guns could not awaken her to word.

PART THREE

1

Lady Elizabeth came into our lives like a perfumed vapour, misting the eyes of my massa, through which he dreamt the treasury of El Dorado. Not that my massa, Dr Gladstone, was a man of need, for he was the inheritor of his father's fortune in Scotland – a tea merchant – and instead of lavishing it on porcelain, paintings and the pursuits of Priapus, he had trained as a surgeon – years of ascetic study – and as soon as he was certified by the Royal College, he abandoned Edinburgh for Demerara, his only motive being pity. I was a child of eleven when he bought me. I know because he tallied my teeth and told me: "You are eleven, young Francis," not only giving my age but also my name, for before I had answered other massas when they shouted out "boy". I marvelled at his cleverness in accounting for me by a mere examination of my mouth, and the name Francis had a kindness to it, so I resolved, even with a mind as yet untutored in the discipline of loyalty, to behave as the son of Dr Glad One, for that is what the niggers whom we moved among called him. "Dr Glad One, tek look at me jigger-foot, Jesu go bless you plenty-plenty"; "Dr Glad One, me belly like it breed worm, please for a syrup." They displayed their cuts, bruises and swollen parts, and he reached into his bag (which it was my proud duty to hold, following him through the canefield) for ointments, vials of liquids and plasters. He dispensed his medicines, not only identifying each but naming each nigger first: "Billy, this is a tincture of veronica, it will increase the celerity of the blood's motion", or, "Cato, this liquor, an infusion of hartshorn and copperas, will strengthen the head and stomach." None of them understood, but such was the mellifluousness of his speech, and the novelty of hearing their names, that they swallowed whatever he gave and seemed to be cured at once. We left the canefield to their singing as they slashed away with cutlasses:

> *Hey-ho-day! Me no care a dammee*
> *is rock me rock in de arm o' mammee.*

It was as if Dr Gladstone had lifted from their minds the burden of work, the bundles of cane that they hoisted on their shoulders to carry to the mule-punt, like the lepers cured and carrying their pallets behind Christ on the path to Gethsemane. Dr Glad One was like Jesu to me; he died when I was eighteen, the seven years in his presence like seven days, too-too brief, but still he had made of me a new world in that time.

Lady Elizabeth, too, came into his life only for a short while, a mere year or so, and also created of him a new world.

I was asleep, dreaming of the scent of sugarcane. I opened the door to a timid knocking, thinking it to be yet another slave in distress, only to be overwhelmed by Lady Elizabeth's presence. A perfumed and gilded vapour! El Dorado self! She wore a sleeveless white dress embroidered with gold-coloured thread, which drew attention to the bright chain around her neck and rivulets of blonde curls which defied authority, for her hair was unribboned and unbonneted. The nakedness of her arms, which would normally cause a polite person to blush, was embellished by golden bracelets. Whiteladies in the colony wore copious clothing in spite of the heat, tightly laced petticoats and shawls, but this one was a picture of indiscretion. The coming months gave me opportunity to assess her figure, but left me in a state of confusion. Her sparse breasts, slender frame and delicate feet suggested a creature on the cusp of transformation. There was youthful delight in the way she threw back her head and laughed, her curly hair dancing in flashes, brightening the dour interior of my massa's surgery. Her face, too, was pristine, and her eyes as alert as a child's. But I noticed, whenever she patted me on my chin in greeting or ran her hand along my face, that her palm was coarse and damp, like that of Miriam, the old nigger who lived at the edge of the plantation, her hut shrouded by haba trees, who supplied my massa with native herbs. Miriam hissed instead of talking. Her nostrils billowed out at each noisy exhalation of breath, for her nostrils were clogged with hairs. It was not the strange music made by her breathing, nor her snakelike way of speaking – head curling towards me and hissing through gaps in her teeth – nor her dismal habitation of straw and wattle, nor the wisps of residual hair on her head, nor the scars on her cheeks telling her tribe, nor the stench of the thick mucilaginous mixture of oil, plantains and gravy which she kept on perpetual boil on the stove outside her hut that repulsed me – though they did – but the feel of her coarse damp palm on mine as she took the money for her remedies.

"Massa Dr Gladstone sah, why me must go to Miriam for? Me go no-more," I wanted to protest, but kept silent out of devotion to him. And shame, for pleonastic Negro corruptions, creolese colloquialisms and numberless phrases which mutilated the English language filled my mouth in those early days. Best to serve in silence. In any case, Dr Gladstone, sensitive as ever to my mood, had explained that our people were convinced of the efficacy of his medicines when he assured them that local herbs were used in their concoction. "Negroes are great naturalists, they believe that whilst God visits them with sickness for their sins, He also provides, in the veins of leaves and the bark of trees, remedies and reprieves. The Negroes have among them wise ones, like Miriam, who study the configuration of stars for clues as to the exact proportion of ingredients to be blended for a particular disease. In the foliage of stars and trees is the unity of God's purpose for man." I was dumbstruck by his assessment of our people and would have fallen to his feet to anoint them but he sensed my gratitude and would have none of it. He steadied me by placing his hand on my shoulder – his smooth, tender palm – and ushered me to the cabinets to rearrange the vials of medicine. A practical man, my master, always containing his emotion, and mine.

Lady Elizabeth changed us, even as she herself was in the midst of change, in between the syrup of youth and the gunge-brew of Miriam's pot. She was radiant in her dress and ornaments. It was only when she left that the dream of divinity vanished with the truth of her coarse damp palm. *Noli me tangere*, I could have said to her, but Latin and knowledge of the Gospels were unfamiliar to me then. I merely shuddered at her touch and grunted some involuntary nigger infelicity: "Tank and praise yee, Missie," or "Dacta Glad One he prapa know herb and dem, you go be alright soon-soon."

★   ★   ★

Giddiness, she said, when she first came, taking out a fan to ward off the heat. And that is what Dr Gladstone confirmed, that she had only recently arrived in the colony and would need to be tempered to the climate, to be "seasoned" as he put it. "Heat and light in such lavish proportions can cause a suppuration of the senses." He cautioned against venturing abroad at noon and advised a broad umbrella and a slave child to bear it. He inspected her eyes, her tongue, and measured her pulse, in odd silence, seeming to hold in his breath during the examination. His hand trembled slightly as he gave her a bottle of pills. "And drink tea in abundance; bohea is best." That should have been sufficient instruction, but the film of sweat on his upper lip betrayed nervousness, so he asserted his professional status by elaborating on the properties of bohea, as he would do to a field-nigger, except his address to Lady Elizabeth was excessive. "Yes, bohea. It animates the faculties, keeps up the vigour of the spirits, expels the cloudy vapours that darken meditation. I do believe it also strengthens a faint appetite and corrects the nauseous humours that offend the stomach. Indeed I have read a learned essay on its other virtues; doctors of eminence claim it as serviceable in lethargies, apoplexies and headaches. It increases the blood's motion by thinning it, thus making the blood fitter to pass all the meanders, windings and circumvolutions of the brain." He spoke all this with his back turned to her, leaning towards a shelf of books as if to locate an authority on tea. She listened intently, with a faint smile, and fanned herself throughout; I suppose to distract attention from her own thoughts.

Later I was to learn that she was once a common moll, plying her trade in the alleyways of London, and that her assumption of a title and widow's status was sheer deceit, but just then, as she departed from our surgery, it was as if a meteor had blazed across the sky, disappeared from view, leaving a vapour of mystery which no tea, of whatever strength, could banish. Dr Gladstone was quiet for the rest of the day, focusing on grinding powders, making infusions, filling his vials. Normally he would have been a font of wisdom, making it his duty to explain to me the application of this or that concoction for this or that malady, and even showing me how to mix the ingredients with exactitude, though at first I was so awed by his solicitude towards me that my mind had little capacity to learn. Why bother to teach a lowly nigger like me when he could, like other massas, just beat and harangue and harass me in bed? I will never know the source of his kindliness. What it was in his childhood and growing up which made him so humane, since he never spoke about himself except in the briefest of references to a Scottish past, preferring instead to concentrate on making medicines. What of his mother and father? Brothers and sisters? I used to daydream them into being, striving to remember my own. My previous massa had in his sitting room a huge painting of the family he had left behind in England. They were as ornate as the frame which held the canvas, and though the tropical weather had made craquelures and bubbles on the surface, their loveliness shone forth. The woman seated at a tea table in the painting I took to be his mother, still in the thrall of youthfulness, complexion a lively vermilion, and the redness of her lips bedewed with a moisture occasioned by some spirit arising from the heart. She wore a cap shaped like a folded handkerchief and a satin gown trimmed with lace. Another I took to be his aunt, given her resemblance to the mother. She too was costumed – in a gold dressing-jacket and pink undergarment. Standing behind them, like a figure of authority and security, was a man, bewigged and cravated, in a short coat of gold lace and waistcoat with long fringes – the father no doubt. The room was lavish with vases and books; in slack moments I would stare at the painting, awed by the display of beauty and learning, and yet puzzled as to how my massa, coming from such an esteemed environment, could behave so uncivilly towards me and his other slaves. The cuff, the curse, the bedtime labours – such coarseness seemed unnatural to the mood of the painting.

And what of *my* mother, what did *her* face look like? My father, no doubt, was just used as a stud, to breed women and increase the stock of slaves, so I cared little to imagine him. But my mother… she carried me for nine months, then was allowed to suckle me for six months, perhaps a year, before I was sold to another, distant plantation (I speculated). My mother could have known me, in her womb, and then at her bubbies, for up to two years. No-one had been acquainted with me for such a duration of time, for I was sold from plantation to plantation, staying no more than a year or eighteen months in each, before landing in Dr Gladstone's possession. This much I knew, for the receipts from various massas were given to Dr Gladstone when he purchased me, and he presented them all to me in a pretty wooden box (the cover bore a painting of a Scottish glen) the last Christmas I stayed with him. It was a gift of myself on paper. I could read what I was worth, what monies exchanged hands. My mother did not appear in any of the documents, no matter how many times I examined them in the daytime or by candlelight. When you are a slave with nothing but odd shreds of paper detailing your cost, all you have is your fancy. And what pleasure I derived in picturing my mother to be as fine a figure as the women in Massa's painting! Though in simple garments, barefooted, bareheaded, her sweetness was evident in her smile, and she had lively eyes, a smooth forehead, and gentle hands. But I was young then and bare of speech; it was not until Dr Gladstone's purchase of a dictionary, which supplied me with the nouns, that I could truly dream my mother.

* * *

I was thirteen when the *Dictionary* arrived, a parcel in a barrel of medicines and instruments sent from Scotland. It was my duty to extract it from the glasses of syrup, bundles of dried leaves, microscopes, tweezers and suchlike. "Careful, careful," Dr Gladstone urged as I tugged at the parcel-string, telling me to unpick rather than tear asunder the knots. "The most valuable commodity in the civilised world," Dr Gladstone said, as I freed the book and presented it to him. He held it up to the light to admire its leather binding. He blew some invisible dust from its cover. He placed his nose to it and breathed in, commenting on the freshness of the leather which had not been tainted by sea air. He made me fetch water to wash his hands, and wipe them dry, one finger after another, making sure to towel between the forks and creases. When this ceremony was finished, he paused for a while as if in prayer, then swallowed reverentially before opening the book. What he saw left him speechless. He stared at the first page, his head moving ever so slightly as he read. He turned the page. Another eternity, it seemed, before he turned again.

That morning he treated no-one, trusting in me instead to dispense medicine. Five years as his apprentice had qualified me to assess simple ailments and to provide relief. The plantation owner was responsible for the health of his slaves and paid Dr Gladstone a monthly salary direct, nothing due for me. Dr Gladstone would give me a few coins which I stored in the wooden Scottish box under my bed. Yes, Dr Gladstone would not have me lying on straw, allowing me my own room, with bed, table, wardrobe and mirror. And I could eat whatever I wanted from the kitchen, not his leftovers, which he made me parcel up for whoever was lucky enough to come to the surgery after meal time. Word spread; there was always a longer than normal queue after breakfast and lunch – niggers with a little dribble from their mouth-corners. Sick only with hunger. Dr Gladstone knew why they came, and when he saw them lining up at the gate, he would eat one sausage instead of three, one egg instead of two, one slice of bread only, and depart from the dining table earlier than usual to make preparations for the surgery and leave me with a free conscience to gather up his leftovers for them. "The loaf is stale, you must fetch another for supper," he would say, lying, for the loaf was only an overnight one, fresh enough for the most delicate mouth but now destined for nigger-stomachs. Out of respect for Dr Gladstone they didn't stampede into the kitchen; each waited his dignified turn for a slice of bread, a lick of butter, sausage-skin, an egg-yolk.

On the morning of the *Dictionary* he treated no-one, nor did he bother with the breakfast I had prepared, so it was feast day for the sick. When all had departed, I took a tray of mango juice into his study. He was stretched out on a Berbice chair, gazing upon the book. He was too engrossed to drink, so I placed the tray to one side and sat down, awaiting instruction.

Dr Gladstone dedicated an hour each day to read to me from the book. "It is my most precious possession," he exclaimed, but relented immediately when he saw my face quiver. "You, too, are precious to me, but you are not my possession," he said in a voice laden with kindness.

"But I belong to you, like table and spoon and cupboard and all the things in your house," I protested.

"You belong to me only as my servant and apprentice," he chided, then turned the pages until he found the right one. "Possession, according to Dr Samuel Johnson, author of this *Dictionary*, means, and I read, '*a thing owned; goods; wealth.*' You are none of these, young Francis, valuable though you are to me; you are beyond a price."

I stopped tears from forming in me. "Yes, Samuel Johnson, a great scholar of unsurpassable humanity, qualities you must aspire to, whatever your present condition. And you too will flourish." I looked down at my bare feet, wondering whether the years in the colony had at last given him sunstroke and muddled his brain.

That evening I stood on the veranda and gazed at the sky. He had told me that we niggers were wise folk, we could read the mind of God in the twinkling of stars, and we could recognise utterances in the way they lined up. All I could see though were full stops everywhere, and between them, blank spaces. Dr Gladstone had taught me, soon after I came into his service, how to read the newspapers. They told of ships and slaves arriving, the tides, the tonnage of sugar and tobacco to be transported across the seas. Ships, slaves, seas: these were real things. Best to read about real things, I determined, than to fatigue my eyes and spirit before a newsless sky. Still, I persisted, wanting to believe in Dr Gladstone and in my latent wisdom, and I stayed on the veranda surveying the stars until a dark cloud passed by and burst open and showered me. I retreated into my room and lay on my bed in wet clothes, wanting to punish myself for being foolish enough to dream that my being could be as great as Dr Gladstone's. On impulse, I reached for my box and counted out the money.

A shilling and three pence it amounted to, all I was worth in the world. Tomorrow I would give it all away to the slaves, together with the slices of bread, the lick of butter, the bits of sausages and eggs. I would go back to being nothing, which is how Dr Gladstone found me so many years ago.

★ ★ ★

I was lucky thirteen when the *Dictionary* arrived. Time passed slowly, one page at a time, at first light Dr Gladstone teaching me words. He made me sit at the table beside him, when before I had served his breakfast and stood in attendance behind his chair. Words were more delicious than food. He picked idly at the plate, leaving a pile for the niggers at the gate. At first I listened intently as he read out the various meanings of words, but after a month or so I became selective, harbouring in my mind only those words which told of my mother. None of the As affected me. I became alert only when he arrived at beauty and declaimed from the book – "'*the best part of beauty is that which a picture cannot express.*' That's Dr Johnson quoting Bacon, a notable philosopher and logician." I immediately recalled in all its minute details the painting in my past massa's sitting room, of his father, mother and aunt in their opulent setting. I had searched the painting for my mother, as I had latterly searched the sky for utterance, but found nothing. Now Dr Gladstone was telling me that my mother's very invisibility held meaning. That she was absent from memory and from record was a measure of her beauty. And there was another word which found my mother in the sightless spaces of a painting, at the very corners and sides where the frame covered over the canvas; or at the back, where the canvas was blank and therefore unexamined by human eyes. "*Imagination: the power of forming ideal pictures; the power of representing things absent to one's self,*" it said in the *Dictionary*. Before, I used to daydream my mother, then scold myself for being unreal, but the *Dictionary* was telling me that she was beyond presence, beyond ordinary sight and recollection and record. I did not believe it. I wanted to, but in the end my box of coins and bills of sale, and the newspapers tallying goods, were definite articles not demanding of faith.

A year exactly, to the very day, after the arrival of the *Dictionary*, Lady Elizabeth appeared and it was as if Dr Gladstone, who had spent a thousand hours dreaming over words, looked up from his book and saw her as a woman beyond capture by paint. I, though, quickly discovered her coarse damp hand and her story, hissed out to me by Miriam, that she was a harlot and that stripped of her make-up she was a pallid moll. She was real, but Dr Gladstone must have seen her in an indescribable light and through an inner eye, for he was soon so intrigued by her that all his waking thoughts became caged birds, desperate to soar into her sublime affection but falling back to ground in self-doubt, heads bruised and dazed beyond medicine. He had often told me about Raleigh, an Englishman who claimed to have discovered mountains of gold in Guiana, which he called the Land of El Dorado. Chimera and illusion, he would say, and laugh aloud as if to claim that he, Dr Gladstone, a Scotsman, sober and practical, was in no danger of losing his head to such folly. "Raleigh found in Guiana mosquitoes, swamps, snakes, a jungle too dense for passage, impassable rivers, poisoned arrows... all God's creation but beyond explanation. For his sanity's sake, Raleigh had to imagine El Dorado, to make existence in Guiana bearable, promising. To this day, all who settle in Guiana hope to stumble upon a deposit of gold beyond ordinary calculation. The plantation owners send expeditions inland, investing their sugar monies in a search for gold. And, given a chance, all their slaves would run away into the jungle with Raleigh's vision in mind. This colony is so full of disease, and to work the land is such a desperate act that people need a dream to survive their days." He would pause from lecturing me to gaze upon his shelves of medicine, perhaps realising that all his concoctions were futile before the flood and drought which bred endless sickness, and the jungle which threatened always to claim back the plantation to beastly chaos. It was at such moments, however, that he shrugged off his despair and returned to his vials with new resolve. "Work, young Francis, you must at least work, even if nothing seems to come of it. If you believe in nothing else you must have faith in work, that some-thing will come from the doing of it." I would open the surgery to the ill, and he would immerse himself in the examination of their bodies, address himself to their real needs, which had to be met with precise, measurable mixtures of syrups.

Work stopped. Dr Gladstone abandoned the truth of Demerara – mosquitoes, snakes, and all the diabolical rest – and settled for the gilded dream, for that is what Lady Elizabeth was. Raleigh, too, would have perished for her, even if he had been privy to Miriam's bad-mouthing of her. Dr Gladstone took to spending the mornings with Lady Elizabeth, beating oars, and at noon they would shelter under a broad tree to picnic. I followed in a small canoe bearing the hamper, and waited on the riverbank while they unwrapped delicacies, uncorked wine, wondering what it was she said that aroused in him laughter, for I was out of earshot of their conversations. The niggers were happy to see their Dr Glad One in festive mood, never mind their cuts and chigoes. They bothered him not; they let him be in his delight, as if they were living out their dreams through him. Too much Jesus in their minds, they sang, when he rowed past,

> *Freedom a-come oh! Massa he a-go*
> *Jesu a-come to take me way*
> *Jesu love me hey-ho-day.*

There was no stopping their faith in Dr Glad One: his pleasure and his plenty were theirs, experienced on their behalf, just as Jesus lived and died for their salvation. Madness! Unreality! I wanted to reproach them, force them to lower their eyes to the earth and behold its barrenness and realise that the hoes in their hands were mockeries; that a lifetime of effort would yield only a few hundred acres of cane, none of the profits from which would come to them. Shiploads and shiploads more of new slaves were needed for each extra acre. Madness! Unreality! I wanted to preach but withheld my tongue for I too was smitten by such, through rapture in Dr Johnson's *Dictionary*.

The book became my solace after Miriam divulged Lady Elizabeth's reality to me. Dr Gladstone took an extended holiday, slave to his enchantress. Without needing to be told, I assumed his role as best I could, preparing salves for the sick. Life stay so. One minute you is busy-busy, next minute you stop work, you laze, you is in the thick of sleep. Dr Glad One stay so. But me too. One minute I talk like how ass does bray, next minute I is medical, naming syrups and ingredients, and on top of all of this transmogrification, there is the *Dictionary* which make me into a steed of words. When ass mate with steed it create mulatto: my mind whiten though my skin stay stubborn black. "You is nuttin but nigger," Miriam would say to me. "And as to that lady, she is nuttin but two-bit bitch." Oh, the bathos of revelation! I didn't mind Miriam cursing me, or rather, reminding me of my diurnal status, my lumpen blackness, which only God could leaven in celestial afterlife. No, it was Miriam expatiating upon the sinfulness of Lady Elizabeth – Moll she called her – which returned me to the reality of earth and bluntness of my hoe-mind. Deputising for Dr Gladstone necessitated visiting Miriam's hovel more frequently to acquire herbs. She harrumphed when she saw me, turned away and went indoors. An earthy and abhorrent hag if ever there was one. Still, she had to be coaxed because of Dr Gladstone's lovesick condition. "Please Miss Miriam, Dr Glad One send for bush-tea, plenty nigger catch cold in recent rain." I heard her scratching around in her hut, fearful that she was sharpening her claws. "Please Miss Miriam, Dr Glad One send for bush-tea, plenty nigger catch cold in recent rain," I repeated. To cajole her, I added, "Only you in the whole colony know the right remedy." She fretted from within her hut, then shouted, "Flattery is for mangy dog; you fool them to stop them biting by saying how they groom nice and fleece-up like lady, when, truth is, lice and flea and dry-blood clog their coat, and in that state they is not 'dog' but 'daag'. You take me for mangy daag or what?"

"No, Miss Miriam, pardon my mouth if it ever curse you so, for you is poodle self, pretty and all," I pleaded.

"You lying through your teeth," she barked at me, and a troolie leaf slipped its moorings from the roof and fluttered to my feet like a graceful, poisonous butterfly. "At least I have teeth to lie through," I wanted to retaliate, but the butterfly looked as if it was poised to squirt at me so I kept silence. Miss Miriam had a reputation for sorcery – a leaf could turn into a butterfly, could turn into a venomous toad at her bidding. She was nature in chaos; her foul words could reverse the order of creation. I recited aloud what I had learned by heart from Dr Johnson's Preface to his *Dictionary*, my prayer against the niggerness that was Miriam: *"When I took the first survey of my undertaking, I found our speech copious without order, and energetick without rules. Whenever I turned my view there was perplexity to be untangled, confusion to be regulated. Adulterations were to be deleted without a settled test of purity."*

"Amen! Amen and praise be!" Her giggle turned into laughter so outright that it seemed to shake the hut, for two more troolie leaves were dislodged, dancing upwards and upwards in a sudden gust of wind, soaring away from sight. When I looked up to follow their flight the sun hurt my eyes. I rubbed them and conjured forth Miriam, for when I regained vision she was at the doorway of the hut. She looked like a tree trunk, gnarled, thick with bark. I rubbed my eyes a second time to get a clearer, human picture but she remained a body of wood. A normal boy would have been worried in the extreme, believing that he was in the grip of nightmare or sunstroke, but I was accustomed to seeing folk who were once human reduced to animal, whipped from slave quarter to cane field and back again; or else, working in the Great House, not acknowledged when they served the massa his repast, being in his eyes no more living than the tray or teacup. No, if Miriam had become a tree her transformation held no novelty to a boy of my experience. True, Dr Gladstone's parenting of me had given me an idea and sensation of what it was to be amongst rational people, and the *Dictionary* promised to make me into a philosopher, but, as yet, I was not fully converted, so could hold ready conversation with a tree.

"Are you mora or mahogany?" I asked, seeking to flatter her again, but she read my mind, knowing that I beheld her as some uglier species of the jungle, thorned and runny-sored with sap.

"Raise your head to the sun; don't stare all your life at your barefootedness! Always raise your head to the sun!"

I did as she commanded, for her speech had the cadence of song. I rubbed my eyes a third time, clearing away the motes encrusted in them which had blackened my sight, making me see the world as one heaving chaos of niggers needing to be stilled by whip and curse. She appeared as a sampan tree, fine branched, filigreed and purple with fruit. The shade of her foliage was a space where children could play as at their mother's frock. "Come, come, shelter beneath me," she seemed to whisper, her voice, once hoarse, a lullaby.

★　★　★

It was so me and Dr Gladstone find family, he first with Lady Elizabeth, his lover, though young enough to be his daughter. And she behaved like a child, sulking, coy, brazen, giggly, demanding adoration, variegated in moods to bewitch any father. It was necessary for the sake of their privacy to vacate my room. "Why not reside with Miriam for a while, whilst I build you a dwelling close by? I will pay her handsomely for hosting you," Dr Gladstone suggested.

A swift dismissal from his household, though delivered with sweet words and a kindly voice. That afternoon I bundled up my belongings and moved to Miriam's hut. I had with me three pages judiciously ripped from the *Dictionary* and secreted in my clothing. Of course Dr Gladstone held me in such trust that he would never have sought to examine my bundle – even if he had not been so besotted by Lady Elizabeth. I took my words with me, expecting them to serve my future convenience, but not realising how quickly. They were put to use as soon as I stood before Miriam. My imagining of her as a sampan tree – scented, benevolent of fruit, protective of heat and sun – vanished when I lighted upon her. She was in her herb garden, harvesting.

"You bring de money?" she grunted without looking up. "Count it out for me, all ten penny."

I took from my pocket a purse that Dr Gladstone had filled with coins and did as she bade.

"Seven days' board-and-lodge money; don't think you can spend one more free hour of food; eat what I give you, you hear? One complaint from you and is out you turn out."

I should have been saddened, even self-pitying, an orphan abandoned by his kindly master into the custody of a creature resembling a horrible tree with vined locks, huge lumps on its trunk and every utterance a shower of thorns. I should have been a self-pitying orphan but found myself shielded from such emotions by the pages folded in my bundle with the same care that I would fold Dr Gladstone's freshly laundered handker-chiefs, but even more so. (Oh, to think that I had given more devotion to the pages than to Dr Gladstone! What had overcome me to show such ingratitude towards him? It was a question that distressed me when he died.) When Miriam turned her attention to me, clutching a posy of herbs, I was not in the least perturbed, for I had already chosen a word for her – elegant – and when I spoke it aloud in my mind she took on the properties of the word given to it by Dr Johnson. Seven days in her hut I would endure, for I had seven words in my armoury to dispel the darkness and scatter the swine in her. To have endured more days would have been to desecrate the *Dictionary* more than I did. And I had been prudent in the choice of words – only those beginning with E – so as not to harvest more than three pages.

★ ★ ★

When Lady Elizabeth first entered our home, Dr Gladstone's mind was evidently confused – the bottle of medicine trembled in his hand – and I experienced a moment of prescience, a foreboding when I felt her palm that I could be abandoned to the coarseness of Miriam's company. That very night, when Dr Gladstone had retired to bed the moon abetted me. A full moon, flooding light into the kitchen, allowed me to read the *Dictionary* without need of lamp, so that when I fell asleep in sudden exhaustion I would not knock the lamp off the table and set fire to our house and precious book. Words, words, words… Lady Elizabeth's entry into our lives made me determined – why I could not explain apart from being repulsed by her touch – to select the choicest words for my salvation. Hours passed, my eyes wilted, my mind spun, then my head collapsed onto the open book, and all the time the moon watched over me, the doting eye of a mother transforming the slave of me into something radiant.

Elegant, excellent, exquisite… some of the words that pro-tected me during my time in Miriam's hut. The vegetables on a broken plate she put before me became expensive meats on porcelain. When she tapped me roughly on the head, signalling bedtime, it was the endearments of my mother's hand. I slept not on straw but in a cradle of swan feathers and woke to sprays of corinna flowers with which she had adorned my room. "Arise sweet boy, time to bathe and dine, the day is laid out just for you," she cooed, wrapping me in a cotton gown and leading me to a stream to be cleansed. Crystal fresh my body, free of scars which were the scrolls of slavery: in Miriam's company I was of now, and new. She sensed my awe and reassured me with explanations that provoked no questioning, for they were the fulfilment of my desire. "I come from nowhere," she said. "I appeared one day which is now. I am now appeared to you. There is no before. Folk say there was a ship and we were hidden in its dark hold like seeds, then we were planted here, growing huge trunks and leaves which became flesh in thrall to the whiteman, human bodies bred to clear the land and turn it into canefields. That may be so, for them, but I am a new arrival, I have no past story. Look, are there any scrolls on my skin?" With the gentlest of motion she slipped out of her frock and confronted me. I was dumbstruck at her nakedness, her firm nipples and rounded breasts inviting me to suckle. She reached for my hand and nestled it between her thighs to feel its moisture. Not the dampness of Lady Elizabeth's palm, but a sensation more luscious, the sap of dark jamoon. "You are enchanting," I went to say, but another word slipped from my tongue, unbidden. "Unblemished," I uttered to my own amazement, gazing at her body, hungry for every aspect of it. "Come, lie beside me," she said, submerging me in her nakedness. The stream ceased its murmuring; the trees lining its bank faded; the birds flew towards the sun into blindness.

Miriam dipped a calabash in the stream and fed me fresh water. I thirsted. She poured more water into my mouth until I spluttered into consciousness. The sun flooded into my eyes. She leant over me and kissed my forehead to shield me from the light. Slowly the land was brought back to life, the trees shivering in the morning breeze, sakis fussing over their nests and the stream noisy with complaint as it tripped over rocks. Slowly the land was brought back to anxiety and hurt. "It is time for you to go," Miriam said, covering my nakedness and putting on her frock.

"Go? Go where?" I asked, looking around as if to recognise some flower or tree which I could name, for the world had become unfamiliar.

"To your master, he awaits you," Miriam whispered, smiling mischievously. She fidgeted with her frock to neaten it. She stood with her hands before her lap, protectively. "To your master," she repeated, and when I looked confused she stooped, drew my head to her bosom. I thirsted again, my mouth searching for her nipple and in a moment of delirium, found it, fastening to it for what seemed a season of eternity.

★ ★ ★

"What's the matter dear boy – you look studious. Was Miriam not sufficiently dutiful to you?" Dr Gladstone asked. It was the end of the seventh day and I had returned to the surgery by prior arrangement. Dr Gladstone was in a hurry to leave me in charge of his patients, for a day-long trip to Belle View Gardens, in the city, was planned, the coach prepared and the riverboat hired. However, his habit of caring for me could not be so easily broken and although Lady Elizabeth was already seated in the coach, fanning herself, distressed by the morning heat, Dr Gladstone stayed a while with me. He looked sternly at me, not out of impatience but to get me to speak.

"Miriam treated me well," I said.

"Good! She is a dear soul and a learned woman; you know how much I depend on her knowledge of herbs. I will send her some extra money. And here's a coin for you to spend while I'm away." He fumbled in his pocket, placed a penny in my hand. "Why so glum, dear boy? A penny will get you a tamarind ball and some mauby." Thinking I was perhaps at the beginning of a fever he rested his hand on my forehead. "You are as healthy as a wood ant. Have you seen how they've suddenly arrived, crawling all over the kitchen floor? Be sure to spread some powder; that will see them off."

I nodded, still concealing my anxiety until the silence between us became brittle. "I called Miriam *unblemished*," I blurted, looking up at him in a plea for help. He was taken aback, unsure of how to respond. He reached to feel my forehead a second time, to confirm my state of health. I intercepted his hand, took it in mine and squeezed it urgently. I was shocked by my behaviour, the intimacy of it. In my years of service he often spoke warmly of me, praising my domestic skills, or commenting, in the company of visitors, on my devotion to him. In moments of sickness he would lie me down, cover me with a sheet, and spoon medicine into my mouth. Never before had I clenched his hand, asserting a human bond between us. Another massa would have taken my gesture as an act of insolence, a claim of equality between us, and after a lifetime of loyal service done to him, would still have had me horsewhipped and sold on. Not Dr Gladstone. He seemed pleased with me, for he squeezed my hand in return, offering solace, urging me to confession.

"So…? It was your kindness to deem her unblemished," he said.

"But I don't know the word, I don't know how it came into my mind like a spirit," I said agitatedly. "I have been stretching beyond my reach, learning more than I should."

Dr Gladstone's demeanour changed to one of sadness. I was accusing him of introducing me to books, especially the *Dictionary*. He could have shrugged and abandoned me there and then to a future of ignorance, but he would not betray his affection for me. He brightened up, laughed at me. "Dear boy, there are all manner of night-ghosts in Demerara, the higue, the bacoo, massacuraman, voodoo jumbies whom they say suck blood or drown you or terrify the soul… So many creatures to feed fear and superstition, and you are haunted by a *word*! You huddle in bed, bury your head under a sheet not because of higue, bacoo and the voodoo rest but because of the visitation of a *word*?"

His laughter restored me to calmness. "It's not the word, Dr Gladstone, it's that it came out of nowhere, as if it always belonged to me, and I don't want anything belonging to me for I am only a slave."

Dr Gladstone tut-tutted at my attempted explanation. "Young Francis, was it not only recently that I told you that you are not a possession? Will you not rest until I set you free? But I cannot, for times are dangerous; a free black youth can easily be kidnapped and spirited away to a distant plantation. For your safety you must stay with me. Or would you prefer to live with Miriam, though you are in my ownership? She is, as you put it, unblemished."

I began to shiver with such force that Dr Gladstone had to steady me by embracing me.

"When did you call her unblemished?" he asked, his voice softened to a hush as if he had read the shame of my face.

"It was in a dream; I drank some bush-tea, it was so strong that I dropped asleep before too long, as soon as I took to the straw bed she made for me…"

"In a dream? Are you sure it was in a dream?" Dr Gladstone asked, but I couldn't answer with conviction. The horses whinnied, wanting to leave. Dr Gladstone puckered his brow and pouted, which is what he did when searching for some consoling phrase to address his patients. Lady Elizabeth called, but he shrugged his head, ignored her. It was a huge show of affection for me.

"Not to worry, young Francis. It happens to boys of a certain age, this kind of dreaming – as a child even to me. It's quite normal, dreaming of nakedness. When I return we will sit down and I'll explain fully. In the meantime take a pinch of nutmeg-powder, swallow it with coconut water, two times before nightfall, and you'll feel chastened by the hour."

"A pinch of nutmeg?" I went to respond, querying his dispensation for I was sufficiently versed in the powder to know that it was for the relief of the bowels. He looked into my eyes, a physician's all-knowing sympathetic gaze, persuading me to trust him; to trust that although nutmeg was no panacea, he was offering it for a purpose, to purchase time until he could counsel me properly. I played along with the game and went to prepare the medicine.

"There's nothing queer when you deemed Miriam unblemished," he called after me. "What you've sensed in her is a beauty covered over by age and toil and parturition – her true self and soul. Sometimes from the mouth of babes comes wisdom." This final effort to comfort me only provoked a new onrush of shame, and I was glad when Lady Elizabeth sent the coach driver to enquire after him and he departed right away, leaving me to tend to the sick.

I paid particular attention to them, to ascertain what was beautiful about them, their "true self and soul". Cato stuck out his hand to gather his vial and calabash of coconut water; although only fourteen or so his wrists were scarred from failed attempts at suicide. Billy's second leg was a stump – an alligator had had the rest when he went fishing and fell asleep, for it was at the end of a twelve-hour shift chopping cane but he was so hungry that he shrugged off his fatigue, took his rod to the canal bank, even in pitch darkness. In the daytime he wrapped a piece of rice-bag lovingly around the stump, to protect it from further malice. At night, he untied the rice-bag and rolled it up for a pillow. Alice, in her twenties, was still of childbearing age but had already bred so many for use on other plantations (as soon as the babies dropped they were taken away, being pre-sold by her massa once pregnancy was confirmed) that Dr Gladstone – fearing for her life – had created a special medicine to make her barren. Alice was constantly sick, weakened by giving birth on a diet of watery soup. Her belly must have revolted; it refused solid food, mistaking a piece of stewed rabbit, the only plentiful flesh on the plantation, for a sign of pregnancy and expelled it before it could settle down and grow breath. Alice needed a stick to walk. There was a throng of such slaves, and I was on the brink of giving up on them and sending them away, burdened by the pity of their condition, when Dido (Alice's last offspring, unsaleable because of chronic fever), gave out the squeaky cry of an infant which, for all its breathlessness, sounded to me like a long continuous howl. It must have been her sixth or seventh visit to the clinic, a measure of her age, six or seven months into life. Dido was howling for a healthy life when she should have given up and died, escaping the future. Dido's determination restored in me the virtue of duty, the virtue of practicality which Dr Gladstone had so often counselled me in, and I refocused immediately on making a linctus for her.

* * *

Cato, Billy, Alice, Dido and a dozen others: Dr Gladstone's regular patients who, however sick during the days, came to life for a few hours of merriment on Saturday afternoon at Miriam's end-of-week ball. I took to going there to relieve my loneliness, Dr Gladstone having installed me in a makeshift hut at the end of the yard as far away as possible from earshot of his doings with Lady Elizabeth. Everyone took food to the ball and they sat on the grass eating, laughing and gossiping. I expected them to be cautious in my presence, given my status as Dr Gladstone's apprentice, but they accepted me readily, indeed welcomed me. To begin with I doubted their friendship, thinking that it was because I brought to the ball choice foods from Dr Gladstone's larder – ham, cheese, pickled herring shipped from England – but after a show of appreciation (eating loudly to savour their privilege, burping to signal satisfaction) they quickly reverted to common behaviour, swapping tales, breaking into snatches of song, bad-mouthing their massa, vying with each other to tell the worst stories about him.

"Massa get catch yesterday with pox, how he groan and clutch he groin."

"Is God give he sufferation and godee; that man is one big sinner, no slave safe from him, boy especial."

"I hear he does bugger you up bad, not so Cato?"

All attention was focused on Cato in mock sympathy, the hush soon shattered in gales of mockery.

"*You* is his boy, is *you*, is *you* is sorebatty," Cato retaliated against his accuser, but the more he protested, gesturing obscenely at him, the more he brought laughter onto himself.

Miriam silenced them with remembrance of Christ. "Leave the boy alone. Poor Cato, he do no nasty business with Massa, and if he do, so what? Which of you will not spread out for extra rations or a morning free from work? Who will throw the first stone?"

"Is true-true you say, Miriam, God does watch over we night and day and God know we is not guilty, only Massa," Billy said. They all nodded and amened at this. A hymn arose spontaneously, Miriam bellowing the loudest, aiming her words at Cato, who stopped gazing at his wrist, looking up at her with boyish admiration. The premature agedness, the constant worry, fell from his face; he became a child again. The hymn gave way to new vulgarity.

"At least Cato is not hanimal, even though he and all of we is lambs of God."

"How you mean? Don't tease we with riddle."

"Is no riddle I telling you but true-true story. Nobody hear how Massa behave? Eh, the whiteman tire out with normal sin, he does fondle and bore sheep instead."

Gasps of disgust, folks spitting extravagantly on the ground.

"Poor, poor lamb," someone exclaimed, and there was another outbreak of amens and a predictable hymn:

> I thirst, thou wounded Lamb of God,
> to wash me in thy cleansing blood.

Dusk fell and the revels began, the agitation of limbs and tin whistles and tambourines aided by home-made rum. Only Miriam was sober. She squatted at her doorway, watching them dance and at the same time rocking Dido in a makeshift cradle of vines and troolie leaves. Dido, alert to Miriam's love, fell asleep, not a wheeze in her breathing. When the moon appeared it caught Miriam in a broad smile, deeply satisfied by the happiness of folk, their reprieve, brief as it was, from the rass-ache and bind-me-belly pain and the endlessness of days. And when the moon appeared it caught me prostrate on the ground, hiccuping out of joy and alcohol, and not wanting to rise ever again.

★   ★   ★

"People is people, we is no different from one another," Miriam said when I woke the next day shivering in the morning dew. "Go wash yourself in the trench, how you skin nasty up with mud; come back for some breakfast." I did as she commanded and returned to her hut to be offered a calabash of dumpling stew. "People is mattie," she continued, the night's revelry provoking in her a love of community which she needed to articulate. It was a matter of pride that she presided over the Saturday balls as a free woman. There was no need to ask among slaves how she became a free creature since everyone knew the fable that she had poisoned her master and mistress many years ago when she was but a young woman, newly decanted from the slave ship into their service. Her appointment was as cook, which she fulfilled to their satisfaction to such a degree that they retained her in the household rather than selling her on. It was when she knew her place was secure that she began to plot her escape. She had brought knowledge of poisons from Africa, the properties of this or that plant readily identified. A little addition to the broth (*Boil braise bake and stew/ pot taste sweet as morning dew/ add a spite to make voodoo/ add gwan-daag and curse or two/ see their skin turn black and blue*) then increases by calculated increments brought to her owners a mild sickness, sickness for a longer period, sickness for weeks, finally death. It was not a continuous process; Miriam was so cunning in her manipulation of ingredients (*One drop one more take your time/ season with a little lime/ wait before you add the slime/ pray God pray God for your crime*) that her owners enjoyed periods of perfect recovery between bouts of nausea. They ascribed their fluctuating health to the climate of the colony, its malarial fogs, water-borne diseases. At no stage did they suspect Miriam, who appeared as anxious about their wellbeing as they were, who made them delicate soups to aid their recovery, bibbing them, insisting on spooning it into their mouths when they were too frail to feed, cooing with joy when the bowls were empty. Five years passed. The lady succumbed first (*If you hear wind and her bowels run/ even I take pity but story done*) and the master was so delirious with grief and poison, and so needful of Miriam's tenderness, that he easily agreed to add a clause to his will granting her freedom in the event of his death and a small sum with which to purchase a plot of land. Miriam allowed a reasonable time to pass from the date of his signature before dispatching him to hell. To begin with she was so proud of her achievements that she boasted of her action to her fellow slaves. They too shared in her exhilaration, glad to see one of their own freed by her own initiative. Any one of them could have betrayed her to the authorities and be rewarded with the gift of a pig or a laying hen, thereby increasing their personal wealth a thousandfold, but freedom was precious beyond calculation and Miriam had set an example that their own children could aspire to. They admired, too, her bubby-swell and inviting hips, sure signs that she would make progress in the plantation. "Hush your mouth, don't boast so loud," preacherman Billy counselled her, not because he was less inspired by her deed but because "Pride goeth before a fall." Billy was an ordinary slave and still a youth, but, by unwearied effort, he had taught himself to read, having stolen one of Massa's Bibles, and it was Billy who took it upon himself to entertain Miriam, his elder, with Old Testament stories, in return for her stew. (She let him, although, secretly, she was intimate with the Bible. She let him as an excuse to feed him to fullness.) He told her about Babylon, the place of captivity, about Moses leading his people to the Promised Land, about Christ whipping the moneylenders who were Jewfolk. He advised her on the Ten Commandments, how to obey them but within the limits of her circumstance. "Kill if you must, but not too much. And tief only what you need. Covet, but only what worth it to covet." The plantation bred brutishness; God understood; He would forgive up to a point. Billy was being practical, adapting God's Ten Commandments to the plantation, ensuring his survival and that of his people. "When alligator bite off me leg I know God was punishing me for changing up his Ten, but God forgive me too. He save one leg for me. If you cross God for good reason He will only bring you a little sufferation. He got no choice. He is God so He got to mash you up a little. My leg was a sacrifice and penance; besides, alligator is God's creation, alligator hungry-belly like me and you."

★　★　★

"Practical people, that is what we is," Miriam tutored me, echoing young Billy, as I ate the dumpling stew. "Once you practice righteousness, not too much though, just enough to get by, God will give you more succour than scourge."

"How you does know the ways of God, how come you wise to Him?" I asked a little ungratefully, since I was eating her food.

She brushed aside my query, calling me a doubting Thomas, which was inoffensive to me because at the time I was ignorant as to who Thomas was. "If I shut my eye and hum to meself, recite a psalm or snatch of song from Solomon, the future conjure up in my mind and I can configure what this body and that will be."

She didn't wait to entertain any more doubting from me, closing her eyes and humming herself into a trance. "Cato, Cato, is you? Come forth boy, don't shy and lurk in shadow, Miriam go mother you a bright future. Cato, you will get new massa, a good whiteman who go teach you craft. A painter you is to be, boy, drawing picture and getting your hand and apron stain-up with dye. Paint will set you free to roam and dream, no matter if your pocket and your belly void. People will hold up picture you make and say, 'Eh, eh, this boy is something else; see how he paint cow in pasture with proper resembling. Cato's cow don't look like donkey or dog, it look like real cow, and that pasture resemble Albion Estate for true!' So much praise you will get, though you stay a slave. The new massa will love you, but without sin." She stopped prophesying, took in a breath and exhaled mightily, the hairs in her nostrils, which used to horrify me, quivering exotically, like the arrowheads of flowering cane.

"Will Cato grow up to paint you?" I asked for want of something to say, for her eyes were wide open, staring madwomanly at me. In truth, staring through me, for she said nothing, sighing now and again, tutting to herself, for the future she had foreseen was not quite perfect enough for Cato. "Oh well, he'll just have to make do, even if dye run dry and paintbrush mat up. God will bring upon him many trials but Cato hand will stay almost steady; it won't smear-up the canvas too much and Cato mind will unshackle and set free and come to know that people is people, mattie all, though one white, one dark, one fat like cow, one fine like brush-bristle that does paint and succour cow into pretend-life."

★ ★ ★

On succeeding visits to Miriam to replenish my store of herbs she would delay my return to Dr Gladstone's surgery not so much by plates of roasted corn and fried plantains, but by extravagant tales of our future lives. We would all escape whatever we were and be transfigured into the unexpected. Billy, she prophesied, would be transported to the Holy Land and meet Mother Mary self. Alice would become a fabled mistress, ending her days as a wealthy woman. As to Dido, Miriam betrayed her motherly instincts towards the infant, her lips trembling as she divulged her aston-ishing ascendancy in life as the godchild of a Scottish aristocrat and liberator of slaves. "And what of me?" I asked to humour her, thinking her at the commencement of dotage.

She closed her eyes and went through the usual performance of humming to bring on a trance. I waited for utterance but nothing came. I waited and waited while she hummed endlessly. "Be still!" she barked when I fidgeted, preparing to leave. "I ain't done with you yet."

"But Miss Miriam, sick folk await me back at Dr Glad One…"

"Be still," she repeated. "Move one inch and I dream a curse on you. You want me to turn you into toad or what?" She frightened me into staying. I nibbled at the last piece of corn, not daring to move. She left me clutching at the husk for what seemed an hour. When she opened her eyes she looked at the husk, then at me, and burst into laughter. "That is what you are, that is what you could remain as," she said, wiping away a tear, for such was the strength of her laughter. The incomprehension on my face provoked more mockery. "You is what you see, a hungry nigger holding a husk of corn. Better to be toad. But worry not, come back to me and I will mother you into something else, something…" She paused, searching her heart for a scrap of generosity.

"You, Miriam, is bile," I cursed her, denying any benediction on her part. "I go grow into doctor, wait and see, and you will be hag always." I walked away but she called after me, breaking my resoluteness, for my legs buckled.

"Is mother you want, but no-one be there for you but me. Come back and I will mother you into something that got no book-word for it, no book-word, you hear."

* * *

Dr Gladstone was gone for days and then weeks, lost in Lady Elizabeth's company and the glitter of the city. Nobody be-moaned his absence but me. The Negroes, so devoted to him, bided their time, bearing up with their illnesses. His previous treatment of them was a miracle in itself and they knew that miracles never lasted. To go to the trench hungry beyond belief, to cast a net and pull up a school of fish, when the day before, and the day before, the water yielded nothing... They dared not rejoice at the catch, in case it was an illusion, and even when the fish lashed out in their hands, they kept silence. Best to accept God's bounty in silent gratitude, best not to grow excited nor harbour ambition that God would keep providing for them, best not to plot plenty for tomorrow's pot. "One day at a time, sweet Jesu..." The hymn wanted to gush out of their throats but they swallowed it, held it down. And if there was no fish, at least the trench-bank was lined with frangipani and all manner of wondrous flowers, Oh so bright you had to shade your eyes; but no, when your belly empty, best to open your eyes wide to devour the lovingness of the flowers.

They endured their illnesses and although I applied myself to their needs, I was truly unqualified to make the correct diagnosis, correct remedies. The medicine cabinets slowly emptied – and the larder. I was forced to seek Miriam's help.

"He not coming back," she said bluntly, and as if to comfort me she dipped a calabash into her pot of metagee, not even making an effort to rescue half-drowned flies from the mess before giving it to me. I had not eaten for the day; she watched contentedly as I devoured the stew. "No massa left, only me," she said, nearly stopping my appetite. "Eat, eat! Ungrateful that you is, you is still kith and kin and me own flesh." She offered some coconut water, chiding me for being so washed white in my massa's employment that I had forgotten my true loyalty, which was to her, Cato, Alice, Dido, Billy, and the rest. Benighted today, true, she said, but tomorrow will see uprising of spirit and staves; all the massas and missies scoot, catch boat to where they belong across the seas, and the land come back to promise and we live by one another. Who is Mandingo don't matter from who is Ibo; who face scar sideways or who face scar longways don't matter; man nor woman nor tribe, we will all be one another. One people, one congress. "So eat what I plant with this hand and put to your mouth, suck up through your thick lips my plantain soup or rabbit broth – even breeze. Yes, breeze, for if the earth parch, punish and nothing grow, I will still cup a little breeze in my palm and feed you."

"It was not because I forgot I was kin that I would not come to you," I protested, so in want of another calabash of stew that I would grovel before her, succumb to her curses or her blandishments. "If I didn't care for Cato and Alice and Dido and Billy, I would not come to you. They need medicine now; centipede and worm will see to them if I don't treat them."

The alarm in my voice and the pathetic dribble of stew down my chin restored her pity for me. She dipped a finger in the pot, located a floundering insect and flicked it away. The insect – an infant moth – fell to the ground and staggered as if in the process of dying. Miriam lifted her foot above it – out of spite or out of a desire to end its agony – but before she could crush it the infant crawled away, rolling over and over, making a desperate effort to free its body of broth. Then, to my astonishment, it found its wings, and in the blink of an eye flew off into the safety of the trees. Miriam rested her foot contentedly. "Is breeze I give it when I raise my foot. I can raise breeze in my hand or with my foot, moth or man no matter, is salvation of life with the nothing I have, the nothing of being nigger."

★　★　★

The slaves arrived at Miriam's house in small numbers to begin with, for they wanted to remain loyal to Dr Gladstone. Saturday festivity under her supervision was acceptable but they doubted the power of the dried leaves and herbs she dispensed. Dr Gladstone had believed otherwise, but in truth, the slaves only trusted the powders and syrups which came from England. A bout of diarrhoea soon put an end to their resolve to wait for Dr Gladstone's coming. Dozens flocked to seek Miriam's help. They took from her resentfully and she retaliated by adding an extra cent to her normal charges, seeing they had no option but to acquiesce. For all her remonstrations about kith and kin, and prospects of a promised land, she still took their money, refusing alternative remuneration like nails, needles, brooms – all, like the coins, stolen from the Great House piecemeal, over a period of years, so as to avoid detection, and then secreted in the hollow of trees or under stones, treasure to be spent in emergencies such as an outbreak of diarrhoea.

"Cash is cash," Miriam said, and when they affected innocence or protest she told them what they knew to be true, which was that money was sovereign, the sole measurement of value. "You, Billy, is worth fifteen pounds, but if Massa ever find out you can read and preach, is one wallop you get, and he chop off your one good foot, and who will buy you then when you can only locomote like a turtle, dragging you belly along the ground? Massa will stop feed you, then you not worth even a bowl of bruk-up rice."

"Massa will never harm me," Billy replied proudly. "I is the best pan-boiler in the colony; he can't make sugar shine like gold without me."

"So you agree with me then?" Miriam asked triumphantly. "You agree that you is the price of fifty loaves of sugar every month?" She paused, looked upon them with such fierceness that many averted their eyes.

"Dr Glad One give all-you title; he call you Billy and you Cato and you Alice and you Dido, but he shoulda name you after how you serve sugarcane: boilerman, weedboy, puntman... No, no, drop man and boy, just name you boiler, punt, weed, rattan, manure. Dr Glad One lie when he make you feel like man and woman and boy, just like I lie when I dream that Billy will grow back he stump and wander the Holy Land, that Cato will grow paintbrush like a third hand and Alice will grow into rich mistress. Nigger don't grow. Only cane grow, so shut your blasted mouth and give me my dues in cash." Disturbed by the commotion Dido began to cry. Miriam watched as Alice tried to rock her to sleep, and her anger waned. "Only Dido I speak the truth, for one day in another life she will be princess, nobody able to parcel and price her up like pigtail or lard."

"Ow-me-Gaad, Missie Miriam, tek pity pun dem! Money run out; tek two egg or bunch of banana instead of coin," I begged her on behalf of the sick. I could have added that the diarrhoea still raged, that her bush medicine was that of a quack, but Dr Gladstone's trust in Miriam's herbs restrained me. Perhaps the medicine was useful for other ailments. Perhaps the niggers still suffered from diarrhoea but the medicine rid them of hookworm or some other taint which would have weakened them further. In any case, there was no substitute, given Dr Gladstone's absence.

Miriam relented but first made me renounce the Devil and his works. "Only a specimen or two of them, not the whole damn nasty deeds which if you list will fill more books than stars number in the night sky, and fat-fat-fatter books than what stack on Gladstone's shelves. Blast only that devil Gladstone and his whore."

"But why I must turn my back on Dr Glad One? He is like father to me."

She scoffed at this, gesturing to me rudely to banish me from her society. Her anger seemed to arouse the wind; it flowed through the trees in a sudden rush of spirit, flattening some of the younger palms. Miriam looked at one of the denuded plants and called Lady Elizabeth's name. "You tell me how kind Dr Glad One is, how he teach you this and that, and never lash, but he still left all of you all, in a second, for a sniff of whiteslut."

I fell into a grievous silence for Miriam's charge could not be denied. Dr Gladstone had abandoned us without warning or explanation.

"*Kind* and *Kin* not the same," Miriam continued. "In the end he is whitefolk and you is –" She looked me up and down, dwelling on my bones and the battered straw hat on my head, trying to arrive at a withering description. "You is kin," she concluded, letting me off lightly, her breath a little breeze lifting my spirit. "Poor Francis pining for Dr Glad One, but Dr Glad One deh pun scunt, he twist and turn and sweat like if is *he* get fever, not the slaves. He gulp and heave as if he drowning in a pool of her molasses. Oh! her sweetness darken his mouth and choke him with glee, whilst the rest of you cut and grind and boil cane to make molasses; you slash you foot, sprain you back, scald you skin when the pans spill, but none of you can get to taste one drop of the sweetness you make, one lickdrop that trickle down her thigh." Miriam paused to concoct a thought as brutal as the process of making molasses. "Burn down the fields, the Great House, slaughter the animals, and let the whole colony of niggers fall upon her and suck each last drop till she turn dry like Sahara, amen!"

I returned home and immediately sought out the *Dictionary* to find a noun to describe Miriam's outburst. Villainy: apt indeed, given her ambition to destroy plantations down to the last massa and mule. I pondered upon the word, then decided otherwise, searching the pages for a more precise formulation of her character. There were many, too many. I could discover no one word which was an amalgamation of her various traits. She was full of rage but was it not rightly so? And was not her resentment of Lady Elizabeth grounded in some truth, given that I myself was suspicious of her touch?

"She bewitch man as only whore can," Miriam had said, accusing Lady Elizabeth of perfumed deceit. Miriam closed her eyes for more acute vision. "I smell her back in Englan. She is wiping away foulness from her flesh, a rag for towel and where she live is dung, and rats everywhere, chewing everything, as craven as she."

Ridiculous! How could England with its mighty galleys traversing the azure main; its bible, dictionary and other learned books; whitefolk themselves, in robes of authority, and of such presence and prestige that artists were commissioned to immortalise them on canvas or in marble for succeeding generations to marvel at their deeds... how could England ever be a dunghill and plantation?

★   ★   ★

Miriam sensed the swelling of doubt in my mind and, at my next visit, sought to lance it by launching a tirade against the English. Such was the indelicacy of her language that I can only cleanse and abbreviate her opinions as follows; (1) The English were worse than cannibals. A select group fattened on the labour of the rest of their tribe, reducing hundreds of thousands to beggary and bone. People scavenged every day in refuse dumps for pieces of food discarded from the tables of the rich. They lived in hovels crammed with unwanted babies. They sold their children into brothels. Hundreds died each day from diseases, their bodies thrown into horse carts and tipped into mass graves, shovelfuls of lime their only benediction. The living sank into forgetfulness by drinking home-brewed liquor. Every full moon or so the rich harvested the most sturdy among the survivors, forcing them into ships sailing to faraway places to plunder gold from the natives. Cannibals were compassionate in comparison: they ate their captives outright rather than subjecting them to prolonged malnutrition. (2) As to the Scottish tribe, they roamed their country in warlike bands, ransacking each other's villages. The English ruled over them, robbed them of whatever they owned, now and again massacring them to keep them obedient. Lady Elizabeth was doing the same to Dr Gladstone, she was born to whore and to rule. She came from the gutter but her beauty set her apart from her pockmarked folk. Her parents pimped her out at the age of eight to various merchants and noblemen. She stole from one, ran off to another, stole from him. By the age of twenty-one she had gone through a dozen keepers, had mastered the birch and unspeakable modes of copulation, accumulating a small fortune in the process which was then dissipated by the costly treatment for a variety of diseases. Still, consorting with her social betters had taught her the arts of conversation, costuming and card-playing, so that she evolved from a gutter-leech into a lady. By some miracle the spores of syphilis she bore within had never ravished her face. Indeed, every bout of illness seemed only to refresh, not consume, her looks, soften her eyes, protect her skin from wrinkles. She remained in a state of perpetual youth whatever her condition below the waist. Fleeing from debtors, and hearing about a land called El Dorado, she inveigled her way onto a ship bound for Demerara, enjoying the comforts of the Captain's cabin. Landing in the colony, she soon gathered news about Dr Gladstone. His generosity had made him the subject of conversations among planters, all chiding him for tolerating slaves who feigned sickness and doling out medicines when a good cutlass-chop would have sufficed.

"So if Missy Lady is so loose and money-sucking, why she not take to bed with rich planter?" I asked at the end of Miriam's harangue.

"Ah, the doctor is a better investment, wait and see," she snapped, dismissing my naivety, then changing the topic abruptly. "And you still pining for your mother? Wondering whether Lady Elizabeth will let you curl up to her bosom and when you wake strip you down and bathe you by clear flowing waters? Oh don't look so faint, is dream you dream last month that you sleep in my body, that I suckle and bathe you. You was lying on straw next to me in deep sleep but still twitching and your flesh stiffen in your pants and you open your mouth and call out a word."

"Unblemished," I said involuntarily.

"Yes, it sound just so; a nice word I can tell. That is what all niggers are like – in the day they curse and bad-talk under the hot sun, tongue sharper than cutlass against cane, but when night time come, and the cool, and the light rain, and they sleep, is such sweet noises come from their mouths. As if they drinking rich broth, Oh the satisfaction! As if they dream of days lazing under a sampan tree, a cloth laid out before them, with flasks of mauby and plates of roast duck, and their children running about chasing butterfly. They dream that the land all around belong to them, to plough with their own free hands, and it have a pigsty and cow-pasture and fowl a-plenty."

"So is dream I was dreaming when I…"

"Yes, little boy," she said relieving me of all shame. "Is your mother was in your mind, not mangy daag like me. Is your mother your nose sniff when you dream hibiscus and corinna. And all little nigger-boys want to wake up next to mother-nipple, and for a mother to cleanse them by clear flowing waters. In your sleep your pants bulge according to fancy. I can read bulge just by looking at it, each different from each. Some dream of suicide and final release from work and they bulge so. Others dream of running away, hiding in the jungle, making a new settlement, and they bulge so, in another direction. Some long so fierce for woman that the bulge bore straight through they pants that is already threadbare. You pine for your mother and raise all your one-inch bamboo-stalk for her, and hope to hoist flag on top of it, but heed: your true mother dead-dead or far away in Africa, so do not hope that Moll will ma you. Is man-bamboo stalk Moll adore, not a one-inch orphan bulge like you."

★ ★ ★

91

Three weeks passed with no news about Dr Gladstone, and the ubiquity of my loneliness and lugubrious countenance (the *Dictionary*, my only solace, furnishing me with the definition of my mood) was apparent to all who met me. "Eh-eh, like mule kick your face, it so bash up", or "bird shit in your eye or what, how you rub and it water" – such were the sympathetic, if unlettered remarks made by my fellow slaves. They urged me to lift my spirits and I retreated into the *Dictionary* to find a term to cheer me, seeing that Dr Gladstone's medicine cabinets were bare. To grin, to laugh, to skip, to clap... Such words were too common to cure my woe, they were for field-niggers who performed them daily, not for one like me, brought up within the high and privileged walls of Dr Gladstone's abode. I did locate a unusual word, "convivial", and walked along the plantation-dam to practice it on the first person I'd meet, but as soon as a nigger approached, his back doubled by a bundle of cane, I turned away in fresh grief – he was an apparition of my future. Without Dr Gladstone's patronage my back would be wedded to cane until death relieved me.

Wedded. That was what Miriam prophesied. "When your massa come back, is like mule pulling cart, she rope and bridle the man and ride him in style along all the roads of Demerara for whitefolk and we alike to curtsy at she. She want we stand at roadside when she pass and for song to break out from we: 'Rule Britannia, Britannia rule the mule'." Miriam rasped her contempt for Lady Elizabeth. I withdrew to my makeshift hut, awaiting real simple word of their whereabouts as opposed to the sop and sophistication offered by the *Dictionary*.

Miriam was a true soothsayer. Dr Gladstone and Lady Elizabeth returned out of the blue in a state of wedded bliss, rings of such shining that Raleigh would have gladly given his life for knowledge of the mountains which yielded the metal. Dr Gladstone had warned me against Raleigh's fancy, urging me to keep my head down rather than lifting it dreamily for the executioner's axe. Now, it seemed, *he* had become Raleigh, unheedful of his own advice, his head still fastened to his frame but his mind deflowered.

"Ow-me-Gaad, is pox she give the man; no mercury will cure him," Miriam sighed when she heard news that Dr Gladstone, when he came home, had to be lifted out of the coach to his bed.

He was indeed sucked of strength, so shrunk that his bones pressed against his skin.

"Malaria," Lady Elizabeth sobbed, dabbing his brow with a lace handkerchief. She was the very picture of romantic grief, her face pale, her eyes glistening with care, her hands shaking as if to slough off the resplendence of gold, her handkerchief fluttering to the ground like Miriam's graceful, poisonous butterfly.

Pox, malaria; others whispered cholera or yellow fever. I knew otherwise.

Miriam scoured her garden for the choicest herbs with which to treat Dr Gladstone. Not satisfied she journeyed into the jungle to find rare mushrooms and sap from magical trees. She gave me stern instruction on how to blend and boil and strain her offerings. "A man so blessed of heart as Dr Glad One we must give our bestest to," she said, all her previous talk of rebellion and the leprousness of being white forgotten.

"I will give my bestest," I promised, but she read in my face a guilt which would hinder my effort.

"I will do it myself," she decided, gathering up her remedies and marching to Dr Gladstone's house with such huge strides that I could only canter after her. Filly and foal, we arrived at the yard where a few slaves had gathered like dejected animals, heads hung low, eyes unblinking. The evening star was early. It hung over the house, and the whole scene took on a Biblical appearance. Dr Gladstone was lying on his bed like Jesu in his manger surrounded by adoring animals. But death bed it was, Miriam knew instantly. She broke down when she beheld him, and Lady Elizabeth, startled by a stranger's sorrow, held her to her breast, comforted her. Yes, Miriam, of reputation mighty, of tongue voluminous, reduced to blubber in the blanched arms of Lady Elizabeth! "Cease, dear one," Lady Elizabeth coaxed, patting her face and offering her a tumbler of rum. The gesture of kindness unbuttoned Miriam even more; she was naked before us, unabashed in her grief. The slaves in the yard, hearing her sob, themselves let loose, braying and groaning in honour of their beloved doctor. Only I was stern of aspect, refusing to cry, remembering Dr Gladstone's injunction to ground myself in the real, the practical. It was not *real* to me that he was beyond restitution; he merely looked wasted and in urgent need of nourishment, like any sick slave. I left them to their wailing and put on a pot to boil. I filled it with the remains of the larder – plantains, eddoes, yam – the food that gave such strength to slaves that they endured nature's rain and blasting sun, and other indignities. Whilst this metagee soup was being prepared I crushed and blended Miriam's herbs, making a paste which I could caress directly into Dr Gladstone's mouth.

He sent Miriam and Lady Elizabeth away so I could feed him in private. Perhaps he did not want to appear slovenly before them, soup trickling down his neck. Perhaps he wanted only me to be present, as an acknowledgement of his special love. Was I special, was I being singled out? It didn't matter. I didn't matter, only he. I was just glad to be in the enclosure of his affections, like days gone by when the two of us spent hours in the surgery making medicines, making conversation, tasting sap from the book – the *Dictionary* – that was more magical than any tree in the Guiana jungle. But I had killed the magic of the book; if Dr Gladstone's life was ebbing away, it was my doing. Not cholera, not pox, not malaria, but me.

Dr Gladstone turned his face away as I offered him the broth. "I have brought sickness unto you. I tore three pages from the *Dictionary*, it's true," I said, hoping that my confession would restore his appetite. "I will paste and repair the book," I offered, but he was deaf to my apology, gazing into space, listening to rain falling lightly against the windowpane, as if for the first time. Yes, the first time, for there was neither fear nor delight on his face, only an infant's curiosity. I, too, stopped being my age and heeded the rain. I, too, gazed into space with strange eyes. After a while I heard a child crying and then a picture of a mother formed in my mind. Foolishness! I banished them as foolishness on my part, denying that I had Miriam's gift of clairvoyance. What was Dr Gladstone staring at? Was he conjuring up his mother and father? He looked so lonely, so far from where he was born, where he grew up, where he belonged. I stood at his bedside, companion to his loneliness, until the light faded, and he fell asleep, eyes still opened.

★　★　★

"One day you will meet him again," Miriam said, patting my face to comfort me as Lady Elizabeth had done to hers. I was expecting tears to break from me, but, against my will, I remained calm. It was Miriam who was troubled, no longer able to pretend she had the fortitude of a mule, enough stubbornness and strength to endure for us, her kin and tribe. Billy, Cato, Alice, Dido and the rest of us congregated at her hut but there was no drumming or whistling or singing or gossiping. She had summoned us to a wake, cooked plenty, but none of us had appetite for festivity. "The dead are the happy ones, not so Billy?" she asked, wanting Billy to recite a psalm to reassure us that Dr Glad One was an infant again, in the bosom of God the Father. Billy remained silent, sitting on the ground, massaging his one limb obsessively. Cato turned his back to us, picked up a stick, studied the earth as if it was canvas, then began to make marks upon it, circles and lines with no particular purpose. Even Dido rested in Alice's lap, making no sound, although her body had not yet been wormed. She looked as hungry as her mother, yet neither sought Miriam's bake and saltfish. "One day you will meet him again," Miriam said, but I too was in no mood for conversation.

"Dr Glad One and me done-done," I replied dryly.

"No, you will, for Dr Glad One single you out for love. The two of you will meet one day, long from now; so many years will pass is like a dream, and far from here, so far that the place you meet him again is like a dream though it name Scotland." I wanted to scoff at her but relented, remembering her power of foresight.

Not knowing how to raise our spirits Miriam attempted a hymn but soon broke down. "I did like that man bad-bad," she said. "Never mind I cuss him up and his bitch…" She wiped the tears from her face and glared at us, daring us to call her a liar, to deny her regard for Dr Gladstone in spite of the bile with which she used anoint his head, and whitefolks, dismissing them as offspring of the devil, deserving not to be rubbed in myrrh at birth but bile, yes, bile, and toad-spit and what ooze from scorpion, what breed in malabunta belly, what snake does loose out when it furious, and baptise them all in a pool where mosquito spawn… Miriam looked up at the sky and noticed, hiding behind an apron of clouds, a half-moon, calf-moon, shy, just dropped, pale with new life, waiting for darkness to announce itself. "Dr Glad One," she gasped, pointing him out to us, and we too were astonished at the sharing of one sky by sun and moon. Billy stopped caressing his limb and cleared his throat to interpret the scene. He began to quote the Bible, about God's abundance, about God's gift to mankind of the earth and seas and the –. Miriam cut him short. "Hush. Hush to what we speak day in, day out. When people talk it does sound so… so…" She struggled but we knew what she meant; that human talk at a time like this was ugly, stupid, sinful. On and on it went, human talk, covering over, drowning out, stifling, stopping all, like shouting from a mountaintop, covetous of hearing only an echo of yourself, bullying all of creation into silence. So we just stared at the sky and at the frail white moon, at Dr Gladstone who was beyond the reach of human voice, beyond our praisesong: *Yuh syrup is sweet like yuh soul; thankee Massa mightily; mine eyes dem see de Laad when me swallow yuh tablet.* Beyond words Dr Gladstone was, all the pages of him torn up, thrown away, only the Scottish box he gave me remaining, with its bills of sale, transfer papers, archive of my movement from one massa to another. One day I too would be freed from wanting to know my name, my mother; freed from the frantic searching of papers for some chronicle. There would be no need for words, not even to call the sun "sun", the moon "moon". When my time comes, let me be content as Cato making circles and lines in the earth for no apparent purpose.

2

Wigs, waistcoats, cravats, breeches, shoes, kerchiefs, all of Dr Gladstone's belongings were given away to the slaves by the magnanimous widow. Only she and I remained of what he was, plus the *Dictionary* ("Take it," she said, seeking to revive my heart after his burial. "Read, learn, it is your glittering future.") and a trunk containing cash and papers relating to Dr Gladstone's inheritance from his father. "Need is banished and with it all the constraints of being," she said, shrugging her shoulders brazenly, throwing off any melancholy recollection of her past. "As to you, young Francis, the constraints of being..." She paused again, searching for an appropriate assessment of my status. I came to her aid by a frank summary of my past and present life.

"Me is mud," I said.

She tutted, raising her eyebrows in disapproval. "You are my servant. You will become learned in the arts of waiting upon a Lady. When I am satisfied by the quality of your performance and when my time comes to be taken before my Maker, a lawyer will be engaged to write out the articles of your freedom. You will be set free as a consequence of duties fulfilled exquisitely."

Lady Elizabeth and I took up residence in the most expensive quarter of Georgetown, the capital city, leaving behind the plantation and all its symbols of low-life: the hoe, the cutlass, the net cast in canal-water for a miracle of fish, nay, fat worms even, for when hunger ransack slave belly anything that throat can swallow taste sweet-sweet. Me and Lady Elizabeth is city-folk now, pretty-pretty clothes we wear, shoes with silver buckles and the two of we ride coach, promenade in city-gardens, me one-two step behind she. Respect is what my face become, whilst she cover face with veil like how widows do, so *enchanting* (page forty-six, column three, *Dictionary*) that when man a-pass, he nod in civility but what the rass-devil really want to do is to drag she behind bush, tear off she veil, suck she full lips more sweet than worm in a season of hunger, but I give him a look stern enough, and the growl form ever so quiet in my stomach like storm a-brew, and as soon as he sense I am her guard-dog he tip hat and gone he gone his way, neither smile nor scowl on his face, for he is become an Englishman again, a picture of composure.

"Her mind high but she get low behind," Miriam used to curse, and not bothering to wait for me to ask, would explain: Lady Elizabeth pretended to be of elevated character but in truth she was as gross as her backside. "Moon a-run till daylight ketch am," was another of her favourite bad-mouthings: just as daylight catches up with a carefree and runaway moon, so Lady Elizabeth's misdeeds would eventually be discovered. It was such a cornucopia of creole sayings that I hungered for in my early days with Lady Elizabeth, for she was determined to wash me clean of plantation dirt so I could serve befittingly to her new condition of widowhood and wealth.

"You Francis, and I, are worth seven hundred pounds a year," she announced, showing no guilt as she tallied to me the sums inherited from Dr Gladstone's father's tea-trading (banked in Scotland but now traversing the seas to our laps) as well as the life-insurance policy Dr Gladstone took out the day before his marriage. "You must learn henceforth to act in a seemly manner, in dress and deed."

So it was superfine clothing for me, satin mostly. I spent hours in gilded idleness studying the *Dictionary* and writing out definitions with a pen she presented to me (a peacock-feathered quill, made specially for me by a skilled slave) together with a sheaf of paper so white that my eyes had to get accustomed to its sheen. She purchased books to stock my shelves – on fashion, cooking, and the arts of conversation. A tutor gave me daily lessons in Latin and in modern poetry; being a rare creature of learning in the colony, he charged a fortune, but Lady Elizabeth merely shrugged, as if to say, "a Lady incurs expenses, such mark her out from lesser folk."

To begin with, Miriam's voice would boom in my mind,

Hogarth: *Taste in High Life*

99

mocking my situation, but it faded as the weeks and months of tuition passed, and my room was transformed into a veritable library. Ours was a grand house built in stone with huge wooden beams and pillars, and a garden with an ornamental pond; it could have been any abode in the English countryside except for the fecundity of the tropical soil, which threatened always to choke the flower beds with weeds, and the profusion of insects invading the house. A small army of gardeners and servants was engaged to keep the savagery at bay. In such purged and protected space was I ensconced with tutor and books. And what curious books the tutor introduced me to, all according with Lady Elizabeth's general instruction: "Nothing dull, sombre, philosophical, but work that amuses." I was groomed in wit and whimsy to the applause of Lady Elizabeth. She showed no interest whatever in my books, not even to pick one up and pretend to examine its title. All she cared for was that I should be made ready to perform for her new companions, the fops, coxcombs, young beaux and planters who flocked to her parties, attracted by her beauty, her money, and the fashionable food which it was my privilege to prepare, aided by a dozen kitchen maids. It was mostly French cuisine. I became expert in the requisite gravies, sauces, pickles, vinegars. My *palais de boeuf en sauce blanche*, *cotelettes de veau farcies* and *epaule d'agneau piqué* (served with *sauce aux epinards* or *sauce de cornichons*, with abundance of a *salade d'haricots* and *artichauts frits*, all washed down with wines, brandy and rum) made me the subject of animated conversation in certain quarters of the city. When I went to purchase stock in select shops I was greeted almost as a celebrity, even by the white proprietors. "My felicitations to your mistress," they would say as I departed, giving me a coin for my own keeping as a way of inveigling an invitation to our "soirées" and "fêtes champêtre" (as Lady Elizabeth took to calling them).

Thrice weekly the dinner parties, a dozen men with Lady Elizabeth at the head of the table, the very image of carefreeness as she leaned over to gossip with this one, chortle with that one. When she threw back her head it was like a shower of guineas, all the men silenced for a moment by the richness of her locks, as Dr Gladstone once was. More liquor was poured, the chatter resumed its raucousness, no-one remembering Dr Gladstone. Nor

Hogarth: *A Harlot's Progress, plate 2*

did they notice the black hands placing and removing plates, their coming and going orchestrated by me, master of ceremonies. Black hands were all they were, being only slaves, but notice was taken of me, and my name was shouted aloud throughout the proceedings. I stood behind Lady Elizabeth's chair, bowing demurely as they raised their glasses and toasted me. "A fine preparation, dear Francis; you are a true disciple of Epicurus," one of the more learned would call out; others would attempt praise in rich language but fail because of their lack of education. They stopped mid-sentence so as not to further expose their dullness, retreating behind a bout of hiccups and pretending to be distracted by the antics of a fellow reveller. Lady Elizabeth beamed whenever my name was evoked, for my virtues reflected upon her, just as standing behind her my ebony presence threw into relief her alabaster skin, the golden ornamentation of her hair.

Is it human to be fickle or is it only massas who convert from unicorn into swine so seamlessly? The question obsessed me when my fortune waned. As the weeks and months of feasting passed, my name was mentioned less and less, until, at one soirée, no one deigned even to notice me. I became a pair of unacknowledged claws scuttling across the table to furnish plates, my French cuisine taken for granted.

Lady Elizabeth, sensing my unease, ordered a new suit of clothing for the forthcoming revelling on the occasion of the King's birthday. It was to start at noon in our garden. Some fifty additional slaves were hired to lay out chairs and tables, to serve refreshments, to make music, and to comfort the guests with specially made fans – dozens of feathers woven into a pattern of red, white and blue. Countless saki, merlas and other native birds must have been trapped and massacred to appease the temper of the guests in the rising heat. The day was to be a memorable spectacle, each guest waited upon by a slave dressed only in a loin cloth so that the rich costume of his superior was highlighted; in the slave's hand a union jack fan of bird-feathers shaped like an oar so that when orchestrated, when all the fans worked in unison, the scene evoked a victorious fleet of British galleys. That each guest was attired as an admiral enhanced the scene, as did the stirring music played by the band, the bassoons and trumpets flaring at the appropriate time, when the oar-fans were raised, lowered, raised again in salutation to a Drake, a Hawkins, a Raleigh. And the Official Artist of the Colony of Demerara and Contiguous Territories was commissioned to record the event.

Lady Elizabeth ordered me to be dressed in various colours, a green pantaloon, velvet waistcoat, turquoise shirt. I wore a silk turban for the occasion, trimmed with lace, and capped with a peacock's feather. My sole task was to move from table to table, not to oversee the work of slaves but the opposite: to be seen by the guests, to be admired, talked about as a mirror-image of my Mistress, a rarity. I was to outshine even the tropical flowers which blazed forth in the garden. As it was, I was barely glanced at. Even the monkeys leaping from branch to branch in the palm trees shading the garden received more attention that I did.

The afternoon's amusement consisted of slaves performing acrobatics, juggling, eating fire. Coins of low value were thrown at them. The guests laughed when they scrambled to retrieve the coins. I spotted Billy among the welter of bodies. I waved at him. He looked at me momentarily but seemed not to recognise me, resuming his one-foot hopping and breaking into a sycophantic grin when a coin was tossed at him. He tried to catch it, failing deliberately so as to fall over and provoke more mirth. He struggled upright and the effort was rewarded with another coin which his fellow slaves rushed to gather up, elbowing him out of the way. I wanted to go to him, to steady him, to lead him from the mayhem and mockery. I wanted to rebuke him by reminding him of his preaching to us, that we must use our cunning to outwit whitefolk and stand tall before them even though appearing to stoop and genuflect. But I left him to perform his acts of self-debasement. He looked thin, surrendered to worry. It had been nearly a year since I departed Miriam's yard, abandoning Billy, Cato, Alice, Dido. Without Dr Gladstone's protection, I wondered what had become of them, what trials they had faced to account for Billy's maimed spirit and the lack of compassion of his fellow slaves shoving him to the ground. Would I have toppled into cruelty had Lady Elizabeth not taken me away to higher ground? Now I was so transformed, in dress and manners, that I was beyond recognition by Billy. I looked away from him, to the monkeys grunting from the tree tops, and I said a silent prayer for the soul of Dr Gladstone, who first saved me from beastly existence. As to Lady Elizabeth, she was even more radiant to behold. I blessed her too for her benefaction, resolving to serve her to the end of days.

★　★　★

The whitefolk who flocked to our dining table I would take revenge upon in Billy's name. They were mostly boors – overseers with little prospect of distinguished employment in England who took up positions of authority in the colony; the sons of planters come to visit their inheritance of slaves and land; government officials; magistrates, who, apart from technical learning, had little to recommend them by way of the cultivation of the arts. Demerara was as much a wasteland as their minds, with no opera, theatre or coffee-houses to nurture gentility, unlike the ambience back home. Dr Gladstone, to feed my curiosity and tutor me in the ways of his people (on reflection, to prepare me for the time when I would encounter them in person and in print) would recall his visits to London, describing the billboards advertising the latest plays or pantomimes by star performers; the clubs where men gathered to discuss poetics and politics; auction houses displaying paintings by French and Italian artists, and sold for lavish sums. Dr Gladstone, being of Scottish temperament, visited such places only briefly, to acquaint himself with the manners and morals of the English; his sole purpose in travelling to London being to purchase the latest medical treatises as yet unavailable in the North.

The attraction of Lady Elizabeth's soirées was that they offered whitefolk a memory of home, an illusion of dwelling in a graceful space; a temporary respite from the colonial condition of heat, disease, and the sheer exhaustion of having to manage their slaves, whipping them out of their tendencies to idleness, surliness. The female slaves might offer some relief, but the male slaves, resenting their women being so available to the massas, harboured anger which could lead to insurrection. Three evenings a week they could escape to Lady Elizabeth's abode, partake of French cuisine and pretend they were men of civilised appetites. They could ape the behaviour of London fops and coxcombs, dress up in defiance of the heat in wigs, cravats, and waistcoats, indulge in rakish banter. And as *maître de table* it was a matter of politesse that I should be praised. But no, these were men of ill-breeding, quickly forgetful of decorum.

My rebellion was subtle, maintaining an air of refinement and my own self-esteem whilst mocking their pretentiousness. I would prepare meats *à-la-Genevois*, with thick Italian sauce but announce the meal as *cotelettes de veau farcies* or some such fancy French dish. *Hachée de mouton aux herbes fines* was in fact polluted with an Italian dressing. Given the gathering's contempt for the Portuguese and the Spanish (failed Empires) I would often garnish so-called French dishes with gravies from these cultures. Needless to say they partook of the food without questioning the integrity of my cooking. Such was my delight in their lack of taste that, at the height of my revolt, I found some of Miriam's herbs (somehow bundled into my possessions when I migrated to Georgetown) and stirred them into the pot. Sick slaves would stumble at dawn towards Dr Gladstone's surgery for a preparation which included Miriam's herbs. Now it was the massas having glutted on them and swollen their stomachs with much liquor, who stumbled into the night towards their carriages. Miriam would have ridiculed the effete nature of my revolt but I did what I could, according to my means. "Why not organise your fellow slaves to poison massas and escape into the jungle?" "You could have raided their pockets," she would argue, "robbed them of their watches, ripped the silver buttons from their coats. In the jungle you would have found pockets of free slaves, those who ran away so long ago that their massas had forgotten about them, or died, and their estates had placed them in the ledgers in the 'loss section'. These blackfolk would have greeted you as brothers and sisters, especially when they saw your cache. Each button would have gained plenty yams, a watch would be worth a plot of land, they would have cleared the plot of weeds and given it to you in a pristine state just for the joy of winding up such a watch, holding it up to the light to admire its sheen, pressing it against their ears to listen to each heartbeat ticking." These were the remarks she would have tossed derisively at me. But I was no ordinary slave craving freedom from mere physical bondage. My mind was not coarse enough for a bloody insurrection. I was catalysed by polite words, not the slogans of emancipation.

★　★　★

Lady Elizabeth was responsive to my needs. She realised that dressing me up gorgeously or letting me display my culinary skills were insufficient to place me at the centre of attention. From now on I was to speak. Once more I was overwhelmed by her feeling for me and rebuked myself for being such a demanding slave. Another mistress would have chastised me with cuffs but I could not relent because Dr Gladstone had set me out on the path of words

To begin with my new task was to recite a short poem or two between courses – verses by Rochester mostly – and when the banquet was over and they lit cigars, I was to aid digestion by a display of wit, their laughter tumbling the food in their bellies, breaking meat down to manageable pieces. I started off by belittling myself to win them over. "Why is a fiddler like an African blackie?" "Because he lives by his bow." Having assured them of my status as a clown (as my recitation of poetry had confirmed my status as a parrot, being able to declaim the words without apparently understanding them), I offered a set of inoffensive conundrums. "Why is a man that falls in the gutter approved of?" I asked, pausing to allow them to wheeze or burp before I supplied the answer: "Because he is admired." Nods of appreciation and light applause became ever more hearty as the evening wore on and the glasses were refilled. "Why is a candle like an atheist?" "Because it is wicked." "Why is a corpse like a man with a cold?" "Because he's in a coughing." "Why is a garter like the gate of a warehouse?" "Because it holds the stock in." "Why is an apple like a good song?" "Because it is encored." I withheld the best for the end when they were drunk beyond retaliation and would laugh uproariously, not realising that I was referring to them as wastrels and dunces. "Why is a bankrupt like a horse?" "Because he goes to rack and manger." "Why is a pen like a beau?" "Because it's feather-headed." These were mild insults. I spent many private hours working up puns for a bolder offensive, eager for the time to come when I could launch them. I would outwit my foes, spike them with satire. My fellow slaves spoke simple broken grammar ("we want be free"); their longing for a blunt brutal solution could only find such expression. I would bide my time, eventually outmanoeuvring my adversaries. *Adversaries*. Deeming them such in itself contained clues to strategy: *adverbs, verse, dare*. Punning – the cunning of letters and syllables – would emancipate us. "Why are perch like fine whiteladies?" "Because they are often taken with maggots." Silence. Then, disbelieving that Blackie could be so brazen as to court blows, they mumbled to each other, wanting to find some other meaning to my riddle. Lady Elizabeth came to their rescue, disguising her nervousness by calling upon the gathering to drink to the anniversary of the defeat of the Spanish Armada.

She criticised me the next morning for my insubordination though she did so mildly. I was preparing her hair at the time, powder, pad and pomade of floral oil laid out before me. The intimacy with which I moved my hand through her tresses, brushing them from her neck or tilting her head this way and that, aroused in me a taste for her. Her hair was a harvest of gold. She belonged to me, I would never surrender her to the appetite of merchants and planters. The very thought of her in their embrace made my black hand brush ominously against her neck.

"You are excellent, young Francis, far in advance of your age when it comes to learning. Dr Gladstone told me you were a prodigy, yes, that is what he called you. He said he named you after a Saint who loved birds, that there was something *light* about you, your mind soared effortlessly… But it behoves us well, young Francis, when in the company of gentlemen, to keep vigil over our tongue lest exhaustion – and I know how our evening banqueting must be vexatious at times, taxing our energies – makes us susceptible to inappropriate expression." Never before had she been so long-winded with me. As my Mistress she could have simply barked at me but she stretched words, modulated syntax to soften the blow. How could I not concede to one so sensitive to my pride? And her use of the pronoun "us", whilst an affectation of the aristocratic class, still bound us together in conspiracy. Slaves pretended to be docile, all the while biding their time, burying weapons, making arcane signals to each other until the right moment came to unleash their rage. Monkey loose, O Laad, mayhem, murderation! Lady Elizabeth and I were more subtle but we too were conspirators in the cause of freedom. Freedom: I suspected that Lady Elizabeth's condition was comparable to mine. I had thought she was favourable to me because I tended to her needs, dressing her hair, arranging the household of servants, managing our budget, and such like. That she insisted on private tuition for me, furnishing me with books and the hours to pore over them, suggested otherwise. It was only in the presence of men that I was able to sense her true need. They dissolved in her company, overcome by the prospect of naked pleasure. They could have adored her (as Dr Gladstone did) as ethereal, a creature starkly out of place in a sick colony, but who in some ineffable way promised salvation. Her very beauty was the hope of Demerara and the dream of El Dorado. But these were men accustomed to trampling a path to power. Beauty could not be appreciated until it was owned, tamed. For all her genteel manners and display of pedigree, they would use her as a common filly, break her in with characteristic violence. And when she would not be penned they would starve her of company and even food until she grew haggard in mind. They would banish her to the attic with an old Negro woman (too old to be useful in the fields) as her attendant.

Was this why she had gifted me plume and reams of white paper, a strategy to resist being penned in, me – slave that I was – to be her protector and liberator? I asked myself this, standing behind her chair, watching the men stabbing their meat. She appeared to be at ease in their company, following their conversation closely, showing amusement when they attempted humour. It was pretence on her part; I sensed a nervousness in her behaviour. Her laughter was as hollow as her attentiveness when they spoke.

I combed her hair and listened dutifully as she urged me to caution, to rein in the momentum of my words. "They are…" She could not find a polite term to describe the men and maintain her own dignity in doing so. "They are…"

"Predictable," I offered.

She fidgeted in the chair, placed her hand to her forehead in a pose of studiousness. Knowing that she was reluctant to offend me by declining my word, I proposed another.

"Men are intransigent," I said.

Her eyes lit up, as if her efforts at planting my mind had borne a rich harvest. A planter she was, and me her land of promise. And yet both of us were slaves to men's appetites. My Mistress and me: planter and slave at one in the same time, like the sun and moon sharing an (un)common sky.

3

Of the many guests to our house two men in particular craved her affections. They were like sun and moon orbiting a promised land, vying for space in the one sky. Mr Basnett was fiery, of late frowning habitually as if hatching plot after plot to reduce his rival to rubble. He was fat with middle age and his bulk made him all the more intimidating. Theodore should have been the corpulent one, being a kindly fellow, but he was a stalk of a man, gaunt in appearance except for a red rose he wore on his lapel as if to lend colour to his face. "One fat like cow and one fine like brush-bristle. Come Cato, come, proper picture here for you to paint," Miriam would have said.

What made their rivalry special was that Mr Basnett was Theodore's superior. Mr Basnett, starting off in a humble role, had ended up as the overseer of a plantation of some three-hundred slaves. Theodore was his accountant. Before Lady Elizabeth arrived their relationship had been steady, if not cordial. Both men were engaged in a profitable enterprise (or so Mr Basnett thought). Mr Basnett was a respectable widower and Theodore appeared to be a confirmed bachelor. No scandal was attached to them, no hint of hidden histories to arouse gossip among the company of whitefolk they kept. Their business was as tidy as their lives. Sometimes they would repair to each other's houses to lounge on Berbice chairs, sip juices, discuss the state of the sugar trade, the supply of African slaves. They seemed contented with their lot, and it was expected (as was normal custom) that having spent a certain amount of years in the colony they would return home in modest, if not abundant wealth; enough to purchase a country house with classical features and equip it with fine furniture.

So much I learnt from the slaves who accompanied them to Lady Elizabeth's soirées. Because I heard no stories of cruelty, I treated them well, seating them close to Lady Elizabeth, making sure they, and their horses, were well fed throughout the evening, even reserving for them glasses of special port when the time came for them to depart. They were ideal guests, seeming to enjoy the dinner table conversations, which were mostly about the misadventures of slaves.

"My boy went to gather honey but in his clumsiness – his knees are gone, he is so old he has to use a stick – he slipped in the mud, nearly knocked over the hive. The bees got him in both eyes; you should see him scoot off like a gazelle, hopping over fences, never mind his stick. I swear, pursued by bees, he was faster than a Stubbs racehorse."

"My lot can be slack, even the whip can't animate them, perhaps we should train up bees as overseers."

"But then I will be without employment; how will I pay my way in the world? Bugger the bees who want to beggar me!"

The wine flowed, toasts were proposed, there was much back-slapping. A slave stung by bees, another toppling into the well, a third kicked in the face by a mule: the narration of such accidents gave spirit to the gathering. The laughter was never malicious, I wanted to believe; no, it was a mode of relief, reminding them of the dangers of their enterprise, the nearness always of human epidemics or weevils which could wipe out their profits over-night. They were men of courage chancing their luck in a hostile landscape, five thousand miles and five months' sailing from the security of home (if ever they could return home, given the pirates, Atlantic gales and French warships).

Our revelries were structured like this, slaves the butt of jokes, masters vying to narrate their misfortunes. It made for a success-ful evening and all retired home relaxed and ready for the next day's challenges. News of a silver-laden ship sunk in mid-Atlantic or of slave unrest in a neighbouring colony stirred their emotions but otherwise they were settled in the routine of work.

Lady Elizabeth was like a sunken ship or slave unrest, at any rate to Mr Basnett and Theodore.

"The trouble with Theodore..." Mr Basnett stopped. He

scowled, resenting the desire to criticise a whiteman before me. He stared into his glass of lemonade then raised his eyes to me.

"Pips," I said, anticipating his rebuke. "Me good-for-nothing slave, can't even squeeze lemon proper." I took up a spoon and scooped three out from the glass, flinging them to the ground as if discarding myself as worthless residue of humanity. Flies settled on the pips. This act of self-abasement only hardened his mood. He looked at the pips, seeing flies gathering at Theodore.

"Massa Theodore sah, he bubb blub cana," I said pouring out more lemonade. "Massa Theodore kala panty-pani."

"What are you saying, boy, of Theodore?" Mr Basnett asked in an intimidating tone.

"Massa Theodore flimie lappa mappa," I said.

"Speak English, boy," he commanded.

What I had said of Theodore was babble, translation being impossible. "It is how we Negroes defuse anger such as yours," I could have told Mr Basnett. "We have learnt it over centuries: when the cudgel is raised over us we issue from the bowels of our mouth a stream of piffle, creative on the spot. Oh the spontaneity of our inventive minds! Having brayed at you such nonsense we then grin stupidly, that famous grin that glints in the sunshine, distracting you for a moment from your cruel intent. You want to laugh instead at our condition, or else you are baffled as to how creatures such as us, resembling humans in every way (head, stomach, feet with toes) should be so akin to mules. Having gained a moment of reprieve, we then let a tear roll from our eyes, our lower lips grow agitated, signalling that we are on the brink of breakdown. Your humour or your puzzlement turns into *pity*, and having converted you to the very essence of civilisation, we walk away to a safe distance. We gather under a tamarind tree, its branches broad enough to blacken the air, and there, in the unseen space, and far from earshot, we laugh at your behaviour to the point of crying, we wipe our eyes and muse over the ease with which we can transform you, and we give thanks to the Lord for another hour of protection. Not all massas, mind you, for some of you are beyond redemption, and the cudgel will fall on our heads as surely as Satan fell from grace: in which case only poison or murder will do – Miriam's solutions."

"Speak English, boy," Mr Basnett repeated, his voice edged with menace. My gambit was working; Mr Basnett would persist in interrogating me and I in turn would answer indecipherably, making such circles in his mind – purposeful, unlike Cato's – that he would grow dizzy and fatigued, especially if I added brandy to his lemonade, at which point of surrender he would begin to confess his feeling for Theodore. Persistence; I could depend on Mr Basnett, for in the months of serving him at Lady Elizabeth's table I had discovered this quality in him. He would eat everything laid before him, even though the food bloated his stomach. He would drink the bottle to the last drop even though his head spun and threatened to fall upon the table. Of all our guests it was Mr Basnett who had to be guided to his coach at the end of the evening; my duty, for he trusted, even liked me on account of my propinquity to Lady Elizabeth.

His consumption was not an act of greed but of persistence, for just as he would indulge his appetite to excess, so (his slaves gossiped to me) he would spend other days in a Lenten spirit, not caring for the welfare of his body. It was because of his wife, they whispered. Newly married, they had arrived in Demerara, lured by the promise of plenty. They were greeted instead by the jungle within which a plantation was being carved out. Jungle and restless slaves: it was difficult to differentiate between the two in terms of the peril to their lives. Mrs Basnett's skin flaked in the sun; freckles disfigured it like a form of leprosy. She threatened to wilt but Mr Basnett was staunch in his support, like a column around which ivy could entwine. They talked of returning to England, but only briefly, for the economic prospect for Catholics there was dismal, especially after the failed 1745 rebellion. Some of his wiser slaves had told me that Catholics were different from other whitefolk; they were like cacti which could survive storm or drought as opposed to the corinna which shed its petals at the first droplet of rain, curling inwardly for protection. Cacti were ugly; corinna, which issued a pageantry of mauve flowers, were a delight to the hummingbird. Cacti, however, were more suited to the Demerara landscape. The slaves used to wonder what it was in the Catholic bible which made the Basnetts such cacti but since none of them could read, the couple remained an enigma. I could have expatiated upon Catholic rituals, edicts and encyclicals, explaining how the Protestants were otherwise, but this would have been harmful to them. Instead of focusing on chopping cane at the correct height, cutlass angled in a certain way to lessen effort, they would have become distracted with the nuances of conflicting Christian doctrines. Blood would be shed as it was at the Reformation, for the cutlass would slip from their careless hands and gash their veins. Ignorance was their best security, so I left them in that state.

The rapid succession of personnel (Anglicans all, lacking in resolve, resigning their jobs, returning home on the first available ship) led to the swift promotion of Mr Basnett from husbandry of the plantation's animals to the overseeing of its slaves. Apart from a handful of missionaries the colony was godless, caring nothing for differences in Christian belief. What mattered was Mr Basnett's ability to show a hefty year-end profit. It was precisely this freedom from discrimination which made the Basnetts abscond from England as readily as any fugitive slave. They could thrive in a new environment where whitefolk were whitefolk as opposed to niggers. But, one night, the dogs howled; Mrs Basnett died. Cholera took her. Mr Basnett retired to the attic, seeking invisibility in its darkness. The slaves could hear him sobbing late into the night. They *pitied* him, the older ones remembering how they themselves had cried in the darkness of a ship's hold. Reviving old rituals they left bananas and a calabash of coconut water outside his door. They grieved even more when daylight came and they found the offerings untouched, against the decree of their gods. Mrs Basnett's soul, they believed, would never find a safe passage across the seas to her ancestral home. They ate the bananas and drank from the calabash on his behalf, hoping that the gods would understand and forgive, for the Basnetts were only whitefolk; they could not be expected to know any better.

None of the slaves had been touched by cholera. Mr Basnett must have concluded that he had been singled out for suffering and like Job he must endure. Why else did he not take vengeance against the slaves? Another massa at the slightest misfortune would order wholesale whippings to calm his temper, the crying of others distracting him from his own misery. Mr Basnett, earnestly Catholic, examined his past for evidence of sinning, for God would not have chosen him otherwise. Torment at his wife's death eased and was replaced by a determination to repair past wrongs. Perhaps he had paid too much attention to his frail wife and not enough to the affairs of the plantation. He had been placed on earth to make it fruitful but had been so enamoured of his wife (albeit spiritually) that he had neglected his duties. The plantation made a profit but perhaps he miscalculated its full potential. He had been too lax with his slaves: was that the source of his sinning? When they complained, for example, of sickness, he would call for a doctor. His error was not in giving them access to medicine but the motive for doing so: he acted out of fellow-feeling, which was as sinful as self-abuse for it could corrupt the morality of the plantation, encouraging the slaves to notions of equality. Yes, he should have provided medicine but solely for the purpose of stopping contagion which could kill off his source of labour and lead to the ruination of business.

The source of sinning, the source of labour: they were intimately connected, Mr Basnett must have decided, after weeks of pondering upon his loss of wife, for why else would he have overturned practices which had become the norm on the plantation? Under the new regime, slaves were only permitted to be sick on the last Sunday of the month, and only in the late afternoon, which is when he employed a pharmacist, not a doctor, to halve the expense. In the past he had granted them freedom from work between the hours of three and seven on the last Sunday of the month. They used the time to catch fish which they would smoke and dry and squirrel away for a season of hardship, or use as the currency of trade. A clay pipe made by an artisan among them fetched three hassas; a hammock made from the bark of maronna was worth a veritable shoal, for it took nine full-moons to weave.

Mr Basnett put a stop to such enterprise. He visited their huts to ensure the claimants for sickness were a-bed instead of fishing in the canal. He stayed seated on his horse for the full four hours, not budging, whatever the weather. Persistence: the slaves admired him for this, grudgingly.

In addition he halved their break for the midday meal; reduced by a quarter-ounce the monthly ration of salt; limited holidays strictly to days that marked the birth and death of Jesus. Such acts of diligence gradually increased profits but he was still not satisfied. Not because of avarice, for the extra money he made was remitted to Mrs Basnett's parents in England to pay for a memorial tablet on the church wall and private prayers for her soul on the last Sunday of every month; Mr Basnett chose that time to make his affairs tidy. No, the productivity of the plantation was all that mattered, for what else was the purpose of his existence? If he had been acquisitive he would have gathered up his wealth, returned to England, built a cottage in a leafy village and retired in gentrified leisure. He chose instead to remain in Demerara, to be faithful to the memory of his wife and to do God's bidding by driving his slaves to utmost industry. He lived abstemiously, riding in an old coach and wearing clothes unadorned with gold trimmings.

Mr Basnett would visit his wife's grave every Friday (the day she died) and sit for hours beside her on a bamboo stool. The slaves watched him from afar, fearing that when his brow creased it was not in sorrow nor in contemplation of the brevity of life, but because he was plotting other means to strip them to the bone. They were correct, for it was during a graveyard sojourn that Mr Basnett, gazing upon the ledger of his wife's tomb and the fluted columns which decorated its sides, decided to employ an accountant, someone more qualified than he to keep vigil over numbers. He interviewed a handful of candidates, all recently landed in the colony, all keen to heap up fortunes. They promised to multiply earnings twofold whilst slashing costs. One, Mr Eliston, in particular impressed him, to begin with. An Oxford-educated mathematician, Eliston spoke of calculus, cashflow, capital consolidation and suchlike, making money into a mystery that only the initiated could penetrate. In the end, though, Mr Basnett settled for Theodore. He was not more qualified than Eliston but he was thin and wily-looking. Eliston gushed like a baroque fountain whereas Theodore was classically spare, laconic to the point of rudeness. Eliston was also a lickspittle, complimenting Mr Basnett for maintaining his slaves in such a state of docility that the foundation was already in place for the erecting of an even grander edifice of profitability. Normally Mr Basnett would have blushed at such praise but since his wife's death his least want was to be flattered. The thought of Eliston flitting about his face like a gaudy dragonfly demanding to be admired, and buzzing, buzzing… Too much, Mr Basnett decided. He had spent twenty years in thrall to his wife's beauty, which shone forth even though her skin had been blemished by the sun; in thrall to the restraint of character, the quietude with which she faced the colony's foul-bodied insects and foul-minded slaves, the patience with which she created ornamental scenes of England with needle or watercolours. Her death drained him of the strength and the will to be startled again by beauty. Compared to his wife, Eliston was a harlot – loud, lush, cunning, a threat to his desire for abstinence. Theodore's sparseness reminded him of his wife. Best of all Theodore did not fuss over the terms of his contract – he signed with a shrug just as Mrs Basnett would dismiss the new discomforts each day brought.

★ ★ ★

Theodore divulged nothing of his past to Mr Basnett (me being his sole confessor). Mr Basnett took him to be English, but a hint of darkness of skin and accent suggested some foreign infusion, possibly from Portugal. In Demerara, the Portuguese were lesser in rank than other Europeans. A hundred or so had migrated to the colony from the more destitute parts of Madeira. By tradition they were fisherman or tillers of the soil, barely more worthy than niggers, but in the colony they were brought into the fold of whitefolk. Over the years they became clerks, small traders, book-keepers. Mr Basnett was pleased that Theodore appeared to have Portuguese in him, albeit only to the degree of an octoroon. It meant he could more easily exercise control over him. As for the slaves, Theodore's entry into their lives created panic. He looked like a stick, a new addition to the armoury Mr Basnett had amassed to punish them with. His meagre frame suggested hunger verging on cannibalistic intent. He would gorge upon them, gnawing away even at the bones Mr Basnett seemed bent on reducing them to. When they met him on his afternoon stroll along the canal dam they grinned even more stupidly than usual or contorted their faces as if preparing to cry.

Theodore confounded all assumptions and predictions. As I later learnt from him, he was from Eastern Europe, a scion of privilege, a relative of the Czar no less, his family owning several estates in Russia and Poland. He was versed in all the arts of refinement, an accomplished gambler, violinist, fencer, equestrian and linguist. He was, too, something of a libertine, entertaining women of all classes in the various boudoirs at his disposal. He relished his reputation for frivolity. Being bred to arrogance he saw the hangers-on who would try to ingratiate themselves with him as insects trying to burrow into gilt furniture. He promised favours but granted none, dismissing one set of sycophants when he tired of them, moving on to new swarms of fawners. Upper-class ladies who sullied their reputation by sleeping with him were abandoned to spinsterhood, albeit a bejewelled one. The lower orders (who were invariably with child, not having the wherewithal to dispose of their souvenir) were compensated with a trinket or two. One night, after a prolonged bout of rakishness, he collapsed on the tavern floor and refused to be moved. He rose an hour later, shivering with such force that his companions believed he was in a liquor-induced fit. It was not brandy, though, which troubled him but a recurring dream. Something evil had corrupted his mind, his family thought, for Theodore no longer cared to frequent masquerades, operas, brothels. They sent for the most learned priests and physicians but Theodore turned them away, spending days and nights by himself, seeking the meaning of his dream (which he later divulged to me).

One break of dawn, he emerged from his room and set off to meet different worlds, equipped with just a pittance of money. He wandered westwards, through Holland and France, earning shelter and succour by teaching the skills of horse-riding or swordplay or by acting as a translator. His patrons, taken by his refined manners, would urge him to lodge with them, but he always moved on. When employment was scarce and his money depleted he slept in the hovels of the poor, showing them, in return, how to load dice, cheat at cards, read the form of a horse so that they could improve their odds at race meetings. The poor flocked to him, not to sponge off him, as his previous admirers did, but out of gratitude for his legerdemain. His wanderings ended in London, but even this emporium of wonder detained Theodore for only as long as it took to find berth on a boat sailing to Demerara. Like Raleigh before him Theodore was drawn to the colony by a powerful and improbable vision. By the time he landed he was just a slip of a man; white and blackfolk alike avoided him in case his malnutrition was caused by some infection. Some took him to be an escaped convict, others a debtor fleeing prosecution. They were not to know that his scragginess and seeming penury were due to an aristocratic disdain of food, of possessions. He could surrender his appetite as easily as he could indulge it.

A strange creature then, but because of his learning he soon found employment as a translator in the courts where many of the legal documents were still in Dutch, Demerara being once in their control. There he bided his time, waiting for the opportunity for elevation to a plantation, his real purpose in travelling to the colony. When Mr Basnett advertised for an accountant, Theodore knew the moment had come. A dream had foretold as much. His curt behaviour at the interview was not because, as Mr Basnett thought, he was laconic by nature, but because, according to his dream, he was assured of appointment. He spent the first three months poring over the ledger books, working the hours of a slave, locked away in the counting house, refusing to be served cooked food for it would mean an interruption of his calculations. He chewed on raw carillas, not minding their bitterness, which would provoke a normal person to retch. The slaves were convinced that he was a madman, especially since he would not be waited upon at home. Two slaves belonged to the bungalow given to him, but Theodore had no need of them. He scrubbed and swept, washed his own clothes, cooked simple food before retiring to sleep, made his own bed in the morning, bathed and dressed himself, before hurrying off to the seclusion of the counting house. When Mr Basnett and Theodore were together, a slave would press his ears to the office door, hoping to hear something useful which could be reported back to his fellows and prepare them for the worst. A decision to work them longer hours was to be expected and could be managed: they just had to cut themselves more frequently and blame the dew bathing the cane for making their cutlass slip. Each cut meant a day's rest, Sunday or no Sunday, so Mr Basnett would be forced to relent, letting them start work half an hour later when the sun was strong enough to suck up the dew. Whatever hours Mr Basnett set would still find them coping, using their wit to outmanoeuvre him. What was unbearable was any scheme to sell off some of the women, in particular those of childbearing age, to another plantation. They were our sisters and our mothers, but to Mr Basnett they were women who fetched a high price in plantations less well stocked than his. They would be put to breeding; in the massa's silken bed or tupped by slaves in a sweaty field, it didn't matter. The new offspring would be sold on, to recoup costs.

But the slave glued to the office door heard no plans being hatched, only Theodore's quill scratching pathways across the page, for it was Theodore's habit to decline engaging in conversation with Mr Basnett whilst in the process of calculations. He nodded to acknowledge his employer, quickly returning to his books, staring hard at one, jotting down a figure in the other, crossing out a few entries from the third, his hands moving between them with the dexterity of a cardsharp. He dipped his quill, writing down figures in this column and that, subtracting or multiplying them, drawing a heavy line underneath them when he was done. Mr Basnett was happy to stand behind him, looking over his shoulder to witness the rapid calculations. He was full of silent praise for his accountant, marvelling at his cleverness, for Mr Basnett was clumsy with sums, taking several minutes to add any numbers with multiple digits, starting over again out of uncertainty. Numbers were like double-Dutch to him. Or else they had a magic to them, the way some like seven or nineteen could not be divided except in themselves, whereas others yielded at the first attempt, peeling off as readily as the segments of a tangerine. As to fractions and percentages he would just give up and call out for Mrs Basnett's help. Since her death, he had thought of sending a slave to be schooled in the necromancy of numbers.

Such a slave could pluck him from despair, rescue him from drowning, brush away the numbers drawn to him like pond-insects. He would reward the slave with an extra yam to supplement his diet.

It was neither the cost of tuition nor yam which made Mr Basnett hesitate. He could not afford to be deemed lesser than a slave in mental capacity. The least tremor to that pillar of subordination on which slavery rested could see the edifice come crashing down. A century of pent-up rage would be unleashed, whitewomen raped, whitemen's heads hollowed out into drinking cups. Whenever a tract appeared in the colony (smuggled in by sympathetic missionaries, usually of Methodist persuasion) proclaiming the rights of man and calling for a halt to the slave trade, Mr Basnett would grind his teeth in a temper. Only those with hearts soft to the point of rottenness could promote the Negro cause. Let the writer be brought forcibly to Demerara, let him be made to experience a canefield infested with rats the size of rabbits, malignant snails, and soil a sanctuary for all manner of insects. Would the writer agree to remain among these? Would he be willing to ship over his fellow Britons and put them to work? Surely there would be uproar in England at the least proposition to employ whitefolk as labourers, however destitute or criminal. Even the inmates of Bedlam and naked lunatics wandering the streets of London would find advocates to prevent their removal from civilisation to the colony. Shelters would be set up to house and clothe them, or fresh straw provided each week for their cells. The plain truth was that sugar was in demand to sweeten the tea of gentlefolk, and only the Negro was sufficient to the canefield, being sturdy of body and deficient of mind. It was men like he, Mr Basnett, who were the true patriots – even though Catholic – enduring the rude conditions of the colony for the benefit of his country. The "rights-of-man" mongers would sell out their country to the French whose territories in the West Indies competed with Britannia's in the sugar trade beside much else. When Mr Basnett dwelt on it, he resolved to give up Lady Elizabeth's foreign fare, but only momentarily, for remembrance of her beauty made him treasonable again.

Double-Dutch, Mr Basnett concluded, pleased with himself that he had employed Theodore to translate the figures into sense. And at what reasonable cost! At the interview Theodore had simply agreed to the pittance Mr Basnett brazenly held out to him. Now, as he watched Theodore sowing and reaping figures, he felt guilty. He decided on the spot to present him with a handful of yams at the end of each week (calendar, not working week; not that Theodore bothered to rest on Sundays, following the routine of the slaves).

A full three months passed before Theodore summoned Mr Basnett to the counting house to summarise his audit and recommendations. The ledgers, the invoices and receipts were laid out on his desk. Theodore began slowly, explaining this column of proceeds, that column of expenditure. He used simple terminology, and, satisfied that Mr Basnett was at ease, almost in a state of repose, he shook him to attention by grasping a book and banging it on the table. He opened the book and pointed ominously to a set of figures. He slammed his palm upon the page in displeasure then glared at Mr Basnett.

The poor fellow was taken aback but before he could recover Theodore battered him with words like fiduciary, equalisation, debentures – words so unfamiliar to him that Theodore might as well have been speaking in tongues. Mr Basnett found himself longing for the days when he was mere manager of the plantation's animals, overseeing the feeding of mules, the removal of ticks from cows.

It was a befogged Mr Basnett who stumbled out of the counting house that morning, only to be blinded by the sunlight. He had to call upon a slave to steady him and guide him home. He threw himself on his Berbice chair. Two boys fanned him, a girl served papaya juice. Mr Basnett felt as exhausted as one of them after a bout of punishment. He fell into a mood of sadness. It was an odd feeling, for never before had he regretted reprimanding his slaves. He had ceased beating them after his wife's death, even though the dictation of the whip was the surest way of communication, and he was bent on improving their productivity. There

felt sorry for him. After much debate, they consented to giving back to Mr Basnett the two hours a month sick-time. They would no longer cheat him by feigning fever (heating kofa powder and rubbing it into their foreheads) or diarrhoea (catching a toad to taste a drop of its spittle). They made their mathematician reckon the figures again, subtracting from the original sums. The new figures were still too high; another conference was called; they decided to forgo three hours every other Sunday. Some held out in disagreement, demanding more hours to be gifted to Mr Basnett, out of fairness to the man. After all, he did provide food, though it was mostly saltfish and corrupt rice, and the two lengths of cloths were cheap cotton. The dissidents won the day, or rather a fraction thereof, for it was finally agreed in a jubilation of backslapping and jigs to permit Mr Basnett their full labour on the last Sunday of every month.

They composed a ditty on the spot to praise their mathematician and new companion, a boy barely twelve years old, completely unschooled and clumsy when it came to performing his duties of weeding the sides of canals, for his mind was elsewhere. How often had he fallen into the water and had to be dragged up spluttering! How often he slipped on horse manure, smearing his skin which later bred boils! He was a useless slave but they conspired to shield him from Mr Basnett lest he be trafficked to another plantation. Whenever Mr Basnett was on a tour of inspection they rubbed pepper oil on his neck first thing in the morning. The vapours would harass him, banishing his normal air of distraction, and Mr Basnett would mistake his agitation for industry. Secretly they performed his work, out of pity, for he was without parents, his father dying early from dysentery, his mother kept behind (hollering to high heaven to be sure) whilst her son was sold on to Mr Basnett. When the boy revealed his genius for figures the slaves were dumbstruck. A month had passed since he appeared in their midst. He had spent his days pulling up weeds along the canal banks or sprinkling cowdung on the rattan, not a word coming from his mouth. The slaves called him "madboy" on account of his blank eyes and to distinguish him from the names Massa gave them according to their afflictions – bow-legs, scar-face, three-fingers (Massa did not bother to bestow titles upon the women). One night sitting outside the logie catching whatever breeze they could, madboy suddenly pointed to a patch of sky and said, "Thirty-one." When they looked baffled he explained, "Thirty-one stars by the light of the moon on the left and thirty-one too on the right."

The ablest among them began to count the stars to the left and right of the moon and after many false starts, concurred. "How you learn to tally so?" they asked but he brushed aside the question.

"Thirty-one is unlucky number," he said. "It is the age of my Ma. She born me when she was nineteen, that too is bad." They fell silent, the women among them swallowing and reswallowing air in grief. "Is a bruk-up daag-bone-and-muck life we come into when we begotten," one woman muttered, unable to contain herself. Madboy would not be drawn into emotion, flinching when she reached to rub his face.

"Thirty-one is the amount of cane you fetch in one go to load punt and you walk there nineteen times till day done."

"Thirty-one? Nineteen? How you know?"

"I watch," he said. "Watch, watch more, wait, what you want will happen."

Their puzzlement turned into a vague fear that madboy had some hold over them much greater than Mr Basnett's. At least Mr Basnett's ownership was legal; he had a safe full of papers signed and stamped, which he would take out when slaves had to be carried to market. Madboy threatened to possess them in an immaterial way. It was their turn to flinch from him when he stood up and picked a path through them to his bed.

"That boy is trouble self; mark what I say," one slave whispered even though madboy was far distant. Many nodded sheepishly, but there was the usual group of dissident voices.

"He is only a child. How can a child tell we to watch when he sway-head and does wander about as if haze in his eyes?"

"He fill with foolishness and all-body know that when you mad is wondrous things you does talk. God does put magic in the mind to make up for not having common sense."

"The boy got magic for true, how he can count!"

The moon drew a covering over herself and her brood of stars,

protecting them from moisture. When stars twinkled, it was because they were sneezing, having stayed out too long and caught a cold. Like all children they resisted when it was time to sleep but the moon tonight was stern, hauling them in, cowling them in cloud. It was time too for the slaves to turn in. Normally, wearied by the day's work, they would fall asleep instantly but madboy had made them anxious. They twisted this way and that on their straw beds until daybreak surprised them with its sudden coming.

★ ★ ★

Thirty-one stalks of cane to be exact! They gathered up what they had cut, hoisted the bundles onto their shoulders and walked the furlong or so to the canal. Instead of tossing them into the punt, they laid each bundle on the ground first, carefully counting the pieces. Thirty-one without fail! And madboy was right too about the loading: it took each man nineteen trips from canefield to canal before the punt was heaped high and ready to be hauled by mules to the factory.

"If one more stick of cane than thirty-one put on your back, knee will buckle over, not true?" madboy asked. They sat in a circle, he in the middle. "And if you have to walk to and fro twenty times, is topple you topple, crack your head on the punt, mule lick you face, lick, lick, but still you not lively. Not so? Rub coconut oil in your temple, fan you, wet your brow and bandage it with banana leaf, only then, after five hours or six, you wake up." The slaves answered him in a hail of loud amens. They marvelled at his talent, no longer wary of his strangeness. "Is baby Jesu born to we even though he black," one woman uttered, gazing up to the moon and the starry beyond. That night they sang a ditty to him, the words seeming to arise from nowhere – just as madboy had come into their company, suddenly, a month ago, his toes caked in mud, his belly pressed to bone like a sail blown back, stretched against masts. The remembrance of ships… Ships haunted their dreams, unavoidable as shadows, but they had survived and grown accustomed to their silhouettes on foreign soil. When they died their ghosts would migrate back home across the seas, but for

128

now they would settle for any sign that tomorrow would be lenient to them. There was something providential about madboy, so they sang for him, transforming him from sickly boy to sainthood:

> Come sun or rain come laugh or cry
> pumpkin eddoe sago and rye
> or nothing to eat mouth dribble and dry
> madboy feed we dream till day come to die.

Madboy sat quietly in their circle unaffected by their praise, the same faraway look on his face. "How you know how much cane weigh and how to gauge we strength?" someone asked at the end of the praisesong. "Yes, tell we, tell we." They broke out in ululations as they used to do back home to rouse the dead to feast with them, laying gourds of boiled corn before the grave. Years, decades, had passed since they left Africa or received fresh news of their villages and though most of the ceremonies and the forms of prayer were lost, memory erupted at critical moments. They sang or stamped on the ground in a certain way, or twined feathers to hang in the doorway to stop an enemy-spirit coming to visit them in the body of a centipede.

"Nineteen and thirty-one is like three and five and seven and eleven and a lot more," madboy explained, his voice grave as a prophet's. "You can't break into them, they so hardhearted. You can't put into them a little pity because you can't open them. You can't divide them, convert one or two of them to godliness even though the rest stay stubborn. And there is so many of them…"

"Is Satan's legion. What we to do? Tell; we obey." He seemed not to hear the chorus of voices, resuming an inwardness as impenetrable as the numbers he warned of. Perhaps he was unable to change their lot. Why show up his weakness by mocking him with their demands? The circle closed around him protectively.

"Let it be," one of them said, speaking aloud what they all knew in their hearts. "Let it be that tomorrow and tomorrow and tomorrow is thirty-one piece cane and nineteen punt-trip and not one drop of pity."

★ ★ ★

Madboy confounded them, as Theodore had done, for before he departed he was to reveal many wonders, not merely the estimation of bundled cane. He taught them, for instance, how to divide a circle, how to measure the angles made by each division, how to translate such angles into a system of percentages, thus arriving at a knowledge of ratio. They could not see the purpose of ratio until he prophesied that one day they would be granted the right to purchase a certain acreage of land and must learn how to divide it up justly, for nothing parted brother from sister more violently than squabbles over land. Massas fought each other constantly over land. The very plantation they laboured in had passed from Dutch to French to English hands. Countless whitefolk killed each other over the centuries; it would take a continent of ululations, each voice at the highest pitch, to awaken them. To treat each other justly it was not enough to master the mysteries of ratio: they must also know their worth in a practical way, for the world was governed by money and to be of the world was to grapple with the principles whereby certain values were placed on certain things.

Madboy changed their lives forever when he taught them how to value *themselves*. He told them that the plantation produced three hundred and ten tons of cane converted into a hundred and eighty hogshead of sugar, each fetching one hundred and twenty-five pounds sterling. Add the mule and livestock which amounted to seven-nine-eight pounds and the sum total came to eighteen thousand plus. Subtract the cost of food, clothing and medicines, say a hundred pounds and seventeen thousand nine hundred or so was left. Which meant that slaves made on average three hundred and twenty pounds each for Mr Basnett. He refined the figure to make extra allowance for the men who worked harder than the elderly women and children. The men were costed at three hundred and thirty pounds each (at the start of the year).

"But Massa buy me for eighty-six pounds at auction. I hear when the hammer fall; how come you put three hundred and thirty on my head?" one slave queried.

Madboy began again, patiently guiding them through a thicket of figures. They were overwhelmed at the new estimate, which was two hundred and seventy-seven pounds per head, on average, once death was taken into account (he discounted the cost of two deaths a year, which lessened the bill for food and clothing, but increased replacement cost, though only marginally if children were bought). He further whittled down the figure by factoring in a total of sixty days lost by illness. Consideration was given to the gradual waning of strength due to ageing and the sun sucking the juices of their flesh.

"Today, this very minute, the balance is a hundred and seventy-four pounds so your collective value is five thousand two hundred and twenty pounds, by what the sugar earn, but each month pare off a shilling for slowing down; at year end, a pound. After thirty years work you grow cripple and worth next to nothing: even your balance can be *minus nothing*. You can barely move but you can still swallow pennyworth of soup and souse. If it take six days on average for you to die, is three full shillings gone from the overall profit, more if you call for bread to dunk in the broth."

The slaves followed his every word. Those who were on the cusp of retirement (or rather, ripe for terminal illness after a lifetime of labour) resolved to speed up their decline, let go sooner than later so as not to lessen the collective worth of their fellows. Others grinned in delight for they were young and useful for years to come and at present were priced extravagantly. Most just looked at madboy sheepishly, embarrassed by their good fortune, wondering whether it was truly deserved. They would work even harder, to justify themselves, even though madboy warned that overexertion would hasten their demise and reduce the substance of body and balance. By telling their true worth, madboy was encouraging them to save their value by guarding against whiplash, disease, scarring when the cutlass slipped because of slackness of attention, and the hundred other dangers to their wellbeing.

Before he parted from them madboy made a final calculation and decree: freedom will come, he said, and on that day they must reckon their worth according to his equations. They must demand compensation for being made redundant: a slave was equal to so much tonnage, whereas a free man was worthless. The authorities must give them cash to offset their unemployment, the fault of which would lie with missionaries and kindly men like Theodore. With the cash they were to buy land, dividing it according to how much each had invested; a measure of their humanity would be the exactitude with which they proportioned the land. After that grounding was achieved they could give away as much of their lot as they liked, to the less fortunate, by their own free will. "Watch, wait, freedom will come. Prepare yourself for when massa day done; practice ratio, learn balance, capitalisation."

★ ★ ★

I never met Madboy (long capitalised, in reverence) and used to wonder whether he was invented by the slaves. Or by my imagination. News about him spread far and wide and it may be that he became more and more talented over time, words embroidered as they passed from mouth to mouth. Madboy was so glorified that he might as well be like the tapestry of Mother Mary that Theodore gave to me; a beautiful piece of handiwork with golden threads and sequins, which he had brought from Poland. One enterprising slave carved images of Madboy out of kumara seeds and bartered them for fish, fresh straw, or a little frolicking at night with different amours. Those with nothing to give had to make do with taking up a stick and tracing Madboy in the earth outside their logie, not a likeness but a cipher of his presence. They made the shape of a broom and a cup, for Madboy had cleansed their souls and quenched their thirst. They had to renew these images every morning for the wind erased them overnight, or impious sheep trampled on them. The more fanatical decided to tattoo Madboy onto their bodies.

The manner of his death convinced me that Madboy was a trick of the mind, for how could someone so heroic end so bathetically? He had fallen into the canal when no one was looking. By the time they retrieved his body, crabs had claimed his eyes. A true prophet was stoned to death, broken on a cross or sucked up by a whirlwind and transported to heaven, not plucked from a canal like a parcel of weeds. For all the prosiness of his death they still transformed Madboy into rich scripture, imput-

132

ing to him the highest principles of mathematics; even the odd miracle, admittedly modest. When a foot swollen by bee-sting eased swifter than normal or a fever passed without medicine, it was Madboy they evoked in praise. That crabs had clawed out his eyes only confirmed his status. In life he was like a blind man seeing but not looking; so too in death, for his vision was inward.

"Pang-a-lang pang-a-lang pang-a-lang/ ring the bell wake up the work-gang," they used to sing at dawn, shaking their hands to imitate a bell's alarm. Now they closed their eyes instead, imitating Madboy, and their new prayer consisted of a jumble of figures, for they had not yet mastered the art of arithmetic:

> *Forty times twelve we sing your praise*
> *almost four hundred it reach, O happy days!*
> *No care, distress, let the work start*
> *and when money heap up on a cart*
> *is so much you value in we heart.*

In Africa, their ancestors had risen at first light to pledge their lifetime's earnings, and more, to the gods. In Demerara they owned little to sacrifice – a few scrawny chickens – but at least they could offer up abstractions. Such thanksgiving took greater effort for it was much harder to work figures in the mind than it was to wring the neck of a sacrificial bird. Madboy had resurrected the need for African ritual, given them new ciphers to worship, new formulae of prayers. He took the place of Ogun and their other gods of fire and thunder. Ogun and the rest had failed them when foreigners arrived in their villages. With one sweep of the sword foreigners had vandalised the idols. They lay broken on the ground and the Africans were converted into niggers, scattered like shards of clay to the far corners of the earth. They double-capitalised Madboy, not in terms of money but, more radically, in language, adding an extra letter to make his name sound more African: MMadboy.

Perhaps MMadboy, given his ability to plot, organise and manoeuvre around figures, was best equipped to protect them, but I still distrusted him.

"There is but one soothsayer: me," Miriam would have said,

thrusting a fat finger at me. The colony, she would grumble, was full of fools and false prophets buzz-buzz-buzzing in poor people's ears all kinds of promises, stinging them for a penny or a piece of patacake, not stopping to preach till they parted with their purse or pulled down their panties. "Me, Miriam, ever ask anything of all-you when I dream? I foretell this one will be beggar, that one prince, and I do it for free. Not so much as mango skin or guinep seed what goat does eat pass my lips. I ever ask even for a sip of sugar-water from all-you?" I imagined sinking my hand into my pocket as she scolded me, wishing I had a farthing to give her, or even a nutmeg, which would stop her mouth in surprise. She would grab my present but still glower at me; any tribute from a slave's hand was bound to be inadequate. Such was the power of her dreams that she deserved (by her own reckoning) the munificence of kings. Bombast and jealousy over a rival prophet apart, I suspected she would have cursed MMadboy out of genuine anxiety over his message, dismissing him for trusting in figures, as I trusted in words. "Cut Massa throat, the only way; no amount of learning will do." Miriam refused to take a long-term, eyeless view of things. "Why I must wait ten years, a hundred years? Why I must endure from one ship and one eclipse to the next? Sun darken, moon darken; me Miriam stay in Massa gaze steady as a nigger with cutlass in hand, for when Jesu cross lean and topple, when sun and moon shut out the light, when tempest drown all, and time come for the world to ruin, is nigger you will still find tending to the cane, the last man and woman standing. But eh-eh, why you let whitefolk eye-pass we so?"

★ ★ ★

Was MMadboy breeding cowardice by taking the sword out of the slave's hand, replacing it with a sum?

"Speak English boy!" Mr Basnett barked, rupturing my reverie.

"Massa Theodore, *sah*, is like sandfly, *so* he stay, scratch up skin, but not for me to *say*, not for me to *see*." Sah, so, say, see, followed by a sigh: I was a picture of stupidity.

Mr Basnett curled his fist, preparing to box me for confusing him.

"Nigger look but can't see, talk but can't think," I said.

He relaxed his knuckles for a moment. "More boy, more" he persisted (as I anticipated) sinking his hand into his pocket as if to hide his intentions or to find a nutmeg as bribery.

"Massa Theodore, sah, bite we like sandfly – ouch, ouch we cry; he lump we flesh, coconut oil can't cool it; we so mad we want mash-up the place, like bull when you poke his balls does charge, bruk up pen, head to the canefield and when nigger see it come, quick-quick they drop cutlass and scoot, plunge into canal even to save them life. Sandfly, madbull: that, sah, is Theodore, in a word, sorry sah, two words."

Mr Basnett was pleased by my estimation of Theodore and furnished me with a shilling. A shilling! Too much! Who mad? He? Theodore? MMadboy? All of we? I poured more lemonade, Mr Basnett not bothering that a pip had slipped in. He urged me to go on, extracting another coin from his pocket, another shilling, O God! I so inspire I say:

"Theodore is like poui blossom on high that the breeze shake, so many petals, white, gold, pink, flutter down, oh so pretty-pretty! They dance in the air; you run to them, raise your hands to catch them before they touch ground, mouth open because you so amaze; petal fall in, joy done! It taste bitter-bitter, burn mouth, more hot than bird-pepper. Spit you spit, scrape tongue with your teeth but the petal paste on, the more hard you scrape, the more it stick. When you swallow spit is then sickness start, belly-wuk, belly-wuk, belly-wuk; you dig a hole and spend whole day squat over it, slacking your guts. Poui bad more than senna; by the time you rise is like all your insides hollow out, barely you can walk for so much weight you lose. 'O Jesu, hallow be your name,' you holler out in pain."

My berating of Theodore and crass punning moved Mr Basnett as readily as the poui petal had moved my imagined bowels. He let loose a series of oaths. He stopped my hand when I went to fill his glass, thinking that in my weakened state I would drop the lemonade jug, break it, bring a lash upon my back (not that Lady Elizabeth chastised me for any such clumsiness, but Mr Basnett was not to know) which would further enfeeble me. A cascade of poui blossoms was indeed an astonishing spectacle, but nothing to match the showering of two shillings upon me and Mr Basnett taking my side against a fellow whiteman. Massa day was truly ending; who would have believed that execrations would be uttered against Theodore in the earshot of a nigger? I myself was taken aback by his outburst, given that he was a committed Catholic. Moreso, one recently widowed should not take God's name in vain and vulgarity, in case God took it out on the soul of his wife, penning her in purgatory until he repented.

Mr Basnett, however, was careless of his fate and that of his wife. He was possessed by Theodore. He leaned towards me conspiratorially. I responded by moving my ear to his mouth. "Murder," he whispered. My head dizzied but the coins in my hand were like ballast and I remained calm as he made his confession. Theodore had converted him into a slave, for he blubbered and spoke to me in broken words. "Speak English, boy," I could have said to him without least worry of punishment. I listened hard to make sense of his confession, nodding now and again to encouraging him to continue. His voice rose to a shriek, as black as any ululation back home, but Mr Basnett wanted to kill, not to awaken the dead. I tried to hush him but he would not heed. "Poison, give to Eliston. He will apply for the job. He will give it to Theodore. Plenty. Pish, ears and noses, make it plenty! You niggers know how to poison in syrup. Swallow, stay till the last drop he swallows, wait, watch, watch till Theodore is done for, and I am free. Free me. Me! Me!" He pressed a third coin into my hand, a crown no less, enough, he said, to concoct poison to kill Theodore tenfold.

"Nineteenfold, thirty-onefold; go for MMadboy's evil numbers," I could have mocked, but I took pity on him instead; *pity*, the essence of any civilisation. Mr Basnett leant forward, his hands covering his head as if to contain his madness, yes, madness, for that is what he proposed. And the madness seemed to have visited him suddenly, just as Dr Gladstone was one day sober in mind, the next day seized by Lady Elizabeth. Just as MMadboy come from nowhere, then drown. Maybe *sudden* is what does happen by nature if you are in plantation and colony. One day we minding cow quiet-quiet in savannah in Africa, next thing you know is holleration, we get catch and ferry out to faraway. Mr

Basnett is a gentle man in England, but as soon as he land in Demerara he start cuss we up and spit. And Mrs Basnett dead out one night without warning. And Lady Elizabeth turn up out of the blue to tempt him. And Theodore come to ruin him (yes, Mr Basnett suspect so; he tell me he hear how Theodore plotting to bankrupt the plantation), and all the time rivalling him for Lady Elizabeth's bosom. To think that in early days Mr Basnett used to visit Theodore's house to converse and quaff, but then death lash him first, lust second, the prospect of ruination third: the glass drop from his hand, shatter, scatter to faraway, his mind too in splinters, wanting to juk out Theodore's life from his body and gobble it, yes, cannibal it, like how when a slave hungry he does wander canal-bank, snatch a snail, poke out the flesh with his longest fingernail, salt-and-pepper it in his mind and swoosh it down.

Yes, *sudden* is a thing I must guard against. I must wait, wait, calculate, I must never do *sudden*.

★ ★ ★

What Mr Basnett told me was the stuff of dreams. Miriam was right – there were too many people in Demerara dreaming; Miriam herself, then MMadboy, then Theodore, and now Mr Basnett trapped in nightmare, believing he could gain deliverance by Theodore quaffing poison. I was to create the fatal brew, which Eliston would dispense in return for succeeding Theodore as the plantation's accountant. Dr Gladstone had taught me to be practical. Raleigh, he said, was the first to dream; and though he lost his head, literally, when King James condemned him for bringing back pebbles to England instead of the gold nuggets he promised, his legacy endured. For centuries afterwards whitefolk came to the colony, wandering through the jungle, abandoning sense, in the search for El Dorado. Me, I would be level-headed, obedient to Dr Gladstone, though he did not heed his own injunction, lured into prospecting for Lady Elizabeth. Gold I would never get. I settled for the crown and two shillings, careful not to make a compact with the Devil. I chose my words in replying to his call for poison. "Nida gwan jiga gena," I said, reverting to idiotic gabble. He himself was already in a state of confusion, on the verge of gibberish. No doubt he took my response as assent, hence the gift of money, but my heart was clean before God and I promised Mr Basnett nothing even as I accepted the bribe. God is God, money is another matter: was that not the principle underlying slavery, for how else could whitefolk justify the trade in fellow human beings? They had to separate prophet from profit, doing God's business on a Sunday and rendering to Caesar for the rest of the week. Like sun and moon, God and money could exist in the same sky, the worship of one not interfering with adoration of the other. Why, therefore, could I not take Mr Basnett's money with a clear conscience, unlike Judas, who mixed up the two and brought the world to the brink of catastrophe? "Abolish slavery, and the world will collapse, nations sink into penury, mayhem and massacre will follow": the planters argued thus, banishing missionaries from their plantations, for missionaries were like Judas, putting God and money in the same column, instead of in different spaces in the ledger books.

I, too, nearly committed the same error. I withdrew to the privacy of my room to count and recount my fortune, pinching myself in case I was in a dream. A crown and two shillings! I was about to give praise to God for this trinity of coins, but caught myself in time. I looked at the coins, seeing them for what they were – they were not blessings from God, they were wages due to me on account of my people's knowledge of poison, which I had no intention of enacting. Still, so stupendous was the sum I couldn't help feeling that I was singled out, that I was like Mr Basnett, except in grief. He hoped I would bring Theodore to grief, as God had called him to suffering by removing his wife. I would have none of it, I would not permit my conscience to interfere with my appreciation of money. I looked again at the coins, translating them into things, for the coins were of this world. Growing up among massas taught me their value. The slaves lived in a community practically void of actual money, hence they needed MMadboy to explain what was meant by worth. Some of the women had more experience with money. Seeing cash pass hands between whitefolk, when slaves or cattle were being traded, they demanded the same from their massa before feeding him flesh – though only the beautiful ones, because they knew their master would not whip them, and scar the bodies he so favoured. The first night's tumble gained them a small copper coin. Though they knew not its purchasing power they reckoned its value by the sweat pouring from Massa's brows, as it would from their own men after lifting two or three bundles of cane. The next night the women demanded two or three coins accordingly. They grew bolder, like snakes that slithered away at the first approach of canecutters but were soon accustomed to the comings and goings. The women coiled up in bed, refusing to slacken until coins of a different size, or a different metal were paid, just as the canecutters flung stones at the snakes to budge them from a safe distance. The coins were bundled in pieces of cloth, according to their size and colour, and hidden under secret rocks, awaiting the day when they could be tallied by someone grown wise among the slaves. Their hopes came to naught; Massa tired of their flesh, going elsewhere to renew his appetite. He beat the women until they showed him the hiding places. He took them, coins of silver, brass, copper, the round ones, the ones with edges, he took them all. One minute they rich-rich, next minute they *minus nothing*: is *sudden* that afflict them.

★   ★   ★

I would not yield to Mr Basnett, only to be cheated by him afterwards. Nor did I need to await the coming of a special one who would lay bare the mystery of worth. A crown and two shillings could buy seven nights of tumbling with the choicest maidens, and a pair of snakeskin shoes into the bargain, six baskets of fish and a slingshot with specially rounded pebbles, five egg-bearing hens, four with a rooster young enough to breed them, three pigs, two calves and a partridge in a pear tree, stuck there by birdlime so I could practice my slingshot against it. Other slaves would yield, driven by hunger, but not me. Lady Elizabeth fed me well, but even if she didn't I would still, in my mind, free the partridge to soar high and higher, beyond the reach of pebble; beyond the reach of anklechain, muzzle, branding iron and all the other instruments which lowered our faces to the ground.

A crown and two shillings should have been sufficient instruments to humble me, Mr Basnett thought; to him all I was worth could be translated into sex-meat, pork, *poisson*, eggs, shoes, slingshot, and a partridge in a pear tree. I resented his underrating of me, knowing that Eliston would be rewarded for killing Theodore with an accountant's salary of ninety pounds a year, board and lodging gratis. Why not train me in figures and when I showed sufficient competency, appoint me as Eliston's apprentice, seeing that I was to be his accomplice in poison? When I mastered arithmetic I still would not cheat him, though it would be easy to secrete a pound here and there in the ledgers, under figures which seemed steady as stone but which with a sleight of hand could be lifted. The columns, too, seemed unshakeable, their bases sunk deep into the earth, but they could be lifted up and money hidden in the holes. Prophet, profit, ledger, legerdemain, poison, *poisson*... The money mattered to me, but the playfulness of words more, for which I knelt at Dr Gladstone's grave, lowering my face to the ground, thanking him for the *Dictionary*. I wanted to drink hemlock (not a nigger brew of kumari seeds – that was for slaves pining for home or punished too far; hemlock was a poison reserved for bookish men wearied of the prosaic doings of other men) but Dr Gladstone would not let me join him. I lived on – the *Dictionary*, the Classics and French cuisine my consolation for his loss.

★ ★ ★

Gradually I come to understand Mr Basnett's madness. There was his wife, the suddenness of her loss. He put on a brave face when he emerged from the attic, but it was a slave's mask. He was already enslaved to everlasting grief. His liking for Lady Elizabeth was, to begin with, a happy distraction, making it easier for him to wear the mask. But, as time passed, as Theodore bullied him, as Theodore threatened to take Lady Elizabeth, Mr Basnett changed. The mask slipped. Hatred for Theodore. Lust for Lady Elizabeth: not carnal, more the need to capture and tame her; or, at least, not to be cheated of her by Theodore.

He was, in truth, a pitiful creature. Apart from the odd lemon pip slipped into his drink I would not cheat him. My haul of a crown and two shillings was the result of honest trawling through my emotions for right similes. Sandfly, bull, poui blossom: Theodore bit into Mr Basnett's mind, ached and broke him; broke him figuratively and literally in terms of his wellness and his wealth. Theodore brought the plantation to the point of ruin, unbalancing Mr Basnett in a double way. His arms seem to shrink to the extent of his diminished worth, the elbow-bones like pointed sticks, though the rest of him was as fatty as usual. Skeletal and shekel-less, even his slaves felt for him; me too, though I was divided for I also relished the ways Theodore had made him into a pun, which could be multiplied or subtracted and still maintain the same measure of delight. But why, the slaves asked themselves, did Mr Basnett not dismiss Theodore upon the first suspicion of fraud? A sensible question, except to those learned in matters of Law. Mr Basnett had readily signed up Theodore to a three-year contract, seeing how poorly he intended to pay the accountant. He even allowed Theodore to draw up the document, signing and sealing it without bothering to peruse the sub-clauses, which, according to practice, were written in Latin. Mr Basnett was ignorant of Latin. To employ an attorney, whose business it would be to explain the sub-clauses, was an expense, however modest, that Mr Basnett preferred to shun. By the time he paid for their translation, it was too late; he had already been turned into a swine. Even if he had done so sooner, the contract would have proven too punitive to break. Mr Basnett was bound to it, or else he would forfeit the whole of a year's revenue from the sale of sugar. Apart from such a catastrophic loss, the owner of the plantation would voyage from England to Demerara to dismiss him in person, maybe even to prosecute and jail him. His reputation would be so besmirched in England that no one would employ him there if he chose to abscond rather than face incarceration. A runaway slave, when retrieved from under or within whatever rock or hole he hid, was tied to a pear tree, faster than birdlime. He could not even flutter when lashed. Slingshots would be handed out to his fellow slaves. Those who found his head were given as much fruit from the tree as they could eat. Only when he was concussed and covered in blood was he released. The Law allowed it, and it would allow for Mr Basnett's punishment should he dishonour the contract. Theodore might as well have tied him to a tree, robbed him of his blood, for Theodore had enslaved him to the letter of the Law. What sealed Mr Basnett's fate was that he had consented to Theodore's management of the plantation. In Court, Mr Basnett could not plead the innocence, clean heart and clear conscience with which I had taken his money (and – in my defence – a much lesser sum than Theodore deprived him of – on reflection an amount almost matching Theodore's weekly salary).

★　★　★

"Do as you will," Mr Basnett had told Theodore, several months before when he had visited the counting house to spend a friendly hour with his accountant, only to be verbally assaulted by him, overwhelmed by a battery of financial jargon. Theodore's extension of the slaves' lunch-break, improvements to their diet, extra holidays, and lessons in reading the Bible made them so grateful that they worked harder, cut more cane, and even made an extra journey to the punt though they were on the point of dropping with fatigue. They burst into song when Theodore approached; they called God's blessings upon him in their nightly prayers. The eldest among them claimed he could re-enact a ceremony offered for demigods, those who were human but possessed the gift of invoking rain to make their crops prosper. No-one believed him, for Africa was distant, but they watched in reverence as he dyed his chest in the colours of jandi blossoms, braided his hair with strips of peepul and danced around the night fire. He shouted out Theodore's name with such force that even the howler-monkeys fell silent, gazing down from their trees with the same bewilderment as the slaves beheld their performer.

Mr Basnett, to begin with, was so pleased by their industry that he didn't blanch when Theodore proposed paying the slaves, in hard currency, a monthly bonus, a sliver of a percentage of revenue but something all the same. It was only when he made plans to open up a shop to be run by the slaves themselves, with all the profits given to them, that Mr Basnett decided to confront Theodore. He cleared his throat, preparing an objection, but succumbed as soon as Theodore waved a book at him. "Adam Smith," he said. "A handbook for the future governance of the wide world, never mind the thousand acres you oversee!" Theodore opened the book, pointing to a set of tables. Mr Basnett looked at the page out of cowardice. The arithmetic made no sense. "Let it be as you intend," Mr Basnett said, hurrying from the counting house.

Theodore set about the construction of the shop. Mr Basnett had expected a hut at the edge of the plantation; he watched in despair the erection of an extension to the counting house, spacious, in solid brick, and roofed securely against the weather. There was even a chair behind the counter for the slave to rest between serving the customers. A straw fan was placed high on the ceiling; with a pull of the rope the slave could cool himself. "He'll soon have them gambolling in the canefield, munching on watermelons and grinning from ear to ear," Mr Basnett muttered to himself as he examined the new building, noting that air-bricks had been placed on one wall, to ventilate the slave even more. His own house lacked air-bricks! That night he raised the subject of luxury to Lady Elizabeth, inviting debate among the company. He lived frugally, but argued that luxury was essential for the cohesion of society. The planters all agreed with him. The more they spent on themselves, the more it benefited the lesser breeds. A coach, for instance, employed a host of hands in its construction – carpenters, craftsmen, ironsmiths, painters and varnishers, and that only for the shell. Seats and harnesses for the horses added leather-workers to the list, goldsmiths to give a splendid finish to the interior. Thirty-forty men and their apprentices; the money trickled down to them. Mr Basnett looked pleased with himself for initiating the conversation which moved from coaches to connoisseurship of wines, brandy and paintings – the last arousing arguments.

"Titian is not worth a farthing more than fifty pounds."

"Fifty pounds! Fie, you call yourself a man of taste! Titian is a veritable genius, no price is high enough to pay for one of his Madonnas."

"I prefer a Pietà myself; brings even a boor to tears."

"What do you say to the Moderns?"

143

"I rank Rubens before Thornhill for murals. Thornhill should be dangled from one of his ceilings, the fees he demands!"

"I hear Hogarth ran off with his daughter."

"Serves him right. Hogarth is vulgarity personified. Have you seen his *Harlot's Progress*?" Some of them hushed up, sinking their forks in the meat in sudden rapt concentration. Those were the guilty ones, I surmised. They kept a print of Hogarth's Moll hidden in a trunk under their bed, valuing it more than the Old Masters (who clothed their women). Now and again, late at night, when the urge took them, they gazed upon Hogarth's Moll by lamp light, envying the Jew who owned her.

Basnett, wanting praise for the flow of debate, beamed at Lady Elizabeth, inviting a fluttering of eyelids, but before she could flirt with him (for every gesture she made in response to him was interpreted as a token of affection), Theodore thumped the table to bring the meeting to order.

"Nothing but saltfish and broken rice reaches the slaves who build your coaches," Theodore said. The stab in his voice surprised them.

"So you are an abolitionist at heart; is that your dirty secret?" Mr Basnett asked, making the company laugh out loud. "A foreigner with dark complexion, a tincture of the Jew in him," Mr Basnett continued, encouraging them to mock Theodore. He looked again at Lady Elizabeth for flattery. She had grown pale at the mention of Jews. Mr Basnett was about to apologise to her for mentioning Jews at the dining table (an act of bad manners) when Theodore came between them a second time. "Adam Smith," Theodore said, turning to his meat and drink as if he had done with the conversation.

Mr Basnett didn't know about Adam Smith, apart from a table of computations Theodore had shown him. Still, to maintain his pride before Lady Elizabeth, and sensing the mood of the company, he frowned at Theodore, gathering his breath for a hiss.

A planter, representing their collective disgust, got up, growled at Theodore, called for his carriage and exited without even bowing to Lady Elizabeth or kissing her hand. The rest of them abandoned their meal and did the same, behaving just as rudely in not acknowledging the largesse of their hostess. Only Lady Elizabeth,

Mr Basnett and Theodore were left at the table. I thought Lady Elizabeth would be mortified, being accustomed to a grand finale, to a flourish of compliments. Instead, a smile brightened her face. She looked at Theodore as if grateful for his intervention which had sent the company scuttling away like so many Judases.

Mr Basnett, Theodore, me, her trinity of suitors remaining at the end of the ruined supper. Not a word passed between us, but in the silence I could hear Mr Basnett's blood simmering. He had felt singled out for Lady Elizabeth's affections. Why was she smiling at Theodore? Someone beneath him in social rank, beneath contempt, the way he antagonised the guests and brought the evening to an inelegant end. Theodore seemed not to have noticed the mass exodus he had caused. He continued eating, in breach of etiquette. Lady Elizabeth did not show displeasure, as Mr Basnett hoped. Her smile was like light shining through the singed wings of a moth. Mr Basnett wanted to escape her presence, but was too drawn to her. He could feel his skin stinging with heat. He thought of hellfire. He should have risen for his soul's sake. He stayed, sinning.

★   ★   ★

What evil had Adam Smith committed, I wondered, the mere mention of his name making gentlefolk behave like canecutters, leaving without so much as a curtsy? Who was he to create such unrest, a prelude to insurrection (I had expected the company to knock Theodore to the ground before they escaped in their carriages)? As to Theodore, having caused the equivalent of a slave revolt, should he not at least have laid down his knife and fork and, if not made peace with Mr Basnett, offered him an explanation?

Mr Basnett would not lower his dignity to seek out Adam Smith among the more knowledgeable planters. It was left to me to educate him, having been told all by Theodore.

"Here," Theodore urged me, "take Adam Smith's treatise, and when you have examined it, purchase it from me. The money is naught but you must pay for it. Remember this always: let a man pay for his needs, do not give to him gratis. He will value the shovel, guard it from rust, bluntness, theft, once it belongs to him. This is Adam Smith in brief. He is the future of the world."

The future! I could have dissented, knowing my *Samuel* Johnson was named after a prophet, one who lit up the future for us to behold. Theodore's *Adam* Smith was named after a sinner from a past so distant-dark that even MMadboy would be unable to count the years. Still, I took the book, to placate Theodore. He had selected various pages for me to read first, using rose petals as markers, as if the book was a billet-doux.

I studied the passages Theodore had underlined, which dealt with the subject of slavery. I read and reread them until I could recite them by heart, if not by head, for Mr Smith's arguments were complex.

"I have it in a box," I whispered it to Mr Basnett on his next visit. "I'll bring it tomorrow."

"Now, fetch it now!"

"But we begin to dine soon –"

"Damn the dinner! Hand it over now. I'll make an excuse to your Mistress for both of us."

"Then tell her you have stomach-ache, you need me to tend to you all night. Say that you trust me more than your own physician, seeing that I was trained by Dr Gladstone." Imagine me giving Mr Basnett instruction! My boldness carried no risk though, Mr Basnett was desperate for my help.

I rode home with him, *inside* the coach, *beside* him. The first few minutes dizzied me, so swift was my ascent in rank. I felt like a freed lark in the glee of rising air. As the journey continued I relaxed, even revelled in my new prestige. I looked at the gilt ornamentation (freshly done, Mr Basnett planning to take Lady Elizabeth for afternoon rides) and persuaded myself that, one day, expenditure on such luxury would trickle down to me. A trickle would do, no need to crave the impossible which would be the whole coach. Practical. Practical. Practical. The wheels rumbled over the pebbled road, sounding Dr Gladstone's injunction. This I neglected as soon as I reached Mr Basnett's abode and was settled in his drawing-room. A slave came to me with a tray of refreshments. I was scrutinising the room, my head swivelling from this wall to that, admiring the finery, more excessive than

our own abode. (Mr Basnett, anticipating visits by Lady Elizabeth, had refurbished the house.) As soon as the door opened and
the slave entered I caught myself, pretended that I was so accustomed to being among paintings and porcelain that I ceased to
notice them. Almost, for I could not quite still the beating of my
heart. Slaves were excessively vigilant, eyes and ears alert to any
sign of danger, like wild animals fearing predators. As he poured
me a glass of lemonade I suspected he heard my heartbeat and knew
that I was a fraud, that I belonged really to the fields. To put him in
his place I raised the glass to the light and, satisfied there were no
pips, waved him away. I could tell he wanted to linger, for he
stooped to pick up a particle of dust from the floor. He straightened
the edge of the carpet, relit a feeble candle, busying himself for no
other reason than to be in my presence. Was he simply perplexed
and wanted to find out why I was so exalted ("singled out", as Mr
Basnett would put it?) Or was he one of those who guarded his
master's property as if it were his own? Did he think that if he
looked away I would pocket whatever precious thing came to
hand? It was hard to tell for he wore a slave's face, habitually blank.
Even I could not read his thoughts. I realised again why massas
were so ready with the whip: their frustration at not being able to
comprehend their slaves. Beat them, just in case they were
plotting! Beat them again when their faces stayed masked! The
slave before me could have been seeking kinship. Or he could have
been the first to report me if ever I so much as whispered a
rebellious word. There were many like him who appeared utterly
trustworthy but betrayed a great uprising, one that took years of
preparation, for the sake of a trinket, the sole use of a slave-woman
for seven nights, a crown and two shillings worth of tumbling.

★ ★ ★

Mr Basnett returned to the drawing room with a maid in tow. He
made her sit beside me. A word whetted my appetite immediately: "pulchritudinous". He winked at me, but my face was stern,
in spite of my liquescent heart. His wink was such an unseemly
act, given the comely youth in our midst. "Pulchritudinous" was
too arrogant a term, I decided, too loud to describe her. She

seemed one who was unconscious of her charm; one, who, when faced with crude propositions, closed into herself, guarding her heart like a corinna flower at a droplet of rain.

The slaves had spoken of Mr Basnett as a cactus, comparing him favourably to the corinna which succumbed to the slightest shower. Muscle, calloused mind, a carbuncle for a soul: men were made into these by the machinery of the factory which yet manufactured sugar as aromatic as the corinna. The maid transformed the room, her presence in itself suggesting that beauty could never be commodified. It was traded like sugar, but the aroma and taste of sugar – the qualities that drew humming bird and spangled butterfly to the corinna flower – could never be captured by ledgers, jailed in a counting house. You could, with the infinite patience of a miser, number the needles of a cactus. Apart from its hardiness, its accountability made it more admired in the colonial mind than the corinna.

"Name her," Mr Basnett said, as if to soften the rebuke on my face. I was astonished by his offer. He was truly in my ownership, allowing me to do what only whitefolk could perform, giving title to a slave. "Bestow upon her whatever name tickles you." My look changed again to needles. By permitting me to name her he was in fact offering me the sole use of her as a seven-night trinket. It was impious behaviour on his part, acting as a pimp instead of penitent Catholic. I picked up a sugarcake, but before I put it to my mouth I spoke a prayer, in Latin, to put him to shame.

My words had the opposite effect, the language goading him to execrations against Theodore who had outsmarted him with Latin sub-clauses. He demanded his poison with such force that spittle shot from his mouth, a drop landing on the maid's face. She remained serene, as if accustomed to being spat upon by men, but I could sense her curling into herself. I longed to be closeted within her, and when the rain ceased and she unfolded, to be released as a scented breeze such as Miriam commanded. Miriam was cactus in appearance but she could awaken airs trapped in bark or rock, perfume them with her breath and send them forth as benedictions.

Mr Basnett's mouth frothed in anticipation of the effect that poison would have on Theodore.

"Open the box, give me ocular proof of it, money will follow." Right away, at the mention of money, I banished all thoughts of scented breezes or beds of petals and produced a parcel from my box (my Scottish box with its pictured stream as shiny as a florin), unwrapping it slowly, slowly, to suggest the price more valuable than the crown and two shillings endowed so far.

"A book! You brought me a book!" His mood changed from anticipation to revolt at the sight of the book.

"If you are to poison Theodore, do it with due diligence. Revenge is sweeter that way," I said. This failed to disarm him. He was like an incensed slave, refusing to lay down his cutlass. I raised my voice to quell him, as solders would fire warning shots over the heads of the rebellious. "This sweetens the poison," I shouted, thrusting the book at him like a bayonet. He was taken aback. I seized the moment by launching a salvo against Adam Smith, author of the book, explaining to Mr Basnett how Smith was a freethinker, a free-marketer, a free-the-slave maniac. Smith was a felon, a foul fellow, a fiend, a familiar, a fallen angel, a flibbertigibbet. Words issued from my mouth, splattering Mr Basnett, but being a cactus he responded sturdily. He was beginning to understand that to destroy Theodore, he must subdue not only Theodore's body but also his mind. Rebellion was not enough – that was for slaves. A full crusade was called for, the total elimination of smutty Smithian ideas and practices put in place by Theodore that threatened the sanctity of the colony. "No need for haste," I advised. "Clock the exact moment, wait, wait, watch, and then your time will come." He agreed, and, one gentleman to another, I offered my hand. He shook it, sealing our contract. *Sudden* – that thing again! One minute he was frantic for poison, the next he settled for a book. One minute I was a slave in his eyes, the next a wise man.

No magus, me. The sole reason I suggested he delayed his combat with Theodore until he was completely versed in Smith, was in expectation of coin. The more occasion I had to tutor him in free-market principles, the more money I could cajole out of him. Mr Basnett needed me to explain the intricacies of Smith's economics, and I predetermined that, at the end of three months or so, I would amass tutorial fees of three pounds. I was selling myself short, Smith himself would have advised me. Given the scarcity of intellectuals in the colony I could command six, even nine pounds. I let it be: Smith reckoned neither on Mr Basnett's meanness nor on my overwhelming need for three pounds. Smith's formulae were deficient in not taking into account the *value* of three pounds to me. The *value* was in the *need* and the *need* was of the *spirit,* not of the *body.* Three pounds would pay for my ship-passage to Scotland (with sufficient balance for boarding and lodging), my mind's destination, nay, destiny, to visit the homeland of my massa Dr Gladstone; to go, on his behalf, as his cultured and erudite ambassador; to tell his village of his grave at the edge of the plantation, shielded by palms; to read out the inscription on his grave, chiselled in Latin; to translate the epitaph for them; to dwell on his saintliness; to show them his medicine bag and tell what cures he provided to us; to sing a Negro ditty in his memory; to hand out to each and everyone of them a calabash of sorrel-drink or the juice of whatever local sacramental fruit was in season. What greater honour could I bestow upon Massa Dr Gladstone than accompanying his spirit across the seas back to Scotland, to final rest? Honour beyond value, though three pounds in coinage?

★   ★   ★

For now I was Mr Basnett's companion, tempering his spirit, delaying Theodore's entry into the grave. When it was time to retire, he himself showed me to the guest room, lingering at the door nervously in case it was not sufficiently furnished. I waved him away, the gesture coming naturally, as if I was born to dominate. The slave who waited upon me in the drawing room came up with a tray of milk and biscuits. He was no longer suspicious, rather obsequious in the extreme, smoothing and re-smoothing the bed-sheet, patting the pillows. Satisfied by his efforts he stood before me, a huge grin on his face, awaiting a compliment or a coin. The grin looked like a scar; I felt sorry for him but caught myself in time, sending him away with neither. Even so, he carried the grin to the door and turned to show it to me once more before exiting. Behind the closed door it might have changed into a scowl but I cared not. He was irrelevant in the scheme of things, of which I was, at present, maestro and Mephistopheles. I undressed and retired to bed, enjoying the sensation of lying under starched cotton. "Cut your coat to suit your cloth," Dr Gladstone used to say, tutoring me to be measured, to aspire to what was befitting to my condition. I thought of his other favourite saying, "A stitch in time saves nine", but in rehearsing it in my mind I felt the urge to rebel. Were it not for Lady Elizabeth's benevolence I would be wearing osnaburg all my life. I deserved silk, not out of charity but in appreciation of my talent. Mr Basnett recognised this, hence the goose-feather pillow and mattress. A surge of gratitude for Mr Basnett was matched by suspicion, even resentment, of Dr Gladstone, who would have a manger as my abode. I reclined in boudoir luxury, my eyes darting with an infant's glee from this fine object to that. With the tinkling of a bell I could summon three slaves to adore me, wise to all my needs. As to Dr Gladstone's stitch-in-time I could rip my nightclothes into nineteen or thirty-one pieces and still have them mended within the hour.

The maid caught me in mid-fantasy about being besuited in rakish silk and waited upon, as a wealthy patron, by artists, musicians, fencing-tutors. My cockiness waned the moment I noticed her. She blushed and averted her eyes. She had entered the room quietly, subdued by nerves. She held up a fan, uncertain as to how to proceed. She was in night clothes so threadbare that her bubbies and the contours of her still fledgling body showed through.

"I am nearly your age" she said, as if to appease my conscience. Mr Basnett had sent her to comfort me. "I know everything," she said boldly. "From the time I small, I learn." She contradicted herself by lowering the fan and looking away. I was baffled by the nature of her boast, then at her wilting into shyness. She surprised me again by sliding into the bed, still wearing her night clothes. "Shall I lie in the light or blow out the candles? I will do as you like."

"You will do my bidding?" I asked, unsure of my status when only a few minutes ago I was at ease with my superiority, plotting to acquire greater wealth than a crown and two shillings; even the three pounds passage-money to Scotland appeared beneath my dignity.

But why should I not inherit the earth? All of it. I placed my

Hogarth: *The Discovery*

hand around her shoulder, drew her to me. She rested her head on my chest, listening to the chaos of my heart. "You are more precious than the whole earth," I said foolishly: there were no right words for the sense of abundance that overwhelmed me. She lifted her face and kissed me. I stiffened, clamped my lips. I did not want to surrender, as I did that night in Miriam's bed (in dream if not in deed), awakening the next day to shame. I was glad that the candles stayed alight, guarding us from mishap.

She stroked my temple and cheeks to relax me. "I have never loved one of our own," she said. The sadness in her voice affected me, I pressed her to continue. She told me that, as a child, she had been seasoned for the appetite of the various massas who owned her, and their friends. She was only intimate with whitefolk's bodies. When Mr Basnett ordered her to my room she felt nervous, original, not knowing what to do, what to expect. Lying in Mr Basnett's house I thought myself cradled in luxury and calculated my worth, but it was she who was the infant, and it was she who was beyond price.

"I could have disobeyed Massa Basnett and not come to you. Punishment would follow, but at least my will would have been unbroken. But in the end I decided to come to you." She lowered her face demurely, then looked up at me with the eyes of a vulture. "I know what to do, how to do it," she said, reaching to touch me. I resisted. Too much *sudden*, so I hugged her to me, counting the seconds and minutes, a time long enough for us both to be lulled into quiescence.

"I have no name," she reared up, anticipating my question.

"Would you like me to give you a name?"

"I can name myself, but you can try as well." Her eyes quickened at the prospect.

"I could give you a Classical name, or a plain one…"

"You choose," she said, coyly.

I decided to impress her. "You can be called Juno, the Roman goddess of the moon. Juno is –"

"I don't like Juno, give me another," she interrupted, screwing up her face in mock-petulance.

"Why don't you like Juno? Let me explain that Juno is the –"

"I don't like it," she said with the wilfulness of a child. "It sounds like June, which is monsoon time and I catch a fever, but even then I have to work the bed."

"Work the bed?" I was taken aback.

"Silly boy, you!" She giggled at my naiveté before explaining herself. "When Massa feel my hot skin he think I am wild and in want. If you see how he grim his jaw like he plotting so many ways to molest me, he can't make up mind how to start and where to –"

"Let it be Persephone then," I intervened, not wanting to hear her confession. "Persephone is the goddess of bounteous lands."

"No, not Persephone, call another."

"Helen? Will Helen do? She was a queen unrivalled in beauty."

She paused to save my feeling, then shook her head resolutely. "I need kith and kin name, not whitefolk," she said, then bringing our play to a close she cast doubt on my integrity. "Why you so beloved of Juno and Helen and them when you is black? Unless the candlelight blind my eye you look black-black to me, no so?"

"You can be Negro and still be Nero; Latin is for all of we," I said, slighted by her attitude.

"Latin? What stay so? It sound like sin, what whitefolk does do, late sin, the last sin when night come. I want kin not Latin. And I don't trust you when you say Juno is this, Helen is that, how you know?"

"I am a youth of distinction," I answered with as much dignity as I could muster. I immediately regretted my rebelliousness for she shifted away, raised herself to gaze more fully at me. I expected scorn, but her voice was gentle with song:

> Negro boy, whisper me a lullaby
> before a rain come and make we both cry

She leaned over me, wiped my eyes as if wiping away tears. "Listen to what I say. Negro don't know Latin and that, only how to parrot." She mimicked a parrot, flapping her arms and shrieking, "Juuunooo! Helllleen! Bad girl Juno, baaad girl Helen, take off clothes, let Maaaasa smackkk you blaaackk backside."

"Sssch," I urged, putting my hand to her mouth. "Mr Basnett will wake up in ire."

"Don't bother with he; I done put a pinch of tapra in he night-time cocoa, he go sleep through quake or typhoon," she said.

"A pinch of tapra? In his cocoa?"

"Don't fret, is for the best, or else he wake up, sleep break two-three times a night, and he call out different name: Theodore, he scream, or Elizabeth with one big sigh, or howl for Hannah. I show you." She imitated Mr Basnett pounding his fist on the pillow, or caressing it, or burying his head into it and sobbing, "Laad-o-Gaad! Gaad-Laad Jesu! Oh Jesu, oh Jesu, bring back Hannah, bring she back one last time!" Such was the genuineness of her imitation that tears trickled down her cheeks and it was my turn to wipe them away. "He is good massa, Mr Basnett, never raise hand or manhood at me, though he mean with food; never mind that; is Gaad make him so. And when he buy me he did save me from the massa before and the ones before who love hot skin."

"Mr Basnett is indeed a gentleman," I said, but she would not be comforted.

"What will happen to me? What will be? When I reach mothering age will I make infant for whiteman, and instead of one, is two slaves will be, and both of we without name?"

I wanted to assure her that Mr Basnett would not sell her on to a lascivious planter, that her belly would remain fallow, but in the future she would be a free woman... I could not, however, bring myself to falsehoods. Instead I drew her to me again, pressing her to my chest to stifle her woe. "Listen to my heart again, listen, it is calling out your name. What does my heart deem you to be?"

She recovered her composure, becoming a child again. "Bram-bram, bram-bram it sound like; what silly name, not for me, howsoever it come free! Even Juno or Helen nicer than bram-bram! You cannot make your heart talk proper Negro even though your mouth talk proper English and Latin?"

It was a challenge I was doomed to fail, being a scion of the *Dictionary*.

"Don't worry" she said, placing her head on my shoulder, nibbling at my ears. "I have Negro names for myself. I name 'blunt-hoe' or 'carrion-crow' or 'food-no-more', 'wait-outside-the-door', 'come-here-you-whore', 'scrub-the-floor', 'what-aneyesore'. I have names for myself, I am all the birdcalls of a parrot."

"You are none of these," I said in rebuke. "You are a corinna flower." The candle spluttered and died the moment I spoke, the unexpected breeze heralding rain. She curled up to me, wanting to be healed, wanting my physician's hand, her skin hot as in a monsoon fever.

★　★　★

To inherit the earth: how paltry compared to the power of Corinna to beguile. Get behind me, Mr Basnett, I should have said, when he proffered coins, calling instead for Corinna. She was beyond me; I disbelieved I could ever make family with her, a crown-and-two-shillings nigger like me. Best to strive for a bounty, out of which to buy her freedom and that of all my kith and kin... if not *all*, then at least Cato, Alice, Dido, Billy. I resolved to remain in discipleship of the Devil for that was what Mr Basnett had become. Once a devout Catholic, taming his urges by doctrine and ceremony, he was now a mere pimp, offering Corinna (and a child at that!) for seven nights in return for my favours. He persuaded Lady Elizabeth to let me visit his house nightly, claiming he was ill (which he was, in truth, being gripped by fanaticism) and needed a slave to read to him, to becalm his nerves and prepare him for sleep. Every night I read to him passages from Adam Smith, explaining the consequences of his ideas. Mr Basnett was aroused to nightly wrath. He barely got six hours' sleep before having to rise to discuss plantation business with Theodore. He grew more and more haggard of mind, demanding the poison *now*, but I always managed to delay the deed by holding out the prospect of Theodore writhing in pain, his freethinking mind destroyed, calling out for water or a kindly slave to bludgeon him for death. "Don't set him free right away, let us prolong the moment. The longer we wait, the better."

The better for all of us, I thought to myself, but especially for me, since Mr Basnett gave me a half-crown every night I tutored him. God bless avarice and those who dream of it! The coins quickly filled the Scottish box. One morning, when Lady Elizabeth was still in bed, I counted my wealth and discovered that I was worth sixpence more than all the money paid for me from birth, to different massas. A full sixpence! I was so astonished that, instinctively, I called out to my mother, to show off my achievement.

Lady Elizabeth found me staring out of my window. "Why so glum, dear Francis? What are you clutching in your hand?" Without facing her I opened my palm to reveal the sixpence. It was dingy to begin with but I had rubbed it excessively in my palm as if to conjure up the spirit of my mother. Now it shone but I had no care to look at it, putting it back into the box without ceremony. Miriam was right; I was a husk of child, I would never become a man of substance, no matter how much money I heaped up.

"Dear Francis!" Lady Elizabeth sighed, but before she could attempt to console me, I said, "Not *dear* Francis! Never, never put it thus, for I am nothing but *cheap*. Call me *cheap* Francis so I can recognise myself."

It must have been the first time I showed rudeness to Lady Elizabeth for she looked as if she had to sit down, otherwise she would swoon. I did not offer my chair to her; she had to make do with the bed. A madness must have come into my head for I heard myself talking balderdash.

"Cheep, cheep, cheep," I said, imitating a chicken. I even got up and lowered myself to the floor, and pretended to strut like a chicken, head leading, body following comically. "Cheep, cheep, that is all, and what a tiny voice I am! Even a parrot excels, it can caw, caterwaul, chatter."

It was when I began to make parrot noises that I remember Lady Elizabeth falling from the bed with such clatter that two slaves rushed into the room, one fanning her, the other picking me up by the scruff of my neck, throwing me unto my bed, throughout which actions I continued to cluck. Lady Elizabeth recovered quickly, reassuring the household that I did not assault her (in tumbling to the floor her blouse had slipped, exposing a breast), that my madness was *sans* malice.

A physician was rushed to my bedside. He felt my pulse, probed my mouth, pummelled my chest, then pronounced flux.

Piffle, I said to myself, being more learned in the science of diagnosis than he. Not flux at all; my mind chafed at my mother's absence, that was the cause. I felt an urge to mock him, for he was being too solicitous, asking me questions about the regularity of my bowels, my pattern of sleep, my diet – no doubt to impress Lady Elizabeth (who, throughout my ordeal, sat on the bed holding my hand) and earn a higher fee.

"Why is a mother like an embankment?" I asked him, thinking to start off in a harmless way.

He was confused, but Lady Elizabeth, knowing my riddling, smiled in expectation of the taunting. After a pause, I answered, "because they are both dams." Three quick barbs followed, making Lady Elizabeth blush and the physician's face twist in alarm. "If your mother takes up harlotry what will be her fate?" "She will be sorely damned." "If you have a Latin mule for a mother how will you address her?" "Materfamiliass." "If a Frenchman rides your mother, what will he call her?" "Ma mère."

I waved him away before he could splutter out a complaint to Lady Elizabeth. "I have taught you language, go and profit from it and let me be!" I said.

★　★　★

A partial and momentary eclipse of the mind was my only malady, but I turned it to my advantage, staying in bed for three days. Mr Basnett, the one who *was* barking mad, was quick to visit, out of concern for me as well as the satisfaction of being in Lady Elizabeth's company. "Poor thing, he looks wan and wasted," Mr Basnett said: being Lady Elizabeth's pet it was in Mr Basnett's interest to pity me and even furnish me with a consoling coin; the higher the denomination, the more appreciation of him by Lady Elizabeth, he hoped. His lavishness, however, yielded little dividend. Lady Elizabeth showed him the proper courtesies and the door. He looked back at me before he left, a silent plea for placing a compliment in her ears. I winked as he did when he presented Corinna to me. I will pimp for you, my wink reassured him. I felt sorry for him, a serial loser. First, the lowliness of his upbringing in Britannia as a Catholic; then a widower; now a crazed soul. The cards were stacked against him; he lacked Theodore's legerdemain to rearrange them.

"Pen me an amorous poem," he demanded one night, after my usual recitation from Adam Smith. "Lady Elizabeth's heart must be mine, only mine." *Only mine*: my lessons were obviously wasted, for the crux of Adam Smith was the abolition of monopolies. But, on reflection, Smith's principles were again faulty, for it could not apply to marriage where monogamy was a *sine qua non*. Marriage was a type of trade, a woman giving heirs in return for a man's largesse, but the exchange was governed by the principle of monogamy; otherwise, were different men to seed the woman's belly, there would be chaos over heirs and inheritances. Encouraging free markets would not work: once a wife was taken, the transaction was settled. No other bidder, however extravagant, should undo it. Only slaves could pass hands and could be bred willy-nilly. Smith's relevance to the whitefolk's world was limited, I concluded, but who was I to compose a counter-treatise? Better to hire my pen to Mr Basnett and be paid extra for the monopoly on my verse.

★ ★ ★

No poet's garret mine, nor loneliness, but Mr Basnett's drawing room and two slaves in attendance. One sharpened my quill, stirred the ink; the other prepared tea. To clear the mind of crudities or languid disposition I requested China, exceedingly expensive given its far passage from another continent and exotic methods to preserve its virtue, but I merited it. To choose a lesser tea would have been to compromise the start of my writing career. Mr Basnett deserved more than doggerel, such was his anguish. A quack poet, dispensing clichés and panaceas would be a disappointment to the memory of Dr Gladstone. My compositions had to be effective. They had to animate the faculties, keep up the vigour of the spirits, expel the cloudy vapours that darkened meditation, increase the celerity of the blood's motion (even now, years later, I could parrot Dr Gladstone's phraseology).

I chose, too, the most expensive desk to work at. Mr Basnett, not yet realising how perilous his finances were, had refurbished the drawing room. Mahogany furniture, linen armchairs with ivory handles, and best of all a new sofa of scented feathers on which he planned to court Lady Elizabeth. His resolve to live frugally after his wife's death had given way to extravagance. An ageing peacock attempting to revive its splendour could elicit sympathy, but Mr Basnett was never a gaudy creature to begin with. A dull, devoted Catholic husband, then a tightfisted widower: how to transform him into an Adonis would be a task even Hercules might have balked at. Just as Hercules bore the weight of the world on his bent back, so I leant to the desk, already exhausted though I had not yet conceived of the first word. I began to doubt my talents. My French cooking was false, my Latin basic, my learning in the Classics as mythic as the stories they told.

I looked at Mr Basnett who had placed himself at the far end of the room. He was fat and round like Hercules's globe.

"Let me be waited upon by Corinna," I said in a moment of inspiration. Not recognising the name I had to wink at him. He clapped his hand and she appeared in an instant.

"Will you sit by the window, let me see you in light?" I asked, shyly, and she obliged.

Fresh quills like oars, my muse Corinna in sight like a ship's mascot, Basnett waiting with rewards for a successful venture: it was time to launch my career. There were many false starts before I could travel from the left margin of the page to the right. I crossed out words. My sleeve smudged the ink. My rhythm was clumsy. There were too many syllables. I glanced at Corinna. She sensed me floundering. With a slight raising of her brow she saved me. Four lines came like a fair wind, and then another four. I stopped, put down my pen, for, given her inspiration, I could have sailed on and on beyond the pillars of Hercules, into unchanted seas. No bard before me to sing of such seas! Best, however, to proceed with caution. "Discipline. Measure. Moderation": Dr Gladstone called to me beyond the grave, reminding me that he was my first muse. I reread the verse, revised it, making it more chaste whilst remaining faithful to Corinna. Although Mr Basnett was patron, and the verse commissioned for his use, it was composed out of my love for Corinna. I owned no gilt furniture, armchairs with ebony handles, expensive sofa. Not even the clothes I wore belonged to me. Verse would be my tribute to Corinna, though never sufficient, for she deserved to inherit the earth. Happily never sufficient, for I would be provoked into writing more and more for her until I became my own little book.

> When turtledoves coo at the rising of day,
> Or the linnet, sweet warbler, wings thro' the grove;
> Just so I and Phyllis together did play,
> Oh! Such is the voice of the charmer I love!
> Her cheek in the rosebud, methinks, I behold;
> Erect as the pine-tree my Phyllis does stand :
> And when the fair lilies their whiteness unfold,
> I long to be kissing of Phyllis' dear hand.

Mr Basnett was besides himself when I recited the verse to him. I, too, was pleased with my conceits, looking to Corinna for accolade. She pretended to brush an insect off her arm, her skin irritated by its bite. She was signalling disapproval of the naming of Mr Basnett's love, the obvious closeness of Phyllis to disease. "Such triteness!" I imagined her tutting. "If you intend to insult him, do it subtly, like slow poison. Besides, verse should lift the spirit. Keep poison and pique for prose." I marvelled at her wisdom, she who could barely read but who could urge such distinction between forms.

Unlike my Corinna, Lady Elizabeth's response was unhelpful to a poet, never mind to Mr Basnett. "He has asked me to present this to you," I told her. "He says he was engaged in his composition for countless restless hours, waking up in the middle of the night to correct a word, going back to sleep, rising again because of a comma being wrongly placed, corrupting the flow of his feeling."

Lady Elizabeth seemed unimpressed by the arduousness of a poet's life. She did study the page, but then said, "The handwriting is pleasing. Did he employ a scrivener?"

"It is his own effort. His fingers were ink-stained when he surrendered the poem to me," I said defensively.

"Then tell him I commend his effort," she said, putting aside the poem and asking me to peel her an orange.

I needed more encouragement from her, to foment Mr Basnett's passion and the flow of florins to my pocket. I tried again to kindle her spirit. "Look how well he has crafted it. Such syllabic intelligence, regularity of beat, nicety of rhymes! To think that his profession is manager of a plantation when his true gift is husbandry of words and moods!" I could have said "stewardship" or "superintendence" of words and moods, but chose "husbandry" to discover from her response whether she harboured any affection for him.

She was not drawn, sucking at the orange like a stubborn child. After a while, she said with a flirtatious smile, "Theodore is teaching me Russian, such a sweet tongue."

"I don't know it." I was taken aback by my own bluntness.

"Theodore tells me the Cyrillic script is like a work of art. He wrote out a line; it was indeed a marvel to behold. Go fetch it, it lies beneath my jewellery-box."

I did as she bade, resentful that Theodore's words should be kept at her bedside, beneath pearls and rubies, whilst my composition was discarded.

"Is it not splendid to the eyes and senses?" she demanded, unfolding the paper for my inspection.

The fact that she had folded it with such care disturbed me. I looked at the script and nodded in as lively a manner as duty demanded. "Truly to be admired," I cooed like the turtledoves in my own verse.

★ ★ ★

Mr Basnett was insistent that Lady Elizabeth should have penned a letter of appreciation to him.

"She was moved by your script; she said it was splendid to the eye and senses."

"Why then did she not write to me?" His tone was ominous, as if threatening withdrawal of patronage. He went further, hinting that he might have to consider selling off Corinna, the plantation cashflow being sluggish. I counterattacked, to protect our wellbeing, and was surprised at the spontaneity of my cunning.

"Surely, Mr Basnett, you forget that your dearest is a lady. Can you expect such a person of breeding to commit her feeling to paper? You must suffer her silence, as befits the noble quality of your romance."

Mr Basnett fell silent, remembering his inexperience of women, especially women of quality. Mrs Basnett was homely, straightforward: there had been no need, in their relationship, for straining after metre and rhyme. She was plain in appearance when he first met her. It was at a roadside stall in the poorer quarter of Bethnal Green. She was buying a new shawl for Sunday worship which was to mark the martyrdom of St Veronica. Mr Basnett was on his way to the tailor, to be measured for a suit to wear at an interview the following week. He was clerk to a cloth manufacturer. The appointment would see him elevated to a new profession, assistant to the assistant to the Deputy Keeper of Hounds, the kennel owned by no less a gentleman and hunter than Lord Bathurst, the King's third cousin. From such a position he could eventually be promoted to service in the Royal Household itself.

Mr Basnett walked briskly, excited by the prospect of advancement. He knew nothing of dogs apart from those which roamed his neighbourhood. More carcass than canine, Basnett thought, a different species to the creatures of pedigree in his prospective charge, groomed and better fed than most of the people milling around the street, begging, bawling out penny ballads, accosting him with cheap goods. Soon he would be freed of them. His whole life had been spent among mendicants, drunks and streetsellers, for he lived with his parents, in an unfortunate area. It was not quite like St. Giles – London's benchmark for depravity, swarming with whores and gin-addicts, where two or three throats were cut every night. Still, decline had set in, especially since the government had employed new constables to clamp down on smuggling. The illegal dues from smuggling financed his neighbourhood; without them beggary would follow and a flux of whores.

It was whilst dwelling on dogs and flux that Mr Basnett first sighted his Hannah. A crowd had gathered around the stall, for St Veronica's day was popular and the trader seemed to be the only one supplied with shawls. Mr Basnett saw Hannah at the edge of the crowd, too meek to jostle to the front. People butted in, pushing her back almost to the brink of the gutter. He rushed forward, grasping her by her waist, just in time to stop her slipping into the stew. She blushed. He apologised for his manhandling of her. "I've come to buy a shawl," she said. "Can I be of any assistance?" he asked, addressing her frock rather than her face, out of bashfulness. It was plain cotton, faded in places. It bore only a single button, at the neck, indicating a life chastened by poverty. His new suit was to be dotted with six buttons. His relative wellbeing made him unexpectedly bold. He presented her with the shawl of her choice.

"Shall I walk you home?" he asked, surprised by his offer, for, apart from his mother and female relatives, he had never before engaged so intimately with the opposite sex.

He could not remember her answer, if there was any, for she may have murmured her assent. He accompanied her to the mouth of the alleyway where she lived; nearby was the Catholic Church, a modest structure set in a warren of houses, almost hidden from sight, as if still sheltering from the wrath of the Reformation. Mr Basnett quickly abandoned his own church to attend Hannah's. He was in his new suit; a little loose around the arms and waist, the tailor making provision for an increase in fatness, but handsome all the same. He arrived an hour before time, took up position in the back pew so he could see her entering. He would rise, bow, and when she showed surprise he would merely shrug, as if to say that his regard for her necessitated his early attendance. A shrug, a wave of the hand, a wink: Mr Basnett preferred to communicate his feelings thus, being a man of meagre expression.

The church filled up, with single numbers, then in a hurry of bodies. Mr Basnett, thinking he had lost her in the sudden rush, began to crane his neck above the crowd but the organ struck up. All stood, and being a service in honour of a Saint, would remain standing throughout.

Afterwards, he waited patiently outside the church as the worshippers filed out. There were women in choice brocades, others wore petticoats too scanty for his liking. Some exposed their neck with unbecoming assurance. It seemed the women had come to church to advertise their availability. One emerged wearing a familiar shawl. His heart raced. He thought of hounds in full chase. It was not his Hannah though. He imagined the pain of the fox being trapped and torn apart.

★　★　★

At the interview he sweated in his suit, and could not explain properly why he was qualified for the appointment. He felt hot and wet and fat, his body and his tongue. He blurted out that he was a Catholic, as if to end his torment. He wobbled out of the room, jobless. The doorman sniggered as he left. When he reached home his mother helped him out of his clothes. She could tell from the numbness of his eyes that he was not to be in the employ of Lord Bathurst, but she hid her disappointment. Her only son, not handsome, far from it. Plump and squat, balding prematurely, though only twenty-six. Still, he could read and write, add and subtract. Given a chance he could rise above his station in life. He deserved to be better than a clerk. Her husband earned a pittance shovelling dirt. He was born in muck and would die from it. Poverty was their lot unless Mr Basnett struck gold, or at least a job that paid more than three shillings a week. Three shillings, enough to feed the five of them, but little left over to be saved for the marriage of his sisters, one twenty-eight, another twenty-seven, their prospects diminishing as each year passed.

His humiliation brought on a fever. He called out for Hannah in his delirium. All night he called out her name. His mother kept vigil, fanning away flies and evil spirits from his forehead, asking three favours from St Hilda, St Anne and St Veronica, one to banish his fever, the second to find him higher wages, the third to bring Hannah (whoever she was) to his bedside. All her life she had prayed, to no avail, so when Hannah appeared at the door the very next morning, it was nothing but a miracle! "I am Hannah," she said, but she might as well have announced herself as an apparition of the Virgin.

Hannah, by merely looking upon Mr Basnett, lifted his fever. She was wearing the shawl bought for St Veronica's Day. Later she was to confess that she had deliberately not gone to church that fateful Sunday because she wanted to shun him, to sap whatever little self-confidence he possessed. At their first meeting he had talked briefly of his destination – the tailor's shop – and of his forthcoming interview. Poor foxes! She disliked any act that caused pain. She prayed that his application to be in Lord Bathurst's employ would be rejected. She had agreed to him attending her church that Sunday, knowing that her absence would so hurt him that he would falter at the interview. There was a loneliness about him which meant he could not survive rejection. She recognised it when he accompanied her home. He was out of step, either a foot in front or a foot behind her, too nervous to walk beside her. He could not form his words, turning his face away when he spoke; partly out of an instinctive inarticulacy in female company and partly because he was holding in his stomach to reduce the appearance of fatness.

★ ★ ★

He often wondered how his fever came to Hannah's attention, drew her to his bed, but could not formulate the question without blushing in shame, so he let it be. Faith triumphed over reason: Saints had granted his mother's wishes. At St Veronica's bidding (she who had brought them together at the stall) they married, Hannah wearing the shawl she had accepted from him, knowing that she would not wear it to church that Sunday but would save it for an eternity of feast days, the endlessness of their marriage on earth and in heaven.

Mr Basnett's mother was already dumbfounded by his recovery from his fever and by his marriage when he came home one day with news that he had struck gold. The cloth manufacturer, his employer, had invested in a plantation in Demerara, the land of El Dorado. Mr Basnett had been appointed assistant to the deputy manager of livestock, and was to set sail within the week.

Mr Basnett's mother cared nothing that this gold was at the end of the earth, six thousand miles away, but Hannah was apprehensive. The marriage was only three months old. To remove herself from her family… then the long passage to a pagan world... Still, she packed up their belongings without fuss and put on a brave face when it was time to bid goodbye. Of course the tears broke through. The sight of her hugging her parents and siblings, and the howling coming from such a tender mouth, made Mr Basnett envious. He expected pity to overcome him but it was otherwise. He suddenly felt angry, at his parents, his neighbours, his country. His parents valued him as a wage-earner. His neighbours only acknowledged him when they needed to borrow. As to his country... his face contorted. Hannah's family took it as a sign of shared grief but Mr Basnett was picking at the scab of his recent humiliation, when his Catholicism was a demerit to the keeping of Lord Bathurst's hounds.

His rage continued throughout the journey to Demerara, the tedium of which only clarified his memory. He had expected tempests and sea-monsters and pirates, which at least would have distracted him, but it was uneventful sailing. It was only on the approach to Demerara, heralded by flying-fish landing on deck and dolphins cavorting like welcoming natives, that the ache subsided. Demerara was calm, the warlike natives (mostly Caribs) long dispossessed by the British of their face-dyes, drums and arrows. His employer had told him that his status would be increased in the colony on account of his whiteness. He had told him this (also about the Caribs) to entice him to the colony, and to compensate him for his modest wages. As the ship docked in Georgetown, a weight fell from him. In the new world, his fatness would matter nothing. No more sneering. He would never again have to answer to his superiors at work when they called out "dumpling" or "sow" and he put down his pen and waddled to their offices. He was a whiteman now, neither fat, balding, clumsy nor self-conscious. Though as a Catholic, he would never become a high-ranking officer in the colony, there were no other obstacles to his progress. Best of all was Hannah, who rescued him from the lifelong bachelorhood he was prepared to endure in England, given his unshapeliness and his taking fright in the presence of women. He could not help his fright; it occurred like diarrhoea, sudden, spontaneous. When it was over he was still not purged, his sense of fatness endured. Hannah, though, had married him despite this.

As they disembarked, he cogitated upon the miracle of her presence. Throughout the journey she had carried herself with a quiet dignity. Complaints were called for because the food was infested with vermin, but she was a picture of meekness as she picked rat-droppings from the meat. He paced the deck, stones in hand, waiting to pelt any rat that emerged. She spent her time in embroidery, or in watercolours, scenes of rills and meadows, remembrance of a green England. Mr Basnett marvelled at the delicacy with which she stitched or brushed. He wished he had her adroitness. He regretted the fatness of his fingers.

She would inherit the plantation, then the whole earth, Mr Basnett resolved, overcome with adoration for his wife. He would labour and accumulate, enough to free her from the weight of need, the excess fat repatriated to their families.

★   ★   ★

"Persist. We must," I said, arranging the papers on my desk. "Women of quality like to be courted and to keep their suitors in worry."

Once all was ready, my muse and Mr Basnett in place, at far ends of the room, I began. A glance at Corinna activated my pen. I imagined the day Corinna would cease to be near me. My mind became fluent with grief:

> *But since she is absent, my vines all impare;*
> *My flow'rs unwater'd, my spade lies reclin'd :*
> *To sow, nor to reap, is no longer my care;*
> *I only plant sorrows to torture my mind.*

"I am as yet an unqualified physician," I reported on returning from Lady Elizabeth. "You must stay in pain a while longer."

"How long?" Mr Basnett demanded. "How long must I be kept on leash?"

"Her heart is melting," I lied. "A full tear fell from her when I read your verse."

"Will she not send the slightest token of her affections, if not an epistle?"

"She will, but we must wait, wait; it will not be in vain, your freedom will come," I said.

Lady Elizabeth had giggled when I recited the lines. I was satisfied, for her rejection would prolong my game with Mr Basnett and keep Corinna at my side. Mr Basnett had mentioned again that Corinna might have to be taken to market if the economy slid into recession. It was a dangerous game, an error on my part could prove ruinous.

"Invite him to tea, if not supper, poor man! He is quite taken with you," I urged Lady Elizabeth.

"You lance his boil," she said curtly. "As to soirées, I am done with them, they bore me. Come dress my hair and cease your politicking for Mr Basnett's cause; Theodore will be visiting soon."

It was my choicest duty combing and ribboning her hair, but mention of Theodore slowed my hand. "I see he has written to you again," I said, nodding towards the jewellery box which was propped up higher by at least two other folded sheets of paper. She looked at me through the mirror, comfortable in being at one remove, even though my hands were fondling her locks.

"Do I notice reproach on your face or do your looks deceive?" she asked. "Are you no longer an acolyte of Theodore? Fie! And he speaks so fondly of you!"

"He is indeed an admirable man, in all respects, my Lady," I said, and when she tried to conceal her feeling by lowering her eyes, I snipped off a locket of hair, palmed it with a dexterity rivalling Theodore's.

"Is Theodore truly as you say?" she asked quietly, and I nodded again in the direction of the jewellery-box.

"He is like a mine laden with ore, beyond Raleigh's wildest dream, but even then he cannot match the glimmer of your eyes." I sighed, unable to contain my emotions for her. My fingers stroked her temple, brushed away a solitary wisp. She indulged my longing, allowing me to continue playing with her hair. After all I was a husk of a boy, precocious to be sure, but hardly in Theodore's mould. I was hurt by her patronage, which was hitherto beneficial to me. I sensed, in the way she looked at me through the mirror, a *commingling* of pity and amusement. The word made me shudder. I braided her hair without the usual care, imagining the two of them lying under a sheet, in the same darkness Corinna and I shared, except that when Corinna arose, she was still untouched.

"Theodore is a lover of slaves, he is not of your rank. Plus he is from the East, with a hint of impurity in his blood," I said, echoing the prejudices of whitefolk like Mr Basnett.

"A dangerous man! Then you should have guarded me from him, young Francis," she scolded, again through the mirror, determined to be a spectator rather than engaging directly with me. "To think what a man of his ilk is capable of, robbing me of my cash, my jewellery and –"

"Pounce upon your virtue too," I added sarcastically, for she was only play-acting. She puckered her brow in mock-alarm.

"You envisage him as a brute, forcing himself upon me?"

"God forbid, but he bullies Mr Basnett; he is favourable to any act of inclemency," I said, whetting her appetite.

She put her hand to her mouth as if in shock. "Bolt the door, shutter the windows," she said, knowing full well that the bird had flown. I tied the last ribbon to the ends of her plaits, tightly, in a triple knot, to frustrate Theodore when next he sought to dishevel her hair in bed. He was close to undoing Mr Basnett, but I would resist, put him to task.

★　★　★

"We must resist Theodore," I advised Mr Basnett. "We should conspire against any move he makes to emancipate the slaves, for that is his ultimate mission." (I spoke in truth, if not in earnest, Theodore having divulged his dream to me). Mr Basnett listened closely as I explained that Theodore was more dangerous than sandfly, poui, or bull. Their assaults were immediate; Theodore was wily, biding his time until the moment came to pounce. "First, he alters the work-hours of the slaves, saying it is to your benefit. Second, he argues that they should be given money to teach them to shop. Third, he agrees that they can purchase their own freedom, pricing them at a rate they can afford. If they cannot manage a lump-sum then he will institute a method of instalments. As soon as one slave has paid for his freedom, he could get a letter of credit and acquire a fellow nigger or two.

> *Three gone in one go*
> *we fly de nest before you know*
> *shake de birdlime from we toe*

My Negro ditty provoked Mr Basnett. I had to be scrupulous in my training of him, striking a balance between the taming of emotion and its untrammelled expression. Like a circus tiger he had to be kept in a state of performance, obedient to the whip, yet waiting to pounce, the tension arousing the appetite of the spectators.

The consequences of failure were unbearable to contemplate. If Mr Basnett went berserk, murdered Theodore and was jailed, then my income as his poet would end. If Mr Basnett stayed sane but unable to turn around the fortunes of the plantation, then Corinna and others would be disposed of to balance the books. Worst of all, in terms of my wellbeing, would be the emancipation of slaves (Theodore's intention). I would lose the respect that being Lady Elizabeth's Negro gave me. I was not free in Law but in fact, Lady Elizabeth's household mine to command – the kitchen, boudoir, dining room and (until recently usurped by Theodore) bedroom, my sovereign property. I would be as worthless as a deflowered maiden if every Negro was set free. Theodore was indeed a rapist in the guise of liberator.

To keep Mr Basnett in balance was my urgent task. I was his adviser, his promised apothecary of poisons, his poet and now accountant of his mental faculties: I merited an increase in fees to keep me in a state of performance. Let freedom come but I must first heap up a fortune to cope with the loss of my mistress, for she would be bound, by Law, to let me go.

She could re-employ me but the bonds of servitude would be broken. Under slavery I was in thrall of her. I was tamed but wanted to be untrammelled; the tension giving frisson to our relationship. A free man gained a wage and nothing else. He was expected to conduct this or that act of service. If he was diligent, he was kept on; if not, he was dismissed and swiftly replaced. Massa or Missie did not invest in him emotionally.

A slave, on the other hand, was longed for from the very beginning, Massa having to place a non-refundable deposit to secure him, the rest payable when he was delivered from Africa to the colony, inspected, passed. The slave had to be first caught and barracooned on the coast of Africa. The passage to Demerara could see him expire from disease and Massa's deposit forfeited. It was a lengthy process throughout which Massa waited, himself barracooned in worry, calculating and recalculating potential loss (especially if he had placed an order for a dozen slaves).

When the ship arrived Massa could barely contain his glee. Horses were saddled, the gig hurried to the Exchange. Potholes in the road or a tree felled in a previous storm delayed him. His heart raced, he had to sip rum from his flask to steady himself. When he reached market there was chaos, two or three hundred slaves in one long chain, yanking it this way and that, one toppling and felling two or three of his neighbours. They had to be unlocked, parcelled, taken to different plantations. That was the most trying part (more than the handing over of the cash in final settlement), for slaves began to fight or wail, not wanting to be separated, a wife going one way, a child another. The children, what trouble! They wept all the way to their new home and for months afterwards. They sickened, not taking food. They died. Massas tried not to buy children fresh from Africa, preferring to breed their slaves and produce a native, plantation-reared supply. There was no choosing though, when times were hard, when their stock was diminished by epidemic or a spate of runaways. Children had to be purchased directly from Africa in the hope that a reasonable proportion would survive.

The anxiety. The expectation. The longing for safe passage. The joy at the ship's landing. The clinking of chains like music. The strain of having to count out the money. The impatience to see the slaves separated. The anger when they clung to each other. The hardening of heart when they begged to remain as a family. Afterwards, such fatigue that the trial of the new females had to be put off for the following nights.

Freedom could never replicate such flows and transactions of emotions for massa nor slave. "Resist Theodore," I urged Mr Basnett with renewed vigour. I bribed him with the locket of hair enfolded in Lady Elizabeth's handkerchief. "Hair is ocular proof of my loyalty," I said, pointing to her initials embroidered at the edge. He panted, salivated. I could hear the clinking of florins, a harmony to the ear. "Time to compose," I said pointing to his chair.

He wanted to pace the cage of his heart, aroused by Lady Elizabeth's handkerchief, but he sat down tamely when I raised my voice. "Something sad I think, moreso than our last verse, with a pinch of self-pity, a sprinkling of complaint." Having chosen the recipe I wrote quickly, giving him the first four lines as *hors d'oeuvre:*

> *While heavy cares affect my tortur'd breast*
> *I do not rest for care, nor do I care for rest;*
> *Yet could I o'er all cares my conquest gain,*
> *While Chloe's cruel all my cares remain*

He was ready for more but Corinna twisted her mouth in disapproval. "Too peppered with the word 'care'," I could hear her indict. I could have argued that my repetition was to suggest other rhymes like "bare", "tear", "fear"; words appropriate to lovemaking, the boudoir become a lair. Or I could have argued that my repetition was designed to wear down Lady Elizabeth. A muse, however, could not be contradicted. "My offering will not do," I told Mr Basnett, screwing up the paper and throwing it to the floor. The sudden picturing of Theodore doing the same to my lady pained me. My hand curled into a fist, like Corinna retreating from hurt, but one by one I freed my fingers, took up my pen for another assault. I would rhyme Lady Elizabeth to the floor, pick her up and lay her on the sofa. In her fatigue she would be mine to write upon, her white skin vellum to my wilful pen. I had thought that Corinna would bring me to ecstasy, but as the first line wrote itself, I knew that Lady Elizabeth was my real mission. Dr Gladstone had begun with her but had died prematurely. As his disciple I would complete his effort to redeem her from the muck Miriam claimed she was. Let Mr Basnett sell Corinna, let me be rid of her, for Lady Elizabeth was my prey. Given the financial state of the plantation Corinna would be gone sooner or later. Best to imitate our massas who changed slave mistresses at a whim. Monogamy to one muse would stale my pen. Moreover I was concerned about by income from Mr Basnett. The locket and handkerchief brought me only two shillings. Two shillings! For a normal slave, such an amount was well beyond the dreams of avarice, but for me, already in possession of many pounds, a mere pittance. "Only an advance, an interim measure," Mr Basnett sought to reassure me. "In any case, you have singular and complete use of her," he added, winking in Corinna's direction. I raised my pen as if to gouge out his eyes. How dare he offer her as part-payment! I was no nigger accepting credit for my favours. I remembered Miriam cursing sick slaves who gathered at her door with their payment of a solitary plantain. Like Miriam I wanted cash for my pharmacopoeia of poetry.

"You can have a portion of her price when I sell," he said to appease me.

A portion? Which portion? Her bubbies a sovereign each? Would an arm and a leg fetch more? Would I share in the profits from her private parts? Such questions were beneath me, but in any case I was wise to the cunning of Mr Basnett's offer. Shylock had given credit but was cheated of his pound of flesh. No Jew, me!

"Let us begin, I have another matter to attend to." Mr Basnett's command broke my chain of thought. "I cannot keep Mr Eliston waiting, he is due at noon, in this very room."

I wrote in anger. I would try to rid myself, poem by poem, of anger. When all rage was spent, my mind would be freed into a pensive mood and in such tranquillity I would begin the journeying towards an understanding of what mattered beyond money, beyond the affairs of the world. In successive days, seven in all, I would seek to destroy the old world, to clear the sky for another rainbow and covenant. I would write in Corinna's presence, pre-empting her loss by sweeping her away in a current of words. I would make of my heart an empty ark.

"Mr Basnett's Complaint", I scribbled as the title, but it sounded banal. I endowed him with a name befitting poesy, not bothering to seek his permission. "Strephon's Complaint" it would be, with Phyllis retained, the idea of pox suitable to my mood.

174

Ye warblers, while Phyllis I moan,
To cheer me your harmony bring;
Unless, since my charmer is gone,
You cease like poor Strephon to sing.
And, hark! The sweet grove is quite hush;
Their grief in their silence appears;
No songster will peep from the bush,
They're all so dismay'd with my tears.

I was brief, Mr Basnett being in a hurry to greet Mr Eliston. Satisfied by the constancy of rhyme, he asked us to leave. Corinna and I reached for the door-latch at the same time. Our hands touched. She knew I would soon abandon her, my verse dwelling on that theme. Still, she stopped my hand as I went to withdraw it, cradling it in her palm. Mr Eliston entered, discovering our intimacy. He raised his head in disdain, smirking as he walked past us. "How charming, sire, to meet you again, and how gracious you are to receive me," he said to Mr Basnett. He curtseyed then flung back his head in a dramatic gesture. His spindly hand fumbled for Mr Basnett's; he squeezed but made no impression on Mr Basnett's fat. "I have been so tortured, sire, so tortured, awaiting your call." He smacked his lips and closed his eyes in a show of grief.

Corinna went to her place in the kitchen. I decided against returning to Lady Elizabeth, suspecting that she was making busy with Theodore. Another month or so and she would have no further use of me. She would settle me downstairs, at the edge of the yard, far from earshot, as Dr Gladstone had once done. She would build a cottage for me, well furnished, but all the same a gilded cage.

I went instead for a stroll along the canal, walking through a meadow of corinnas, through rosebush and hibiscus, wanting to be careless of their perfume, wanting to be careless, too, of the songbirds high up the sampan trees, and the sequins of light upon the water's surface like the gown of a fairytale princess. The loveliness of the place was its cruelty. It was noon, and I needed to sweat, the punishing sun reminding me of my status as a slave. The niggers were sprawled under a cotton tree at the corner of the field, some sleeping, some chewing on stalks of sugarcane. At this hour it was indeed a sweet grove to them, and the warblers – doves, larks, kiskadees – brought cheer with their harmony. Theodore had forbidden work for a full hour whilst the sun was vertical. When it tilted to an angle of ninety-five degrees (they had more or less mastered MMadboy's measurements) it was time to rise, having first drunk a quart of ginger ale each, provided *gratis*. They were unsupervised, resting and rising by their own will, Theodore having converted the driver into the ginger ale maker, replacing his whip with a ladle. He was in charge of mule, wagon and barrow. He had to ensure that the refreshments arrived in the field fresh and timely and the barrel cleaned of dregs afterwards, with the same discipline he once exercised over the slaves. "Thankee Laad, thankee Theodore, sah," each said, raising the calabash to his mouth.

A sweet grove, birdsong, ginger ale, a benevolent master, but these only agitated me. The picturing of Lady Elizabeth in the gross clasp of a lascivious Pole banished whatever repose I hoped my stroll would bring. I wanted to slip into the canal unnoticed, as MMadboy had. He must have travelled far from the time he had been captured in the Niger valley, which is where most of Mr Basnett's stock believed they came from (they had no documentary proof, only word-of-mouth stories, dimly remembered, from their forebears). I surmised MMadboy being sold to the Yoruba nation, then to Arabs, then taken North, walking in a slave coffle to the coast. There was hardly time to gasp at the first sight of the sea when some Spaniards fetched him off to a ship bound for Brazil; they held him in the harbour for a month, then changed plans, selling him to a British merchant trading in Demerara.

But what did all his journeying matter, and all the learning he acquired on the way? MMadboy chose the canal. The Negroes hymned his corpse, asking to be remembered to this relative and that when his spirit returned home. Not quite trusting him, seeing how distracted he was, they cleaned his eye-sockets of the odd shrimp that had nestled there. That way he would end up in Africa, not get lost in another foreign clime. Another foreign clime! Oh God, to think there were such never-ending regions, our tribulations never-ending!

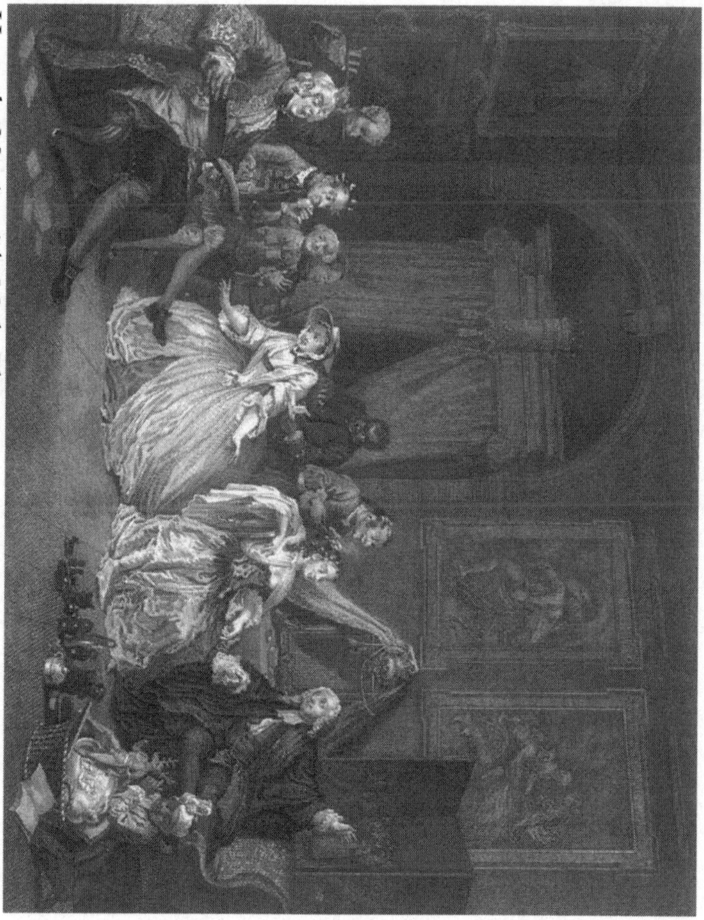

Hogarth, *Marriage à la Mode*, Plate 2

When I returned to Mr Basnett's home, there was a letter waiting for me, as expected, from Lady Elizabeth. "Cherub, stay a while longer with Mr Basnett. The roof leaks, a week's repairs are necessary." I had never before seen her handwriting and was starting to believe Miriam, that once upon a time my Lady was a common moll. The vowels curled each like a scimitar, I was sure of Theodore's penmanship.

Mr Eliston was in an armchair taking tea in delicate sips. In my haste to leave the room and part Corinna's hand from mine, I had not noticed that he wore curlers in his hair. He spoke to Mr Basnett in a voice as tiny as the tea cup. Mr Basnett was in full throat, drowning out whatever Mr Eliston was squeaking at him. The two of them were like ill-matched warblers. I stopped my ears to their singing, knowing it was antiphon to the Devil.

When it ended, Mr Basnett pressed a purse upon Mr Eliston, then embraced him with such bulk that I feared for Mr Eliston's bones. Would his heart be stout enough to poison Theodore (for that was the bargain struck)? I doubted it, especially when Mr Eliston flapped his gloves with a limp wrist and kissed them before putting them on.

"Adieu, adieu, and a thousand more," he lisped.

They left me to myself in the drawing room. I sat at my desk planning to continue my verse. The ink had nearly dried in the interval. My quill scratched the page but the noise was appropriate to my chafing heart. I looked at where Corinna would sit. Misery moved my hand.

> *Each flow'r declines its sweet head,*
> *Nor odours around me will throw;*
> *While ev'ry soft lamb on the mead,*
> *Seems kindly to pity my woe.*

> *An innocent lamb is my dear,*
> *As sweet as all flow'rs combin'd;*
> *Her smiles like a summer can cheer,*
> *Ah! Why was she made so unkind!*

I paused to find a suitable Classical name for Theodore.

Unkind she is not, I can prove,
But tender to others can be;
To Satyr my Lady makes love,
And only is cruel to me.

★　★　★

Mr Basnett ate a hearty supper. Normally it was me who would slice my meat and chew it with a satyr's satisfaction. Mr Basnett would prod with his fork, play obsessively with a single pea (Theodore's head), turning it this way and that way before stabbing it on a prong. In our three months together at the table he partook of little, yet his fat remained his steadfast companion. "Who will rid me of this turbulent pest?" he would suddenly ask, looking up and only then seeming to notice me. I bent my head to the bowl, supping on the Devil's broth. Let me finish my meal in my own time. When I was done, I would burp and rub my belly, feeling the first effects of niggeritis. A slave would lead me to the drawing room. Mr Basnett himself would pour me a brandy, sitting opposite me, awaiting work. A sip, two sips, a mouthful. Only when the glass was replenished and I felt within my belly the wealth of nations, would I begin the evensong's lesson, chapter and verse from Adam Smith; Mr Basnett humming to himself as if preparing to hymn.

He was not his usual self tonight, making the slave remove the plates whilst three dumplings were still left on mine, not to mention a juicy carrot swimming in fish-sauce. Filling, if not as delicious as my own cooking, but I was now above such menial occupation. My fork went to chase after the plate and was left in mid-air, for the slave was swift.

We took up position in our armchairs. I sulked. The slave offered a fig but I cared not for it, wanting my dumplings and juicy carrot. Mr Basnett peeled his, sucked at its heart.

"I am exhausted, today's composition has taxed me quite," I said, hoping he would excuse me from further exercise in verse.

"Oh? It seemed to come easily from your pen."

I should have been disappointed by his rebuttal but I found myself beaming. "Do you think so? Was I effortless?" I asked, forgetting my plate, fishing instead for compliments. He did not oblige, his mind flitting elsewhere. I consoled myself with a thought that a poet's vocation was a solitary one. I had only just commenced mine; it would take a little while to accustom myself to the scorn of patrons and the apathy of the reading public. "Do you think my writing is free of encumbrances?" I persisted.

Mr Basnett brushed aside my question as if it were an irritable sandfly. "Eliston's the proper man," he said, and began to soliloquise on the qualities of his assassin. I could have tiptoed to the kitchen, finished my food and tiptoed back, sauce dripping from the corner of my mouth even, without him noticing, so engrossed was he in Theodore's downfall. He stared into space so intently that he could have been a connoisseur transfixed by the beauty of a painting, astonished by the strokes and flourishes of the brush... except, of course, that Mr Basnett was a vulgarian, the pictures on his wall forgeries of Hogarth's *Marriage à la Mode*. "Yes, Eliston is the correct man," he concluded, thumping the brandy-table and overturning the bottle. I scrambled to save what I could. "Let it be, there's liquor a-plenty," he said. He who was at the brink of penury puffed out his chest in foolhardy boast. "Tomorrow night you will arrange a soirée in my house. Persuade Lady Elizabeth to be my honoured guest. Invite two dozen, chief among them Theodore. Place him by my side so I can better study his features, before and after the potion is drunk. Prepare it well and choose a suitable wine to accompany it. Now avaunt and quit my sight, I need to be alone." He closed his eyes, exhausted by his ambition. "And take your slut with you. Use her well, it may be your last chance," he shouted after me.

Not a wink of sleep all night, *sans* Corinna. I refused to call upon her favours though tortured by my decision. The first (and last) time we slept together I managed to sublimate my urges by dwelling on the Classics. Latin freed me so that when she rose she was not my spoil, my slut, but my muse. Money, mother, Miriam, medicine, massas, manumission, metre, muse: I lay awake striving to list the elements of my life, to avoid dwelling on Corinna's body. I put mother first, but quickly replaced it with massas. I tried putting money at the top of the list, switched it with Miriam. I changed my mind and gave priority to medicine. In the end, money at the start and manumission at the end quietened me down a little. My mind soon became restless. I invented another distraction, matching the ancient deities to my present and my future. Was it Plutus or Saturn who was best at money? I chose Saturn. The rest were easy to deify. I left mother for last. There were an abundance of choices, from Juno to Vesta, but I would not name her, remembering Corinna's indictment of me as a Negro in borrowed clothes.

★   ★   ★

"Renounce your foreignness, you are Negro not macaw," she urged. "Let me look at you, to discover what a Negro is. I have never –"

"Ssssh," I interrupted, drawing her closer to me, kissing her forehead. It would torment me to hear about her intimacy with massas' bodies. She would not cease, though. It was as if I had presented to her (by my black presence itself) her first chance to confess.

Mr Basnett had made of her a present to me but it was otherwise. I put an imaginary grill to my ear through which she could speak. I wanted to be at one measure removed from her, just as Lady Elizabeth dealt with me. To behold a Negro body, to caress it, to learn to love it: this was her only longing, she said. She had never looked upon herself, not even when bathing, the soap in her hand being a welcome obstacle to touching her flesh nakedly. A mirror was as foreign to her as Latin. Now and again, after heavy rain, she would go to a secluded spot at the edge of the canefield, to a pothole filled with water. She would kneel and gaze into it. The wind ruffled the water. She appeared elongated, her face, her neck. Mosquitoes laid spawn where her eyes were. A toad flopped into her mouth. Her sense of being ugly, dirty, distorted, was confirmed. She left happily, knowing that to yield to the next massa was to yield nothing to nothing. And yet she wanted to break out of such self-denial.

Her longing for the apparition and the actual feel of a Negro body was all she disclosed. "You have not sinned nor am I a priest," I said. I went to kiss her forehead again. She raised her lips to mine. I tasted her breath, and tasted again, wanting more of her. She went to peel back the sheet. I recovered, staying her hand.

When the world ended, only then would we inherit each other, bride and groom *commingling* forever. For now, I would remain chaste. And resilient, for when the day came for her departure and sale I would not howl like the dogs serenading Hannah, nor sob into a soiled shawl. Grief was too high a price to pay. I would bide my time for the afterlife. Moreover, my pen beckoned; I could not afford to be broken.

"Wait, wait, we must wait," I said, stopping her from seeing me naked. To my dismay she obeyed. She had let her nightdress slip from her shoulders. She drew it up, snuggled up to me. I rubbed her forehead and her neck, wanting my touch to ease her suffering. Francis the *saviour*! How I wanted to be otherwise… "Dodo, dodo, close your eyes, adieu," I said, rocking her body, mothering her to sleep whilst longing to *savour* her, lie upon her, press her into the mattress until she was as flat as a flounder, bathe her in sweat as piquant as one of my best sauces.

★ ★ ★

Better to dream, better to imagine me, and me her, I told myself, working up emotion for another verse. Imagination, rather than experience of a world, which was like insect-spawn in a pot-hole. Neither muse nor mother existed; I was free to conceive of them, summon them to receive God's benediction and my gift of rhyme. God and Francis were of one purpose, to redeem Negroes from being items of commerce; from being bargains into a state of blessedness. Bargain to benediction – a huge progression, but I was equipped with *The Dictionary*. Whitefolk words, to be sure, but of no consequence if my borrowing had a noble cause and I could express myself beautifully. Mr Basnett was a massa, yet was void of eloquence. He needed me to put whitefolk words into his mouth and nigger poison into Theodore's.

Mr Basnett entered as if summoned by my thinking. He sat at his accustomed spot. I twiddled my quill to keep him waiting. He wanted to inherit Lady Elizabeth now, to hell with the afterlife. His presence, even at a distance, cast a shadow over my page. But my courtship was with beauty, not a moll's muck. I looked at him spitefully, but it was necessary to purge myself of such emotion, for my mission was poetry not prose.

I noticed that he was dressed differently, a cravat hiding his fleshy neck and the bonnet on his head tilted rakishly. He must have rubbed a lotion on his cheeks for they were ruddy, and its perfume attracted flies. His intention, obviously, was to deliver the verse personally to Lady Elizabeth, the ink still fresh on the page. I pictured him kneeling before her, holding up the page, smiling suggestively (God forbid, even winking!). Would she believe his progress from stodge to frivolity? An erstwhile fat, bald, squat fellow turned into a lissom rake? She would seethe with suppressed laughter, especially if he took out her handker-chief from a pocket nearest his heart and mopped his brow with a flourish, making sure her initials showed. I was moved to defend him – my patron; my Lady too, for she would be so lost in hilarity that her bladder might lose restraint and she in turn become a laughing stock in the eyes of her slaves. "Don't make yourself an object of ridicule," I said to Mr Basnett, struggling to control my anger, for apart from being my benefactor, he was manager of two hundred slaves and therefore deserved to be spoken to respectfully. He was adjusting his cravat in a hand-held glass, pouting in the manner of Mr Eliston, trying out a coquet-tish, then a cruel look. I was glad he did not hear me, distracted by his rehearsals for the assignation with Lady Elizabeth. I could have hurled a series of accusations at him like brickbats to a bad actor; or worse, like God's utterances on Judgment Day, but being neither critic nor priest, I desisted. Let someone else accuse him of no longer visiting Hannah's grave, preoccupied instead with his lust for Lady Elizabeth. He now neglected to remit monies to her parents for church prayers. He was a lapsed Catholic, if not an outright atheist, for many a time he would suddenly rise from his chair, execrations pouring from his mouth. The slaves, not understanding his expressions, thought he was in a fit. When he collapsed back into his chair, froth at both sides of his mouth, they rushed to fetch towels, fans, sidyam juice,

Hogarth: *A Rake's Progress, plate 2*

anything to revive him. I knew he was not prey to seizure but to a deeper distress. He cursed God for his childhood, his youth, the mockeries endured. He damned God for giving him parents who showed him no love. Hannah had been compensation, but cancelled almost as soon as it was offered. The colony was not El Dorado but a place of disease and baying dogs. Worst of all was the coming of Lady Elizabeth to tempt him, then Theodore to block the pathways to her heart like a thousand potholes, a forest of fallen trees. Poor Mr Basnett wanted to be Bacchus or even a lesser rake, but it was not to be. He tried to rid God from his mind, blackening it with curses. He failed, for his Catholic faith was a cactus, too painful to uproot. No, Mr Basnett was not an atheist, the term was too brutal. I searched the *Dictionary* and found one to my liking: "apostate"; it had a soft sound to it and was close to "apostle", suggesting, in changed circumstances, that Mr Basnett could revert to piety. I resolved to renew my efforts on his behalf and took up a missionary's pen. "To Phyllis", I began, then thinking of Hannah, I added a clause. "To Phyllis, in a grave mood." I wrote the word "salvation" in the corner of the page to remind me of what mood to evoke and to stay me if I was tempted to stray because, like Lady Elizabeth, words were beguiling. They robbed you of will, hauled you this way and that, took you to a mountaintop and vista of delight only to dump you in a pond of despair, your ankles weighed down with clichés. Salvation would find a place somewhere in my composition, even at the expense of metre, for Mr Basnett's soul was in need of it.

> *What a prude o' th' sudden? Pr'ythee, girl, why so coy?*
> *Your beauty, untouch'd, does your beauty destroy:*
> *What tho' you have charms? Here's a noise and a rout!*
> *If they're not to be us'd, 'twere as well be without.*
> *So, in spite of your pride, say all that you can,*
> *Your true salvation is to give joy to man:*
> *No more of these whimsies, good-nature to smother,*
> *Nor punish yourself thus – to torture another.*

The ink was barely dry when Mr Basnett snatched up the paper and hurried off to Lady Elizabeth, leaving me and Corinna alone. I resented her presence. Although no words passed her lips I could hear Corinna charging me for conspiring with Mr Basnett to sell her for my own profit. True, Mr Basnett had given me charge of her, making me a deputy massa almost, but that was not to habituate me to cruelty (as Corinna supposed, or so I suspected). He was just glad to abandon his household, not just his pen, to my care. To begin with the house slaves were pleased to be unsupervised and I was equally pleased to let them be, for it gave me more time to prepare for versifying, burrowing through various volumes of tea-table miscellanies for inspiration. The hierarchy of the household was altered too by the elevation of Corinna. Once a junior kitchen-slave, her sole domain a sink with a dozen pots and pans, she now had freedom to roam in any quarter because of her acquaintance with me. "I am the instrument of your freedom," I could have claimed, breaking the silence between us, but it would have been a claim as hollow as my compositions for Mr Basnett. I dismissed her instead, as Lady Elizabeth no doubt would dismiss my verse. "Have you no work to do? My pen is rested; there is no need to remain," I said to Corinna, waving her away. She rose, went to the door, then turned back and curtseyed, her mockery of me complete.

The drawing-room-boy entered with my customary lemonade. Was he, too, laughing secretly as he poured me a glass? "What's your name, boy?" I asked in as gruff a tone as I could summon. In the three weeks stationed in Mr Basnett's house I had never bothered to address him. Now was the time to stamp my authority on him, on all of them, before their secret laughter turned into Corinna's open mockery.

"They does c-c-c-call me t-t-teaspoon, sah."

"Teaspoon? Doesn't that strike you as an oddity? Are you making light of my question, boy? If so, you will feel the weight of my hand!" The words thundered forth, leaving me bewildered. Never before had I threatened violence to another. Teaspoon was even more taken aback than me.

"No s-s-s-sah, n-n-no sah, it is t-t-t-t-truth I talk. 'Teaspoon' mostly, but s-s-s-s sometimes I does answer to 'saucer' or 's-s-s-s-sugar-bowl', because I in c-c-c-custody of them things."

186

The Classics, as so often in the past, came to my rescue. Recovering my composure, I looked sternly at him and said, "From now on you are Alexander the Great, you hear? Not Alex nor Alexander but the full title. Now go away, stay outside the door and await my call." He did as I commanded and when I shouted "Alexander the Great" he entered, but only at the third summoning. "You are a slow learner," I chided him, but he seemed too happy with his new name to take offence. "Let's practice again," I said, sending him out of the room, ordering him in, repeating the exercise until I was satisfied he was master of his title. "Now Alexander the Great, I want you to gather all your fellow slaves before me within the hour, that is all of them, all." He nodded as if to acknowledge that I meant everyone but Corinna.

Shortly afterwards, I was telling them, "From today and whenever Massa Basnett is away you are to take instruction from me." They began to shuffle and murmur as soon as I finished speaking. I remained calmly in my chair. Someone began to ask a question about Mr Basnett but ceased immediately when I took up my pen and wriggled it between thumb and forefinger as if taking measure of a stave. "I will examine the performance of your tasks shortly," I said, nodding to Alexander the Great to shepherd them from my presence.

It would be six hours or so before Mr Basnett returned, I calculated. Lady Elizabeth would keep him waiting in the salon for half-an-hour before she deigned to appear. Another half-an-hour for him to pluck up courage to recite his verse, and she would proffer some polite remark before making an excuse to take leave of him. The next two hours would see him hidden away in his gig, roaming the plantation, starting off for the city before taking another direction – he would make any journey to give him time to still his heart, to come up with some plausible reason for Lady Elizabeth's abruptness, to scan and rescan the verse for any explanation of her behaviour. He would stop at the shop Theodore had set up. The slaves behind the counter would run out with a cordial, but Mr Basnett would demand rum, and more rum. Though drunk, he would still be scared enough of Theodore to pay for the liquor before being helped into his gig.

Six hours in which to anticipate his moods over the coming

days. He would still demand verse that begged, or bewailed, or blasted her with curses. Best to prepare them whilst he was absent, without distraction or harassment. A few false starts gave way to a melancholy strain, my own longing for Lady Elizabeth finding exact form:

> *As noble Strephon walk'd in yonder grove,*
> *Lamenting fickle Phyllis' faithless love,*
> *The wind, in whispers, seems to soothe his grief,*
> *And feather'd songsters strove to give relief.*
> *But all their fond attempts were vain,*
> *So fixt, so rooted was the pain.*

Corinna, sensing my mood from afar, entered the room. I softened to her immediately. "Come to me," I whispered. She approached and I stood up to greet her, raising her forehead to my lips.

"A Judas kiss?" she asked, moving her face away.

"Not now, not in this place," I said.

"Why not now? You have enough money to buy me. Massa supplies you lavishly," she said.

"His money is sinful. In another place our love will be untainted."

She thought for a moment as if remembering her image in the stagnant water of a pothole. "You are right. I will go far from you and wait. I will wait for you. One day it will rain and rain and never stop until the earth is cleansed. You will come then."

"My friend Billy was a preacherman. He spoke of that time when God will make the earth new again. Lion and lamb in one grove. There will be a rainbow in the sky; you will reach for it as ribbon for your hair," I said.

"I'll be pretty for you when you come, a rainbow in my hair. My bubbies are ripe for you but I will wait," she said, withdrawing from my arms so I could better view her body. We could have rushed to bed, feasted on each other, gazing upon her nakedness and my own before renewing our embraces. Instead I reached out to stroke her neck, her breasts. I traced the contours of her thighs, wanting to find a crevice to explore, to feel my way into her body.

She slackened, inviting me in, but then she stopped my hand. "I will not be sent to market forever. This very hand of yours must prepare a decree for my emancipation. Let it remain wedded to the page until then." She pressed a quill to my palm. "A plate of sprats, a mutton chop… I am more. Your poetry will deliver me from being threadbare. I will come to you robed, six buttons no less adorning my gown. You will be still when you undress me, your hand patient and your heart, and when the last button is undone and the frock slips to the naked ground, let sky crack, let tempest come, let earth insurrect and there be deluge, but on that last day, in the glow of lightning you will behold the Negro who is your bride and soul. You nor me won't want body then, the whip will see to that and the years of threadbare will wear we down to we soul. On the last day there will be no glutting for flesh, only for the glow of me and you."

★ ★ ★

Flesh it was, in the form of Mr Basnett, who returned later that day, nearly falling into my lap. He was sweaty and covetous. Rum dizzied him. He stood before me with bloodshot eyes.

"Steady, man," I cautioned as he tottered into my arms. The inkpot fell. "Look what you've done! The carpet's ruined, and my verse!" He stood up, moved to the sofa, but slipped again, this time crashing into an embroidery table he had made, with his own hands (guided by the plantation's carpenter) as a birthday present to his wife. He stared at the broken furniture, the only furniture he had ever made, which was to last for centuries, a fitting memorial to their marriage. I expected him to howl, but he had already cried too long for Hannah and was now too numb for emotion. I shouted for Alexander the Great to support Mr Basnett to the sofa. I screwed up the paper and gave it to him for disposal. The verse was not worth saving. I had spent the hour scribbling without interest, my mind distracted by Corinna's eschatology. The earth as plantation would come to an end, the overseer cease licking his tongue and whip on Negro flesh, for nothing left to eat, he done eat all, no body left, not even bone. Like worm that infect host and, instead of moderation, the worm gorge and regale till host dead out, worm too. Corinna said that when that happened Negroes would revive as soul and show themselves by the light of thunderstorm. What foolishness! "You are another false prophet," I could have said, but she embodied hurt, and was on the brink of being sold to another plantation, another swarm of admirers. Unlike Corinna I had no intention of waiting for a spiritual freedom. My just deserts were but a few years away. I fully expected a purse proud enough to purchase her freedom whilst her body was still lush, and there was land in my name to build a new house.

Still, her vision of the bodiless was attractive, given Mr Basnett's rankness.

"Fat. Fat. Fat." He prodded his belly, his neck, his thighs, bewailing his fate. Alexander the Great, thinking it unbecoming to witness his massa in distress, left the room. Corinna was in her usual sedate poise, her chair at a respectful distance. I thrubbed my fingers on the desk, awaiting a moment of calm when I could address him.

"So Lady Elizabeth rebuffed you? Was it before or after you recited the verse?" I asked. Mr Basnett couldn't remember, he had lost his nerve and started to sweat as soon as she had entered the drawing room. A sense of humiliation, as at Lord Bathurst's interview, paralysed him. She spoke something and he stuttered a response. I pressed him for more information. All he could recall were the words "dough", "lump", "puff", "lard".

"She was not speaking to me but to my fat. She might well have called me a hog or hippopotamus," he moaned.

"Fie! My lady is too mannered for such! If she wanted to berate you she would have said you were oleaginous or pinguid. Are you sure she wasn't referring to a cake she had baked badly? Was there a burning smell coming from the kitchen?"

"The kitchen? The kitchen?" His eyes rolled in madness. "The kitchen didn't bother me, it was the bedroom. I swear Theodore was in there, hiding betwixt her sheets, having done my office! Now and again I heard a noise…"

Mention of Theodore in my lady's chamber was a stab to the heart. "Was she in a state of deshabillé? Were her plaits undone? Was the rouge on her cheeks smudged, the pearl-powder moist?"

My fusillade of questions met with no response, Mr Basnett preoccupied with the thought of Theodore's advantageous body.

"He is nimble, he is quick, pokes her with his candlestick!" Basnett said. I admired his rhyming but caught myself from drifting off into airiness.

"But a snake, too, is lithe, and a centipede," I said, to comfort him and myself. "We must rid her house of such encumbrances and remortgage it to our own affections."

"Chop the snake and the centipede in half before they harm her! Shall I get a slave to waylay him in the dark with a dozen cutlasses?" Mr Basnett asked.

My jealousy of Theodore waned immediately, for money was at stake. Theodore had to be guarded against any impulsive action on Mr Basnett's part. The plot had to be drawn out until the last page of Adam Smith was perused. "No cutlass," I commanded. "Let us abide by our original plan, which is poison, but only on my say."

"Let us ply him with it now," he urged, but a stern look from me was sufficient to subdue him. He slouched deeper into the sofa and fell asleep. The sweat subsided, and the stink. It was only then that I remembered that Corinna was still in the room. She was weeping quietly, her hand pressed to her mouth. The talk of murder had shocked her.

"It's only said in jest," I tried to assure her. "It helps to leech the bile from his blood, otherwise your massa would go mad. I am his physician, that is all."

"You are none such," she said, her face set in sudden anger. "You are worse than a quack, you are a complete counterfeiter."

"The money is for you," I said weakly.

"I will not be bought with an assassin's coin. Have you no regard for me? Is your love for me so impious?"

Her question (or my translation of it) trailed off into a painful silence.

"I will win your heart with my pen. I will compose such verse that the public will clamour for me, and the King will grant me a pension, as he did Dr Johnson." It was too late, no amount of hyperboles would move her. She had decided I was a fraud. She had arrived at the truth of my character. I expected her to leave the room, leave me to loneliness, but she stayed. She stared at me, not to transform me into stone or salt but into lightning, in the glow of which I could recognise my compact with sin but also her longing to redeem me from such bondage.

★　★　★

It was imperative that Mr Basnett be freed from himself. He took to drink as soon as he awoke and remained in a stupor until put to bed. The slaves looked to me for direction but my initial fervour in being Mr Basnett's deputy (*de facto* if not *de jure*) gave way to fatigue. I had to concentrate on Mr Basnett's health, to restore him to reason and revenue; my own equanimity was dependent on such.

"You take control of the household," I begged Corinna, but she would not. She had lost faith in me. The accusation of murderer was inscribed on her face, no cajoling on my part, no promise of new poetry could alter her mood. She had become a cactus in all its vicious bloom. "I have committed no murder," I said, but she shuddered at the word, covered her face with her hands to hide from me… Or was she hiding from herself? Was there something monstrous in her past which I had not yet fathomed? I brushed aside the question as a foolish one, reminding her instead of the tenderness of our first (and last) night together. I reaffirmed my love for her and my ambition to free her. "I will borrow the money from Theodore. I will go to him promptly." She remained stubborn. Her attitude towards me had changed so dramatically that I was left with no choice but to appoint Alexander the Great as Manager. He was a simpleton, and by the time he stammered out instruction the household would have already gathered a day's dust. The slaves, without supervision, would simply slink off to hiding places, the household would be barbarous by the weekend.

I rode in Mr Basnett's coach to meet Theodore. He greeted me at the gate, showing not the slightest sign of surprise at my new status. He led me to his drawing room, calling upon the driver and postulant to follow us.

"Nice breeches," he said, fingering the satin. "And your coat is superbly stitched."

I thanked him for praising my appearance, giving credit to Mr Basnett's generosity. "And it is Mr Basnett's credit I've come to discuss with you," I whispered, for the two slaves had taken up chairs, waiting for lemonade. "I must converse with you in strictest confidence. Send them away."

Ignoring my request, Theodore filled their glasses and greeted them with genuine warmth. "How are you, Robin? It's been a while since we shared a cordial together. And what of you, Moses, is your stomach still troubling you?"

They drank in one quaff. "Like the Lord we thirst," Moses said, and Robin chimed in something from the Gospels about thirsting after righteousness. Theodore hurried to refill their glasses.

"Robin and Moses are trusted fellows, as are all the Negroes on this plantation. Anything I say of Mr Basnett concerns them, they will stay." He went to recline on his Berbice-chair. He looked red-eyed, on the brink of sleep, though it was not yet noon. "The counting house," he sighed, pre-empting my speculation. "This last week has been taxing, literally. All the accounts had to be tallied, for the Governor demanded his annual levy earlier than usual." He yawned and rubbed his neck as if to loosen a cramped muscle. Robin and Moses, without instruction, went up to his chair and began to massage his shoulders. Counting house or Lady Elizabeth's boudoir, I wondered. Was it she or the Governor who taxed his energy? Did she seize him with a whore's ardour, empty his purse? He closed his eyes as the slaves massaged him. I looked around the room for evidence of foul play, a tribute of a stocking or a billet-doux, but apart from books, and a silver candelabrum, it was bare. Not a mirror, not a painting, not an exhibition of glassware. Theodore's life was truly as lean as the slaves had disclosed to me, but for the rose fastened to his lapel. My admiration for him revived, I scolded myself for my jealousy.

"All good fellows, Robin, Moses, Simon, Lucie, Peter..." He reeled off the names of Mr Basnett's slaves, telling me of the virtues of this one and that, all the while caressing the rose on his lapel as if to indicate the beauty of their character. I was surprised by his intimate knowledge of their lives. "People are the treasury of any land. Not the mines nor the mahogany forests, but people themselves," he said, looking accusingly at me. He had obviously discovered my plot to acquire a fortune at Mr Basnett's expense. I tried to mumble something in my defence but he stopped me. "Do you know why the boy you mock as Alexander the Great stutters? It's because he's been in fright from the time he was born. Fright of breaking a saucer, fright of being lashed or deprived of his bowl of plantain-soup. And Corinna, whom you court?"

"What of her?" I blurted out, ashamed that he had found out about our relationship.

"What of her? What of her? You have spent weeks in her company and yet not understood her plight?"

"The monsoon fever…" I mumbled.

"No, dreadful as it is, her condition goes beyond monsoon fever. But you yourself must find out why every day she lives is done in guilt."

"Will Mr Basnett sell her on? He keeps threatening to do so."

The pity in my voice moved him for he sat up, easing the black hands from his shoulders. "I came here because of a nightmare, which has left me sleeping since. It came to me in Poland. I was in the midst of glitter and golden calves. The dream dug out my eyes. I was on an endless journey, first through orchards and grasslands which gave way to swamp, then to softer earth, which suddenly collapsed into emptiness. I fell backwards into a pit, backwards, backwards, blindly, a bottomless pit…" He paused, for his breath had left him, and he covered his face with his hands to hide from me. When he recovered he divulged to me the apparition which had visited him in his drunken sleep: his sight returned and he beheld the Virgin Mary being assaulted by a thousand black hands, black faces spitting at her. They stripped her, dragged her to a hilltop where they nailed her hands and feet to a tree, screaming 'Jew', 'Jew', 'Jew', as the hammer rose and fell. One man sharpened the top of a cane-stalk to spear her groin. He, Theodore, had known of the African trade. He had even been tempted to invest in it when he toured Paris and was introduced to a set of merchants on a mission to raise revenue to monopolise the Demerara route, by building a fleet of twelve ships. He declined, being more engrossed with Parisian flesh and the new opiates on offer. "When I left Poland it was to pursue a new calling, it was as if God had given me a new name and promise of another reputation," he said, unfolding more of his story of the journey that brought him to Demerara. When he finished he gestured to the view from the window, of canefields and slaves. "Soon it will be over, and I'll be able to wake up. I have bought the plantation from Mr Basnett's owners for Lady Elizabeth. When the contract arrives and I sign it, I will have bought my freedom from nightmare, brought dreams to theirs."

★　★　★

Madness! Unreality! Everybody airy: slaves practising ratio; Miriam hatching folk's future, me dreaming to make money, Mr Basnett pining to kill, and now Theodore, a new Christ who will emancipate all, mistaking a whore for the Virgin Mary. I was convinced that his scheme was inspired by Lady Elizabeth. Such was his infatuation with her that he had purchased her a plantation (albeit with her own money) which would be converted into Arcadia, she ministering to a congregation of happy Negroes. He had struck first, anticipating Mr Basnett's plot. He had reported Mr Basnett to his superiors, told them that the business was in ruin because of Mr Basnett's incompetence. The owners panicked, agreeing for Lady Elizabeth to buy the estate at a discounted price. Mr Basnett was to be dismissed and returned home in disgrace.

I would have none of it! Theodore's freeing of the slaves and his marriage to Lady Elizabeth would be my undoing. In my distress I turned to Miriam, undertaking the long journey by road, then through jungle path, to her hut.

"Is long," she said, not looking up to greet me, her hands busy peeling eddoes.

"Is long for true," I mumbled apologetically.

"Your good clothes will spoil in this heat and green, go inside and change."

I entered the hut to find a shirt and short breeches folded neatly over a chair. I had left them behind when I had boarded with her, years before. She had secreted them in a sack under her bed, the husk of my childhood. She laid them out on this morning of my homecoming.

"They fit?' she asked, addressing the eddoes.

"The seam split," I said.

She looked up at last, only to laugh at the sight of me stuffed in breeches, my belly bursting out from the shirt. "Sit," she said, pointing to a spot on the earth. When I sat the breeches gave way completely, and she laughed again as I hurried to cover my nakedness. "I done see your lolo already," she said, brushing my hand away from my crotch and giving me her knife. "Here, you finish peel the eddoes." She watched, tutting at my clumsy handling of the knife. "When last you do work?" she asked. "When last you boil water?" When last you eat eddo soup?" There was no need to answer. She knew the extent to which I had become foreign, combing and teasing Lady Elizabeth's golden locks my only vocation. "You have to leave her, and soon, now even, or else the Devil will nest in your groin, eggs will hatch beaks to rip you apart. A lustful Negro is a fearsome creature and can bring ruin to the whole of creation, so is stopcock for you and lock all your nasty thoughts in the box you keep your coins and bills of sales in, lock it tight-tight-tight, to save the universe."

"But Miriam, that is not why –"

"I know why you come to see me," she interrupted. "That is why I warn you that to want your mistress is to want the whole earth, which you can never inherit howsomuch you meek, for you is a veritable Negro. You can get a quarter-acre here, a quarter-acre there, to plant pumpkin, and wife-girl to help, or wife-boy since woman scarce, ships only bringing over mostly man-slaves, and overseer covet any girl born in plantation so none left for you, for you is low-low down the ledger, even less you is than eunuch, you is no-lolo. Dr Gladstone name you Francis but better I start call you sore-batty and you learn now to hearken to that title."

"But Miriam, that is not why –"

"Shut your mouth and listen to me, Mr Sorebatty, plus I can make ointment to ease you up when you come to take man-wife. You come here to talk about your Missie, Theodore and Mr Basnett. Look into the eddo soup, you will see what will become of them." She stirred the pot to get clearer vision. "The sex sweet, sweet bad, Theodore and your Lady!" She began to mimic their lovemaking. She sobbed, grunted, then let loose a deafening cur-howl. She beat her heart to bring back her breath. "Yes, the two of them concur, proper. They forget all about you. You, Mr Sorebatty, left outside the door, scratching at your sorrow of fleas."

"What am I to do? How can I rid myself of Theodore?" I asked.

She moved her gaze from the pot to me, a pitiable sight. "It will not last," she said, beckoning me to move my head to hers. "Let me whisper what will transpire. The trees have ears, they will tell the birds and the birds will chirp out the story to the wind, and the wind will gather the clouds together, and the clouds will blush in coy or glee and their veins will burst, rain will fall for days and weeks, red rain, like the whole of land and sky haemorrhaging. Miscarriage everywhere, fish, turtles, humankind. So haul your head to me, only you must hear."

Madness! Unreality! Miriam elaborating a simple tale into eschatology, a simple tale of no pertinence to the world outside the plantation of slaves and mules and fevered massas. Still, I moved my ears to her lips in case her prophecy was of conse-quence.

"Whomsoever Moll touch spoil in the end. Youth like new tree-bark will soon flake; worm and weather will fail it." As she spoke, her hands imitated the falling away of flesh, and I imagined an earth littered with the skeleton of trees. Her hands suddenly changed, making new movements as she explained Theodore's folly in wanting to convert Moll into true Ladyship. He knew her shame as a London whore but was himself disgusted by his rakish past, his use and dismissal of countless maidens, country girls especially, simple-minded, needful of coin. The city lured them in droves. They stepped off wagons to be greeted by his open purse, which, in truth, contained little, for his pleasure was in the power to promise but cheat. They would perform any act for him, each night lewder than before, but when the week ended they were still bonded to him, for he delayed their dues or lessened it on a whim. The more they begged the less he gave. Miriam clenched her fist to convey their desperation. "Theodore come to we to cleanse heself, that's why he teach Jesu to every slave and want loose we. But the Lady can't cure, the disease she carry is beyond salve, howsoever he lick her skin or make her drink his milk and sweat. And she herself will tire of him." Miriam flung open her arms, acting out the moment Lady Elizabeth would discard Theodore. "Like what he do to Mr Basnett, so it will be done to him, amen! He wrap Mr Basnett in the shawl Mrs Basnett marry in, now motheaten from the stay in Demerara, and put him like a poor man's parcel on the boat to England, back to his mother." She paused, folded her hands over her breast, twined her fingers into a knot of shawl. "Tire of Theodore she will, every day how he trying to transform her, how he oppressing her with his love, his guilt, how he planning to make her happy and free we up. Tire of him, the pity, the penitence, like how you does get fed up with a person just convert to Jesu who harass you, day in, day out, with good news, about how God got happy plan for you, when all you want is to lie quiet in your hammock, catch a breeze whilst you decide what day-work will be: the same as yesterday and the week and year before, but you still lie there, dreaming that when the herbs grind, cassava peel, pot boil, floor and yard sweep-sweep-sweep, fowl feed, dutty dig, that when all this is doing something catch your eye-corner, you look up and see a king-fisher swoop towards a pond like it catch fire and must dowse but the orange-flame feathers too fierce for the water; it dip again and again but the beauty of the greenish-blue and orange stay fast, as if it is a painting Cato one day will compose. Or mayhap your shovel disturb a skap-nest underground; look how the yellow ants pause, blink at the sunlight, then scoot for the nearest shelter; grains of yellow a-flow such as what porknockers pan the river for. You lie in your hammock thinking of what mystery the day will bring, when a God-sick and just-baptised nigger come to simplify you with happy Bible plans. Plan 1: Don't craven, don't call His name in vain, and your prize is heaven. Plan 2: Repent, get plenty forgiveness, and your afterlife is sure. Plan 3: Kneel, pray, ask meek for your daily bread, and your reward will be salvation. But I don't want one plus one plus one is three; keep your trinity, is the flash of a kingfisher and a stream of yellow ants I long for, to stop my breath, speed my blood and bram-bram my heart even for the briefest moment. When you catch yourself and return to work, is like rock roll off your back, your hands and body as light as bird and ant. And if whole day you squat riverbank and sieve, and catch not a fleck of gold, well, no matter, your mind done see kingfisher and yellow skap, your mind done free… But I forget, what is it you ask, boy?"

"I ask what will happen to all of we, Lady Elizabeth mostly, and Corinna?" I expected Miriam to screw her eyes and launch into some lunacy, but she turned away from me to tend to the pot, scooping off froth, adding firewood. Her huge arms disguised her frailty, for she dropped a heavier faggot. I went to retrieve it but she stopped me.

"Let it be, for so will Mr Basnett fall," she sighed, "and Theodore, and all of we, and dirt block we eye, mouth, nose, cover we over, one big grave, story done. How we end don't matter. I can tell you Mr Basnett put in ship and sail back in shame to whiteman country. Or else pirate kill he halfway, or in foul storm he wash overboard for shark to feast. I can tell you Theodore go back to the East, Poland or whatever it call: he does wear rose to remind him of how, over there, his life was once all sparkle and play. But as soon as he land back home, somebody will stab-stab-stab he, and Theodore bleed to death. Somebody still take him for a sinner – a relative of a Christian girl he waylay and make her belly swell, who wait for his homecoming, sharpening the knife for the time when he can revenge upon the Jew. Pole-folk don't make joke with Semites, they smite you for touching their women, so mayhap a hundred blades greet Theodore, one each for every Christian girl he convert to his nasty ways." She paused to picture Theodore's demise in a flurry of daggers. "Still, I sorry for Theodore, he do good in Demerara, but the Pole-folk don't know, they only remember how he corrupt wife and daughter."

"You can save him? You can dream a different epilogue for him?" I asked. He was my rival for Lady Elizabeth's affections but he deserved a more graceful exit. I would have had him return to Poland as a penitent, disburse his ancestral fortune to the poor, as he gave to us his generous heart, and be adored as a saint. They must curtsy to him, not curse.

"Jew and Christian story hark back to when the earth born; a simple moor like me can't change it." She sucked her teeth and spat on the ground, addressing a dragonfly that had settled there.

It gathered its will and took flight, its golden wings reminding me of Lady Elizabeth's aureoled hair bare to the sunlight. "You ever see a yellow dragonfly? Never, but I can make most things soar and glitter except she and manfolk," she said of Lady Elizabeth and her suitors. "Plus I tired of white, waking and dreaming; white wear me down, what happen to them let it happen; I worry for my own, my only children, you, Billy, Cato, Dido, Alice. And how my heart crack when news come that MMadboy drown! His true name was Theophilus…" She bit her lips, held her forehead in her hand. After a while she recovered, her body shuddered, casting off her gloom. "My last pickni and blessed child! Harder than plantation slavery, harder than starvation self and seven Bible plagues is when your own child perish and you still linger on this earth. God just take him and God just turn me into Job. I rebel. I gather herbs to boil and drink and die and join MMadboy but I desist. Desist, you hear; you know what that mean?" Her voice rose. She was speaking not to me, but to the dragonfly which was now high above the sanpan tree. Closer to God, it would take her utterance to Him. "Desist" was in my dictionary but her appeal was to a higher text, to the Word itself. "I desist because of kin left behind, my children, who need me to dream for them, even though I fail. So don't ask me about what will befall whitefolk, ask me about kin, how I born Billy on a rice bag, MMadboy in a cot of canal reeds, Alice on grass by a calf-pen, Cato in bright cloth that run, for my waters break and they wash away the dyes, and when I lift up Cato to the sky he is all the colours of a sunset. As to you, I was drinking a calabash of tea and watching a monkey playing on the treetop when you plop out and surprise me! 'Manu' I title you, though you answer to Francis. The name come straight away for 'Manu' is African for 'magic'."

★   ★   ★

Miriam, our mother! Progeny of different slave-fathers, each sold upon birth, or bartered, to gain Miriam's freedom. The account of how she had poisoned her owners and freed herself by such cunning was merely a fable. It was us babies who were her

Durer: *Virgin and Child and Monkey*

benefactors, she now confessed. "Massa give me two pounds and more, each time belly swell, or bags of rice which I sell."

Why tell me now? I pondered, as she explained how she took up habitation at the edge of the plantation, to better watch over us.

"What about MMadboy?" I doubted. "He said his mother's age was thirty-one; she died then."

"His tallying was so much talk, he didn't know nothing, he only fool all-you with a little sum-making he learn when I beg Massa to house him seven years in the counting-house, where it warm and mouseless, for he born sickly, damp and death trying to nibble away at he." Her voice dipped, she swallowed hard to contain her emotion. A tear big as a bumblebee rolled from her cheek. "I was a wandering whore, visiting this plantation and that to breed. All of you drop in different estates throughout Demerara. When Billy come I collect my money and run away to another plantation. I make child there, collect cash, and gone elsewhere. I reach nineteen pounds and thirty-one pence when Theophilus born, he was the special one. Straight away I go back to my first massa, beg mercy, give him my purse, take a tumbling and a licking, and he loose me. God bless Dr Glad One for putting my case for Massa buy up all of you, bring you to one field where I can watch over you."

"Dr Gladstone!" I said, confused and angry that his name was being dragged into Miriam's yarn.

"True-true I curse him for being white, but Dr Glad One give me family, he advocate for me. But gwan, me done talk, story done. Story done-done."

She pressed her lips together, the blubber melting in the sun, gluing them shut forever.

★   ★   ★

The gig set off for the city, taking me back to the surety of my place in Lady Elizabeth's mansion, but I stopped it barely a mile from Miriam's hut. I stepped out to steady my breath, my thoughts. It was only then that I realised that in my haste to leave I had neglected to change into my finery. I looked at the ripped shirt and breeches of my boyhood, wanting to cry, but a contrariness seized my mind. I had to sit, then lie flat for the laughter hit me like a hurricane. I held my sides and rolled on the ground, calling out my original name, Manu. It was only when the image of Dr Gladstone suddenly entered my mind that I stopped, rose up, brushed the dirt from my rags and re-entered the gig. "Where the road comes to a fork, travel left," I instructed the driver, resuming my authority. There was no need to, for I was his superior and his face would have stayed expressionless whatever my antics.

It had not been my intention to visit Dr Gladstone, though he still resided close to Miriam, at the other end of the plantation. I had thought meeting Miriam – journeying back to a past best forsaken – would be arduous enough without having to face Dr Gladstone as well. I walked the few hundred yards from the road to his grave, stumbling more out of guilt than from the thick grass clogging the path. I prepared a greeting but as soon as I caught sight of the grave the words fled my mind. It was not the weathered and broken structure, weeds sprouting from the cracks, which shocked me, but the imagining of him weighed down by earth and stone, in everlasting silence. I tried to remember his face, how he would narrow his eyes and pucker his lips as he examined a slave, his breath held in concentration, exhaling loudly once he decided upon the remedy. I looked up to the coconut and cuckrit trees encroaching on the grave, many choked with vines, thinking how alien the land was from the Scottish vale and brook pictured on the box he gave me. How often had I imagined making my way along pebbled streets, across a pasture shaded with beech, then over a green hill to a valley, in the bosom of which his village nestled. A dragonfly distracted me in its sudden flight from the grave. It must have been the same one I saw at Miriam's, for its wings were golden. She must have sent it to make my words soar and glitter, but I found myself mumbling to him, trying to make sense of her prophecies.

"I am as ragged as when you first bought me, in a torn shirt and pants," I said, to assert my servitude to him, even beyond the grave. Without giving him a chance to answer I continued: "Miriam said you brought us all together, Billy and Cato and Alice and MMadboy and me, under one massa, in one plantation when before we were scattered like shards of clay throughout the colony." My eyes swelled as if stung by Miriam's bumble bee, but I wiped away the tears, knowing that Dr Gladstone disliked acknowledgement. He deemed it his duty to mend the broken, that was all.

"As to Lady Elizabeth, she and I live in great concert," I continued, choosing my words carefully lest I betrayed my tenderness towards her. What an insult to Dr Gladstone, me aspiring to succeed him in Lady Elizabeth's bed! I kept quiet about Theodore too, though a less offensive matter on account of his whiteness and breeding.

"As to Massa Basnett," I continued, "he mess up the estate so Theodore and Lady Elizabeth will buy and run it according to the precepts of Adam Smith, your countryman. God bless all Scots folk for their knowing and mercy. Lady Elizabeth will give out plots to each slave to grow and cultivate and sell and bide time till daag-day done and freedom come. See how we will attire then, pantaloon and leather shoes and women in party finery, and we so swallow sidyam juice sweeten with rum that we dance till we drop and when night fall we peel off we cloths and cool off in canal, plunge in, splatter-splatter and cavort till dawn catch we."

As soon as I finished I regretted what I had said, for Dr Gladstone was a man of sobriety. "Don't fret," I blurted out to him. "Is school I will set up as soon as they catch their senses. I will prepare them for freedom by teaching them the *Dictionary*, starting with A for abacus to encourage counting and calculated thrift, and by year-end they will get to Z for zeugma, so they will encounter the mystery of language, how conjunctive does work and what is the intransitive. They will realise how language stay, how it does congeal then suddenly conjugate, how it turvy and yet straight, true and seeming, yeaing and naying in one breath. They will understand zeugma for I will take them to a wide sky when sun and moon occupy it at once, each having governance over the other and yet complete strangers. Between abacus and zeugma and sun and moon is our true and seeming destiny. When our tongue become bond-slave to English, baptise and yield in worship to it, then it is we done cuss, done bad-talk massas, beshrew missies. When all that badam-bam and bruk-up spirit leave us like legion, the first light of freedom will fall on our forehead like fresh expression. Blessed be blackman, he will describe the earth anew and share it with lion and lamb, fish and fowl and whitefolk."

I had worked myself into such a froth of idyll that I had to retreat from Dr Gladstone's grave. "Steady yourself, lad," I could hear him ministering to me, my father and physician to the end. The sea-wall was a short ride away. I stopped there for a while. The afternoon heat made me drowsy; I fell asleep in the gig, dreaming of Corinna. Then a loud knocking, the wind banging at the gig's door. I woke up to a perfumed vapour which gilded my eyes, as at the first meeting with Lady Elizabeth. I looked out to the sea, to a ship going from the colony, the stink of its slave-hold now perfumed by sugar, so that by the time it reached England there would be no trace of me, only the story of El Dorado, story done-done tell a thousand times, about Raleigh and all them, so who will remember, much less record nigger-me?

Only nigger-me, gifted with Dr Glad One's book. I must *persist* with learning to write. I must grow old slowly to become a massa to the craft; years and years will pass till I craft this fable. No *sudden*. No bouts of lazing, reclining in tall grass, munching on a watermelon. No sudden, nor no sloth, but I must wait, wait, one Samuel-word at a time, by and by the page fill up, then tear it up, start again, start again, again, till I turn ink into gold and paper into Corinna's glow, and there I am writing in the air, my pen a wand, and see how the air speckled in gold and such enchantment that my words can restore Dr Glad One to breath, for I is Manu, you hear (I shout after the ship), and Manu mean "magic", you hear (I shout after Dr Glad One).

Yes, he hear! Grave crack open, new life come.

EPILOGUE

"To begin at the beginning," the old woman said to Manu, "I was a maiden tending goats in my father's field, or feeding pigeons, I can't remember which, when an angel appeared – a fat glowing thing with wings – and whispered words into my ear, and before I could catch my breath, come to myself and cry foul, the angel shrunk to a sunbeam. I blinked, opened my eye and it was gone. Soon my belly started to swell, the words turned to flesh, and my father beat me, beat me, calling me a whore, unmarriageable, no longer worth a dowry of a dozen cows, for he did not believe it was the angel's doing. You see my nose? It used to be slender but the blows flattened it, and my jawbone too. But I didn't cry, and I didn't care if the villagers cursed me, closing their doors when I passed by. I kept company with my father's goats and pigeons, they never chastised me but blessed me with their cooing or glassy wondrous stare or gift of grain – yes, the pigeons would drop one seed or two at my feet and the goats would butt against the guava tree until fruit fell, leaving one or two for me. Until it was time, and I was chased away to the forest, a rice-sack my bed. O, the pain and the bleeding, but the boy was born and all that mattered was he. I hugged him to me, I wiped his face clean, I sang to him, I made him a bed of poui petals. Happy days! And my breasts were running over! Such a gentle boy, I thought, not greedy to suckle, not a groan from his mouth. He slept and slept and slept…"

The baby was stillborn. She was not to know, being a simple village girl, and bereft of company. Two days she bathed him, played with him, moving his lips to her breasts, coxing him to feed. On the third day she was entitled to return home, even though to face the wrath of her father. Surely he would soften at the sight of the child, and her mother would run to peel the customary peach for the newborn, shower him with ancient blessings. She spent many hours weaving cara strips into a blanket and making a cot from dried reeds and the rice-sack. She set off for home, only to be chased a second time, for when she peeled back the blanket to reveal her proud gift, her parents screamed. The villagers rushed out, looked at the boy and broke into wild behaviour. "They wanted to tear him from my arms. I gathered him up and ran away. They followed, pelting me with curses, charging me with bringing misfortune into their midst. I entered the safety of the forest. I stayed there for endless days, tending to my boy. I laid him out in the sun each morning on a fresh bed of poui petals, singing to him, brushing away insects, but feeling sinful afterwards, for the flies and mosquitoes only came to hum at him, their way of making lullaby. For all my care his eyes vanished, his flesh turned to husk. I put him in the rice sack and set off to find a sorcerer who could bring him back to sight and fulfil his limbs, for one leg had shrunk to nothing, gnawed by the sun. I followed a star that was furthest away from my home; it led me mostly to bog and rock and deserts, idle and rough quarries and hills whose heads touched the sky, but I was patient for my son's sake, and once, when my tongue was shrivelled, the star brought me to a pasture. I was on the verge of dying when a fat man appeared from nowhere, fat as the angel who had visited me, but he was without wings for he wobbled when he walked. He took me into his arms that night, permitting me to place my sack of son under the bed. In the morning he gave me a small wooden box full of coins, asking me to stay. I declined the coins but took the box and placed my boy in it, for he had withered to its size, and I needed to guard him from rats, which were everywhere, no matter how much we pelted them. The box was painted with trees in a meadow and a crystal stream, and my son was snug within its beauty. Yes, I stayed out of gratitude for the loveliness of green, remembering the forest which had harboured and let me give birth within it. The fat man fed me, dumplings and cassava, until I grew stout as cedar. I bore him many children, we were, simply, happy. When dust fell, his work done, our revels would begin, the agitation of limbs and tin whistles and tambourines, children of various ages dancing and rocking, whilst me and the fat man hiccupped out of joy and alcohol, prostrate on the ground and not wanting to rise, ever again.

Still, I did, for the child called from its box, suddenly, in the midst of our party. He wanted company, he wanted to come to life again. I mourned for a month, for I would have to leave kith and kin behind in search of a sorcerer. The fat man understood. He was the very picture of benevolence. He gave me a purse, wrapped a shawl around me and sent me on my way. He howled like a pack of dogs. I nearly relented but the boy called out again. 'I will come back soon,' I promised, my ordinary words wholly inappropriate for the occasion. I wished I could summon poetic utterance to convey the stab of emotions as I forsook my children for a dream and star."

Deserts, savannahs, rivers, she said. Mule and boat but mostly by foot she wandered, to save money. There were thousands of folk, singly or in caravans, heading in the same direction, to the same destination, but in such a hurry that few stopped their cart to offer her transportation. Some thirty days trudging brought her to the point of collapse. She fell towards the stony earth, she said, but a hand saved her, coming from nowhere to support her. When she revived she reached for her rice-sack to make sure the child was secure. It had fallen some yards away. Her feet were unsteady so she crawled after it, becoming a child herself. The rice-sack was intact, the box unbroken, her remaining provisions of pulses and dried fish in place. She looked up to the stranger who had saved her. He held out his hand to bring her upright but she declined. He offered to lift her bundle, but again she denied him, scrabbling in the dirt and broken stones to gather the sack to herself. "*Noli me tangere*," she growled, the words like the stranger coming from nowhere, outside her own understanding. The stranger stepped back, politely. She looked up at his smiling face and regretted her unfriendliness. She started to apologise when he interrupted her. "I can take charge of your passage to the promised land and to the very spot upon which the star glimmers," he offered. "I can hire vehicles to convey you there speedily and in comfort." He spoke softly. He kept smiling and she was tempted to surrender when she suddenly remembered the visitation of the angel. He too had whispered kind words into her ears, telling her that she was a picture of loveliness, that she was chosen for salvation. Nothing but sorrow had ensued.

"You lie!" she cried. "I am done with angels. You too are one of them."

"I am a simple man, Eli, son of Samuel," he said calmly, not rising to her temper.

"You are none such! Your wings are folded behind your back, but I can still sense them. Hook-nosed you are, that is why you confront me, not daring to turn your face sideways. And what large hands you have, enough to gather up the whole world. Get behind me you – you –" From the froth of her mouth the word short forth, splattering his face. "Jew!"

He wilted like a corinna flower touched by rain and then vanished altogether.

★   ★   ★

"What is a Jew?" she asked Manu, but the wisdom of his village and that gained by travelling were inadequate for an answer. "The word came out of my mouth as if I was its familiar but I am ignorant of it," she murmured. "There are so many things to know and not to know…" She looked out from her umbrella to a vacant sky. "How did you know what to fetch me?" she asked suddenly. "Are you the magician I am seeking? The stones must have hidden other stores but you brought back a cot of reeds, cowhide, rice-sack and painted cloth…" She stared at the reeds and began to cry. Manu went to comfort her but she rejected his embrace.

"Not you! Not any of them! They tried to assault me or bribe me with offers of free passage but I made my own way here. Only the fat man has touched me, I am the bearer of his children."

Manu withdrew, suppressing his instinct to ask after their names. She turned her attention again to his presents. She sat upright, face stiffened in concentration, then she lay back with a sigh. "In truth I have forgotten. So many seasons, so many changings of the night-sky, I have forgotten them all. There is only me left and my boy…"

"Where is your boy?" Manu asked.

"What is that to you? You are not here to abduct him?" She spoke with unexpected strength. Manu believed the threat in her voice. She could be possessed of the arts of sorcery, though insufficient for her child. He lowered his head in a show of meekness. Again she relented, softening towards him. "The boy is buried under an olive tree, not far from here. When the magician comes I will free him from the earth, but for now he is asleep, and the sun cannot shrink him further nor can it fade the colours of the box he shelters in. I chose an olive tree, for its fruits, when they fall, will anoint the spot, keeping it liquid-fresh."

"Your choice is wise," Manu said, but she did not respond to his offer of conversation, withdrawing into herself to dwell on the disappearance of her other children.

★ ★ ★

"Sometimes they come back to me," she said, "one by one, or in twos, but the truth is I don't know them, their names, their new ways of speaking... A black boy was the first, a flock of birds circling overhead like a halo. 'Ma,' he said, burst into tears, and clung on to me. There was a woman with him, a lovely apparition, golden bangles, sunbeams in her hair, pale skin. 'I have become his mother in your absence,' she said, kindly. She drew the boy to her, pressing him to her lap. I looked hard but couldn't recognise him. What could I do? I stroked his face, blessed him, blinked, and they both vanished along with the birds. I only recall him now because he resembled you..."

She paused, lips trembling in distress.

"And the woman who had taken charge of my son, she kept asking me whether I had seen her father, who left on some ship, never to return. But I couldn't help her..."

Once more Manu reached out to touch her face, but she spurned his tenderness. Her grumpy spirit revived, this time edged with self-pride.

"I may have left them but they still seek me out! 'Ma, Ma, Ma' they all bleat. 'What happened to your leg?' I asked one man who hopped up to me. He was accompanied by a retinue of pale-skinned people who attended to his every word, bowing when-ever he looked at them. 'I am Billy, yes, Billy, your son, and I am also worshipped by many as a holy father.' He gestured to his followers who immediately knelt and broke into reverential song. 'Holy?' I asked, looking him up and down for some sacred sign but I couldn't see any. He was an ordinary black man, fat lips, flat forehead, broad nose; it was only that one leg was missing, the stump of which was wrapped in a strip of rice-bag. 'I sacrificed it,' he said, then launched into a story of how an alligator bit it off but he still managed to retrieve it from the creature's jaws with the help of two angels who appeared out of thin air. The angels stilled the alligator by simply spreading their wings before it. The alligator surrendered the leg meekly. The angels offered to sew back the leg, but all of a sudden, he, Billy, decided otherwise. 'No, give it to another, to someone more needful. It is God's will that the leg should be taken from me; the alligator is God's instrument. It has the sharpest teeth in all creation; God sent it to remove the leg in one swift act, so that I would feel no pain. There is no pain, so take the leg and depart.' The angels did as he bade, flying off with the leg to sew it on to another soul, and before too long a crowd turned up to praise Billy, to care for all his needs. 'Isn't life miraculous? One moment I am a simple fisherman throwing my net into a canal, the next my life is changed by an alligator, two angels and a throng of disciples.' I listened patiently to his silliness, remembering my own encounter with an angel, and was about to ask what a powerful man like him wanted of a destitute like me; why the need was for a mother when he had a family of a thousand and more: but before I could a young woman broke from the congregation, ran up to me, wailing. 'Canal, canal, O the horror!' She fell at my feet, clasping them so tightly that I struggled to steady myself. I blinked to make her disappear. The cripple and his disciples did, but she remained. I blinked again, again, but she was still there. I was compelled to hear her story before I could be rid of her. She told me she had drowned her brother in a canal. All the years with their massa who had whipped them until the boy went mad. He would sit in the field counting the blades of grass. At night he would count the stars. If she locked him indoors to stop his habit, he would pull out a tuft of his hair, separate the strands and count them. The boy no longer able to work, their massa would condemn him to punishment and prolonged starvation. She took it upon herself to save him. She

David Wilkie?: *Billy Waters*

chose the right moment when the mist lifted and the sun was radiant. She led him through a meadow of corinnas, through rosebush and hibiscus, wanting to be careless of their perfume and lush display, wanting to be careless too of the songbirds high up the starapple trees. She could not help but be moved by the mystery of the place, at once lovely and cruel. The sequins of light upon the water's surface made it a gown such as a princess wore in the fairytale she overheard her mistress reading to her children. Below, though, waited watersnakes. 'I push him in, splash, splash,' she said, her language broken by grief. 'Splash, struggle, splash, then when his belly full of water he sink, and I left alone, wishing I did give him a hug before I push him in, a hug big enough to wheeze his breath. I left alone but the blue-saki and doves were trilling and the corinna flowers sugaring the air, and the place so beautiful! I went back to the canal to search for him, but he float away or trap below; all I see when I bend over the water is my own face. How I hate my face! Since then I never look upon myself, or else I gaze in pothole where mosquito spawn just to confirm that I is ugliness self.' The memory of the drowning broke her, but then anger arose. She stood up to face me with accusations. 'Where were you when Massa put us to trial? You ran away with a rice-sack and our father sold us into slavery. He pined when you left, change from being a fat man into a stick, took to liquor. He drank away all his money. One day a stranger came. I remembered his spindly hand and his curtseying and his gloves and his polite manners and his buzzing around our father like a dragonfly. He offered pieces of silver, our father agreed, me and my brother were taken away and sold to Massa. It is you who is to blame for killing your own son!'"

Manu wanted her to stop punishing herself by such recollection of her children, but she persisted.

"'Killing my own son!' I was speechless, on the point of fainting, when a woman and child rushed up to brace me. 'Alice! Dido!' I said, involuntarily. How their names came into my mind when I couldn't recollect the others, I know not. Apart from the names, everything else about them was unfamiliar. Alice looked frail, perhaps weakened from the long journey. She leant upon a stick studded with gems. She wore a silken cloak and gown, the child too, trimmed with lace. And what dainty shoes, not at all stained by the desert sand! And pearl necklaces! And handbags, stitched in gold, with emerald studs. And they were cleanly scented, like cow-milk. 'When you left, all the family dispersed in different directions, in search of you,' Alice said, the tenderness of her voice bringing such relief from the rancour of the previous woman (who still hovered vaguely, at the back of my mind). 'The temple of love which was our home was pillaged and set afire by barbarians. They killed our father, a spear punctured his belly, he shrunk to a sack of skin. Then wolves ate him. They set fire to the temple which he had built on his own, such a masterful carpenter!' She sighed at the memory, clasping Dido's hand protectively. 'We had stayed behind, Dido being a sick child, but fled when the barbarians came. We journeyed through villages, cities, across rivers and seas, asking after you, but no one recalled you passing that way. Except Eli, son of Samuel, chief Scribe of Judea.'

"A cry slipped from my mouth at the mention of the name. Alice went to hug me again, and Dido too, but I pulled away from them. 'I know no Eli, son of a Scribe, but for a moment when he entered my dream, to spoil it,' I told them. 'I had fallen, I lay on the earth dreaming of dying, but Eli came with promises. A curse upon his kindness! I didn't want to be revived! Look at me now, mange that I am!' It was Dido's turn to cry. Alice dabbed her eyes with a handkerchief trimmed with lace and initialled in gold lettering. 'We cannot speak badly of Eli, son of Samuel, for he saved us from loneliness. It was he who sent us to Lord Gladstone, to a new family.' She let the handkerchief fall to the ground. 'It was not Lord Gladstone's wealth we valued but his compassion. Do you know of him? Has his reputation not spread this far?' Like the others she unfolded her own story, just as bizarre. In their wandering through the world they reached a harbour by the river in a place called Demerara. It was packed with merchants examining their goods. The scent of the sugarloaves drew them to the warehouse, for they were on the verge of starvation. Their eyes were so weakened that they did not see Eli approach with a handful of oranges. 'Come in out of the hot sun,' he said, leading them to the shelter of the warehouse, to a room which was his office. Alice was suspicious as to his motive for helping them, but he simply said he was against slavery, being a disciple of Adam Smith. He was preparing to close down his business in Demerara and return home. Before Alice could ask who Adam Smith was, a group of planters approached Eli's office and Eli quickly hid them in a closet. He hid them there for a week, thinking them runaway slaves. There was already another refugee in the closet, a boy bright with jaundice, his face a yellow glow. He was dying; gripped by new fevers and infections he seemed to change colour every day.

"When the next ship departed for London Eli placed them in it, with money and clothing and a letter to his friend Lord Gladstone, the Lord Chief Justice of Scotland. Poor many-coloured boy, he didn't last a day on board, though the surgeon tried his best to revive him with sago and rum! He was wrapped in a plain cotton sheet and surrendered to the sea.

"A spacious and ornate coach took them North to Lord Gladstone's estate, in the Edinburgh countryside. They marvelled at the rills, the purling streams, the glens, the meadows, the tartan attire, the bagpipes, the shortbreads, the thistle, the harp, the leaping salmon, the haggis, the deer, the battlefields, the black sheep, the fishing boats, the copious alcohol, the grunting speech, the ceilidh, the huge graveyards. They marvelled at Lord Gladstone himself, his ruddy complexion and fat jowls which reminded them of their father, but also Lord Gladstone's robes, ribbons, swords, fashionable velvet coats of blue trimmed with silver lace, waistcoats of black silk with fringes, white stockings, hats with gold edging, full-bottomed wigs, cambric handkerchiefs, ruffled shirts, silver-mounted pistols and snuffbox of tortoiseshell. In the Hall hung huge paintings, of naval battles, landscapes, noblefolk.

"He was a recent widower, and lonely, in spite of the dozen servants attending to his every need. He took to Dido instinctively: though black, Dido had a high forehead, slender nose and fine lips, which bore resemblance to Lady Gladstone. 'He treated us exceedingly well, we became exalted members of his household,' Alice boasted. 'A mere month after our arrival, he passed a judgment in the highest court ordering the freeing of all Negro and Irish slaves in Scotland. We were present in court, sitting in the front row. He winked at me, raised the gravel, bang, freedom! O, how I ululated, spoke in a strange tongue, swooned! He came down from his high table, lifted up Dido and placed her in the witness box to play with a doll he had secreted in the pocket of his robe. And he gave me a pearl necklace strung with golden calves, look! O happy day, and the years afterwards, in his care!'

"Her eyes lit up as she paused to remember her benevolent patron. How I wished to share in Alice's bounty, hug her, kiss her forehead and feet, utter fine words, but I was too versed in cruelty for such. All the years of journeying, stung by centipedes as I slept in straw, desert scorpions, sea-snakes, churlish men, and hungry, always hungry, me; the dead boy in his pretty box my only solace, and the prospect of a sorcerer. By the time the star brought me here, I was poison-self. So I couldn't embrace Dido and Alice, share in their fortune. Poison, not fine words came from my mouth. 'If you were enjoying such a bejewelled life, why bother me, why bother with me?' I hissed at her with such ferocity that spittle escaped my mouth and settled on then. They began to wilt, their image growing fainter and fainter. 'We came to make you proud, to tell you that we are your richness; that though you left us in our youth, we grew up to be the wondrous beings that Lord Gladstone made of us. We came to gild your eyes and spirit so you can forgive yourself the suffering you endured. We came for your forgiveness…' Alice had summoned up all her strength to speak words and so resist disappearance, but the spittle of my contempt overcame her. I reached out to retrieve both of them, but tumbled in a blank page of air. I got up, I ran as fast as my feet could take me, to the olive tree, hoping to find them there in the sacred space so we could form family again, me, my children, my dead son, with tambourines and tin whistles and sorrel juice and platters of fruit, but no. No, no, no, no, no! Only me, and the husk of my child."

Manu reached to support her, a third attempt, and this time she let herself lean on his shoulders and her tears soaked into his flesh, restoring life to it after his barren travails.

★   ★   ★

Manu lay under a black-eyed bruised moon, lopsided as if swollen from a blow, but luminous still, defying the urge to die. When he was satisfied she was in deep sleep he withdrew from her embrace, covered over her nakedness, gathered his belongings and walked to the olive tree, remembering the taste of her flesh, aged, yes, but the wrinkles still the faintest tributaries of nectar. He thought of ancient rock, easily overlooked but for the prospector of sharpened sense who could intuit within traces of gold. With the point and sharpened tip of his tongue he, Manu, had prospected and discovered nectar: the gold secreted in the kernel of her agedness.

He dug up the box and retrieved the husk of boy, covering him with the painted cloth, protecting him from the night-chill. Under the olive tree he performed his ceremony, with vials, calabash, lama brush. Never before had he revived life, but his hands moved strangely, blending sidyam juice with the venom of watersnakes in unknown proportion, and new incantations came from his mouth, new words of such unknown cadence that life rushed into the boy with the force of tears that had fallen from his mother and soaked into Manu's flesh. The boy rose in an instant, shook himself clear of imaginary dust and skipped away in normal childish glee to his mother, following a path made by moonlight. It was as if he had never known that he had withered. The boy just arose, shook himself and scooted off, not even blinking in the sudden light, not even waiting for a name, innocent of being buried in years of darkness.

The commingling with the mother, the ceremony of resurrection, the joyful child… Manu was so exhausted he fell asleep under the olive tree, not bothering to gather up his vials, calabash, brush. In his dream he dreamt he was skipping after a star with the glee of a child running to its mother. He was moving through orchards and grasslands when his feet became tangled in sudden swamp, which yielded to even softer earth, then collapsed altogether. He fell backwards into a pit, backwards, backwards, a bottomless pit. The whole of his being shook and collapsed inwardly, reduced in size to the point of a nail; a nail that would seek to puncture life itself, light itself, because it was human to do so whilst still marvelling at life and light, and creation seemed to thrive on such alternation of adoration and brutishness. As he fell, images flooded his mind, of the marketplace plump with melons, children taunting cattle with sticks or squealing in the pleasurable canal, women giving suckle whilst grinding corn, men weaving nets or plotting which pebbles to throw next in the game of pukka, a youth harvesting a gift of yams for his beloved, she making dyes to adorn her face, a beggar breaking the back of a rabbit and skinning it whilst it was still alive, fields freshly sewn with fena seeds or sensational with corinna, hibiscus, poui flowers, and behind these, the tall trees which stood sentry around the village, guarding it from sandstorms and fierce tribes and the beyond where the ancestors lived in a realm of unknowingness.

All of creation was there – beautiful and brutish – except he, Manu, disobedient to the will of Elder and Sorcerer and tradition, and now, like the ancestors, falling so unfathomably deep that he was neither moving nor still, neither sensible nor in dream, screaming as if on the point of a nail but without sound, without the release, the relief, the closure of words.

ALSO BY DAVID DABYDEEN

Slave Song   ISBN: 978 1 84523 004 3, 72pp, £7.99

Slave Song is unquestionably one of the most important collections of Caribbean/Black British poetry published in the last thirty years. On its first publication in 1984 it won the Commonwealth Poetry Prize.

At the heart of *Slave Song* are the voices of African slaves and Indian labourers expressing, in a Guyanese Creole that is as far removed from Standard English as is possible, their songs of defiance, of a thwarted erotic energy. But surrounding this harsh and lyrical core of Creole expression is an elaborate critical apparatus of translations (which deliberately reveal the actual untranslatability of the Creole) and a parody of the kind of critical commentary that does no more than paraphrase or at best contextualise the original poem. Here, Dabydeen is engaged in a play of masks, an expression of his own duality and a critique of the relationship which is at the core of Caribbean writing: that between the articulate writer and the supposedly voiceless workers and peasants.

This new edition has an afterword by David Dabydeen that briefly explores his response to these poems after more than twenty years.

Turner   ISBN: 978 1 90071 568 3, 84pp, £7.99

David Dabydeen's "Turner" is a long narrative poem written in response to JMW Turner's celebrated painting "Slavers Throwing Overboard the Dead & Dying". Dabydeen's poem focuses on what is hidden in Turner's painting, the submerged head of the drowning African. In inventing a biography and the drowned man's unspoken desires, including the resisted temptation to fabricate an idyllic past, the poem brings into confrontation the wish for renewal and the inescapable stains of history, including the meaning of Turner's painting.

"A major poem, full of lyricism and compassion, which gracefully shoulders the burden of history and introduces us to voices from the past whose voices we have all inherited" – Caryl Phillips

The Intended   ISBN: 978 1 84523 013 5, 246pp, £8.99

The narrator of *The Intended* is twelve when he leaves his village in rural Guyana to come to England. There he is abandoned into social care, but seizes every opportunity to follow his aunt's farewell advice: "...but you must tek education...pass plenty exam." With a scholarship to Oxford, and an upper-class white fiancée, he has unquestionably arrived, but at the cost of ignoring the other part of his aunt's farewell: "you is we, remember you is we." First published almost fifteen years ago, *The Intended*'s portrayal of the instability of identity and relations between whites, African-Caribbeans and Asians in South London is as contemporary and pertinent as ever. As an Indian from Guyana, the narrator is seen as a "Paki" by the English, and as some mongrel hybrid by "real" Asians from India and Pakistan; as sharing a common British "Blackness" whilst acutely conscious of the real cultural divisions between Africans and Indians back in Guyana. At one level a moving semi-autobiographical novel, *The Intended* is also a sophisticated postcolonial text with echoes of *Heart of Darkness*.

Disappearance   ISBN: 978 1 84523 014 2, 180pp, £8.99

A young Afro-Guyanese engineer comes to a coastal Kentish village as part of a project to shore up its crumbling sea-defences. He boards with an old English woman, Mrs Rutherford, and through his relationship with her discovers that beneath the apparent placidity and essential Englishness of this village, violence and raw emotions are not far below the surface, along with echoes of the imperial past. In the process, he is forced to reconsider his perceptions of himself and his native Guyana, and to question his engineer's certainties in the primacy of the rational.

This richly intertextual novel makes reference to the work of Conrad, Wilson Harris and VS Naipaul to set up a multi-layered dialogue concerning the nature of Englishness, the legacy of Empire and different perspectives on the nature of history and reality.

The Counting House   ISBN: 978 1 84523 015 9, 180pp, £8.99

Set in the early nineteenth century, *The Counting House* follows the lives of Rohini and Vidia, a young married couple struggling for survival in a small, caste-ridden Indian village who are seduced by the recruiter's talk of easy work and plentiful land if they sign up as indentured labourers to go to British Guiana. There, however, they discover a harsh fate as "bound coolies" in a country barely emerging from the savage brutalities of slavery. Having abandoned their families and a country that seems increasingly like a paradise, they must come to terms with their problematic encounters with an Afro-Guyanese population hostile to immigrant labour, with rebels such as Kampta who has made an early abandonment of Indian village culture, and confront the truths of their uprooted condition.

Our Lady of Demerara   ISBN: 9781845230692; pp. 288; £9.99

Drama critic Lance Yardley is only 30 but is already a seedy wreck of a man, spending his nights in the back streets of Coventry looking for prostitutes. A working-class boy brought up in a broken home on a council estate, he has sought escape in literature and through his marriage to an actress, the great-granddaughter of a 19th-century Englishman who made his fortune from the sugar plantations in Guyana. At first Elizabeth attracts Yardley, but their differences of class exacerbate the mutual hatred that grows between them. Later he is drawn to a mysterious Indian girl, Rohini. She seems shy, but sells her body to customers when her boss goes out of town. When she dies suddenly, the victim of a strange and violent assassin, Yardley decides to decamp abroad for a while. He goes to Guyana, not least because he wants to learn more about an Irish priest who as an old man has been a priest in Coventry, but as a young man had worked as a missionary in Guyana. The priest's fragmented journals seem to offer Yardley some possible answers to his own spiritual malaise, but the Guyana he discovers provokes more questions than answers.

Ed. Kevin Grant
The Art of David Dabydeen ISBN: 978 1 90071 510 2, 231pp, £12.99

In this volume, leading scholars discuss Dabydeen's poetry and fiction in the context of the politics and culture of Britain and the Caribbean. The essays explore his concern with the plurality of Caribbean experience; the dislocation of slavery and indenture; migration and the consequent divisions in the Caribbean psyche. In particular, the focus is on Dabydeen's aesthetic practice as a consciously post-colonial writer; his exploration of the contrasts between rural creole and standard English; the power of language to subvert accepted realities; his use of multiple masks as ways of dealing with issues of identity; and the play of destabilizing techniques within his narrative strategies.

Eds Lynne Macedo and Kampta Karran
No Land, No Mother: Essays on the Work of David Dabydeen
ISBN: 978 1 84523 020 3, 236pp, £12.99

The essays in this collection focus on the rich dialogue carried out in David Dabydeen's critically acclaimed body of writing. Dialogue across diversity and the simultaneous habitation of multiple arenas are seen as dominant characterics of his work. Essays by Aleid Fokkema, Tobias Döring, Heike Härting and Madina Tlostanova provide rewardingly complex readings of Dabydeen's *Turner*, locating it within a revived tradition of Caribbean epic. Lee Jenkins and Pumla Gqola explore Dabydeen's fondness for intertextual reference, his dialogue with canonic authority and ideas about the masculine. Michael Mitchell, Mark Stein, Christine Pagnoulle and Gail Low focus on his more recent fiction. Looking more closely at Dabydeen's Indo-Guyanese background, this collection complements the earlier *The Art of David Dabydeen*.

All available on-line from www.peepaltreepress.com